WHILE SLEEPING WATCH

KIP MORGAN

∞

First Printing

3/25/2025

This is a work of fiction. All characters herein are solely the product of imagination. Any resemblance to persons living or dead or otherwise is purely proof of the Universe's humorous proclivity towards that synchronistic weirdness known as accident.

DEDICATED TO

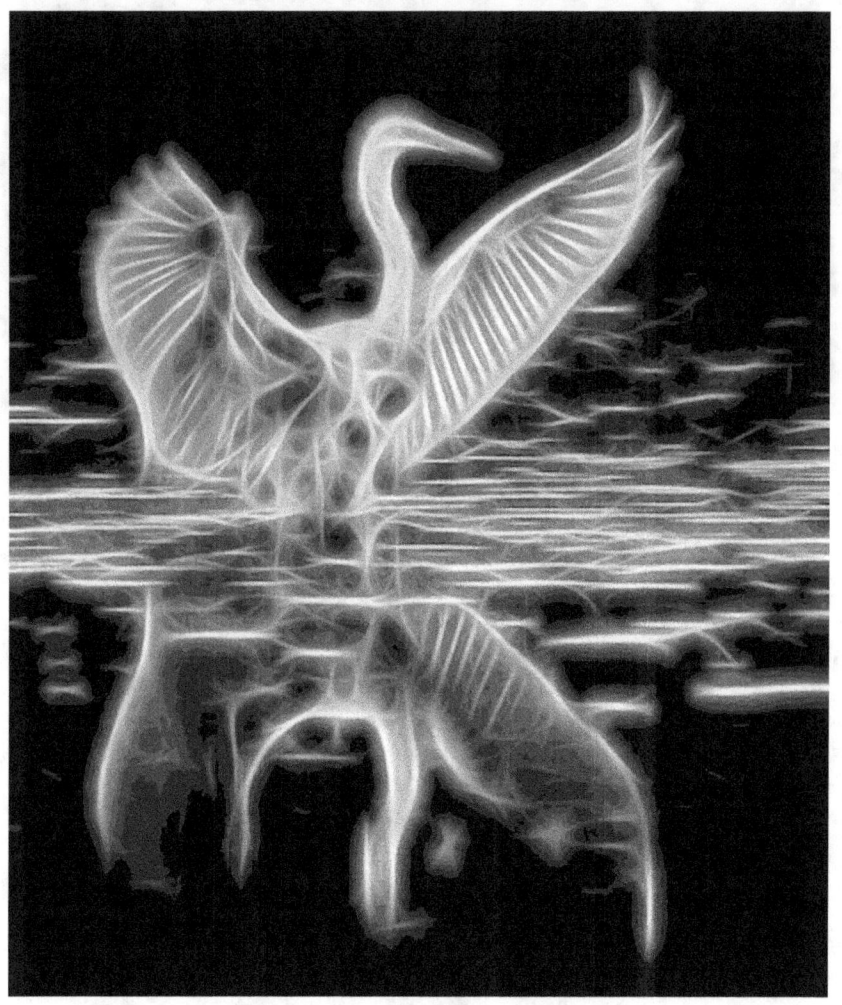

**ALL OF US ENJOYING
A MOMENT TOGETHER**

Our dreams are as full of life,
As our feelings are full of meaning.

CONTENTS

CHAPTER 1
The Dream

"Look to your experience of sleep to discover whether or not you are truly awake."

Tenzin Wangyal Rinpoche

As Bunzy lies naked on a cold rock slab bleeding to death, he thinks back over all of the things he did that led him to this moment.

It all starts on a lovely warm summer evening with fireflies dancing in a dark hardwood forest alongside a highway outside of Peoria, Illinois. After drinking dinner, Bunzy Ringer cruises down the road in his cool new car, a shiny black Chrysler Mohican coupe.

He thinks. *What a beautiful piece of iron this is, all smooth feminine curves and awesome macho power. When I stomp the gas pedal down, I feel the lunge in my crotch. Oh man, how could I stop any of this when it feels so fine?*

A huge, striped tent appears in a field on the right side of the road. It is lit up like a Vegas casino and announces, "Good News".

Bunzy's drunk, not stupid, well maybe a little stupid too. He parks in a big, mowed hayfield beside a bunch of other vehicles. Walking along with a noisy crowd, he stumbles toward the tent.

At the entrance on the right, a big rawboned farmer wearing an uncomfortable banker's black pin-stripe suit grabs his right hand with both of his strong, calloused fists and vigorously pumps Bunzy's arm up and down.

The farmer declares, "We're glad that you made it Brother. We didn't know if you would come or not." He points with his head towards a plain, but lovely woman in a pretty floral-patterned dress standing to their left.

Bunzy smiles a goofy, vacant grin at each of them, one at a time but says nothing. He can't remember their names. He can't even remember where he knows them from.

"Thanks," he says. His head bobbling like the heads on the springs of those souvenir dolls people stick on the dashboards in their cars. He walks on past the farmer and the lady into the tent.

A dense feeling of high expectations mixed with friendly smiles and sweat fills the place. Folding chairs have been set up in an amphitheater style. A big stage has been built up front out of fresh-sawn lumber. The floor is covered in clean sawdust. At the rear of the stage a large, black gospel choir in gracefully flowing, long white silk robes jumps and sways, singing as exuberantly as God's own tabernacle choir. A full-sized, white, big-city orchestra with a tuxedoed conductor backs them. The tent is filled with a rich, magnificent, epic-movie music. Hope, beauty and love surround the crowd. The people have been swept up onto their feet. They clap and sing.

Bunzy wants to sing along with them, but he can't remember the words. The song seems familiar, but he can't quite remember where he's sung it before.

Hundreds of people, eyes shining, surround Bunzy. They rock with joy as they sing. Everywhere Bunzy looks people sit or stand in front of all of the chairs.

Then he spots an empty seat near the back between a slender attractive blond woman in her mid-thirties and a distinguished older gentleman with almond shaped eyes.

Bunzy slides down their aisle, claims the vacant chair, turns to the woman, and introduces himself, "Hello, my name is Bunzy Ringer."

He offers her his hand.

She shakes it and replies, "Hi, my name is Susan. I'm very much looking forward to hearing Brother Michael's message tonight."

Just as Bunzy is about to ask her about this Brother Michael whom she seems to like so much, the music reaches a crescendo. The crowd turns towards the entrance at the back of the tent. A handsome man in a black silk suit and a beautiful, tall slender woman in a long flowing white gown enter. They walk down the center aisle smiling and waving. The man shakes hands. The enchanting woman with a Mona Lisa smile calmly strolls through the people carrying a large bouquet of red roses.

The man bounds onto the stage, turns and offers the lady his hand to help her gracefully ascend the platform.

He smiles at her, then walks over to the podium, raises both of his hands in the air and shouts, "Brothers and Sisters, I feel it. Do you feel it?"

The people roar back, "Yes! Yes! We feel it Brother Michael."

He walks out to the front of the stage and continues, "It is wonderful to be alive and to be here tonight with all of you good-looking and delightful friends. Tonight is the night. Everything that you desire is going to be delivered. Everyone is going to make it to the promised land. Every wound is going to be healed. Every injustice is going to be made right. Every wish is going to be granted. We are all going to be happy, healthy, wealthy, and loved. Brothers and Sisters are you ready?"

The audience enthusiastically shouts back, "We're ready." Here and there in the crowd, men loudly encourage the handsome, charismatic speaker by shouting, "Tell it Brother Michael,"

Michael steps out on to the very edge of the stage, leans forward into the audience and in a confidential tone quietly asks, "Do you want to know the truth that will set you free?"

Bunzy along with the rest of the crowd answers, "Yes, Brother Michael, we want to know the truth."

Michael raises his hands above his head, jumps back away from the crowd, slamming his hands forward and thunderously proclaims, "Wake up!"

A great white light flashes from his palms filling the tent with a glowing warm radiance. In this light Bunzy hears words and in those words he hears a message in a language that is bigger than any speaking he has ever done.

The white light, the words, the raw energy blasts Bunzy over backwards. He falls down into the sawdust.

As he strikes the ground, he wakes up in his bed in his bedroom back home. He stares out through the sliding glass door on his right side at gorgeous pink, orange, yellow and white flowers glowing in the morning sunlight.

He vigorously pats his body. He rubs his eyes, his face.

He says to himself, "I'm here in my bedroom. It was only a dream."

Sitting up, he wonders, *what did that marvelous man say? I don't remember. I have to get back into that dream, back into that tent. I have to hear that message again and remember it this time. I have to know what was communicated in that flash of light.*

He enters the family breakfast nook and sits down opposite his wife Isabel. As he slugs down a shot of blue-green algae from Klamath Lake in Oregon and drinks a hot chocolate made from fresh squeezed almond milk, baby Thai coconut juice, raw cacao, and cordycep mushrooms, he asks himself, "How can I get back into a dream? Where are my dream memories?"

Staring across the table, Isabel, his wife, asks, "What are you mumbling about over there?"

Bunzy tells her, "I can't remember my dreams."

"Yeah, so what? Few people do. When most people wake up, their dreams go away. No big deal. That's just the way it is," she tells him.

"Well, I had this incredible dream last night in which this guy said wonderful things. I want to get back into that dream and hear what he has to say again."

"Too bad. It can't be done. Besides dreams aren't real anyway."

"That honey bowl in front of you doesn't seem any more real to me than the guy in my dream seemed to me last night. There are answers over there. Important things are happening in the dream worlds. I want to know what that man said. I'm going to find out."

"I didn't even know you had questions."

"I didn't either until I heard that guy speak."

"Bunzy, you're going crazy. You've become deluded by a dream, a hallucination. You shouldn't confuse dreams with real life. Dreams are just dreams. Let it go."

"I don't care what you say. I'm curious. I know what that man said is important. I'm going to find a way to get back into that dream."

"Whatever. I hope you enjoy yourself, Crazy Man. I always knew you were lazy and not the brightest bulb in the store, but now you're crazy too? Bunzy, if you weren't so handsome and charming, I'd take the kids and leave you. You're such a fool."

"Well hang on Babe, we're about to do some amazing things."

"Bunzy, I don't know if you're an idiot or brilliant or just plain lucky. Maybe you're a little bit of all three. What I do believe is that you're living in a state of grace. A great mystery seems to surround you."

■■■

Unable to forget the 'good news' dream, or to shake the desire to enter the dream world and learn what is going on over there, Bunzy watches movies and reads books about dreams and dreaming. He does internet research and listens to podcasts. He believes great adventures, great ideas, great moments of wonder hover just beyond the veil which hides his dreams from him. Remembering them is hopeless though. The more he struggles to recapture their memory, the more they recede.

A few days later in the evening, as Bunzy sits in the coffee shop at the Mystic Moon Bookstore sipping a mocha, facing Isabel whose long legs, smoldering eyes and deep knowing peg him to life on this Wednesday night; a big black cat surprises them both as it jumps off of a chair behind Bunzy. He shivers feeling suddenly cold. Watching the cat, Bunzy's eyes fall on a poster tacked in the middle of a nearby bulletin board which he hadn't previously noticed. It is an invitation to "the Dream Jam, a non-invasive learning event about dreaming". The flyer promises a unique experience.

Bunzy's hand astonishes him. Without any conscious command from his mind, it leaps across the distance between his body and the bulletin board, grabs the poster, rips it off the board, folds it up, and stuffs it in a pocket.

He thinks, *that was odd. I guess I'm going to this Dream Jam thing-a-meroo.*

Bunzy asks Isabel, "Would you like to go to the Dream Jam event the poster talked about? I think I'll go."

Isabel answers, "Sure. I'll go too. It could be fun."

On Saturday evening Bunzy and Isabel arrive early at the Hope Center for the Dream Jam. They're sitting in seats 7R and 7S. The auditorium is nearly empty, but there is a man with almond shaped eyes sitting next to Bunzy on his right and an attractive slender blond woman on their left on the other side of Isabel.

Bunzy is about to lean forward and say to the woman, "I know that we know each other, but I can't seem to remember from where," when the man on his right turns to him, extends his hand, and says, "Good evening, sir. My name is Tilopa Rinpoche."

Shaking his hand, Bunzy responds, "My name is Bunzy Ringer," and gesturing to Isabel with his left hand, adds, "this is my wife, Isabel." Rinpoche and Isabel smile at each other as if they're old friends. While they're exchanging pleasantries, Bunzy studies Rinpoche.

When their conversation lulls, Bunzy says, "Forgive me if I seem rude, but I can't tell where you are from. You're wearing a Western suit and speaking English really well, but you don't seem to be an American."

"It is my pleasure to forgive you, Bunzy, and an even greater pleasure to meet an important person such as yourself."

"Me 'important'. I'm afraid you have me confused with someone else," Bunzy tells him.

"I'm not talking about the you that I'm sitting beside. When I called you important, I was referring to your future self," Rinpoche informs Bunzy.

"The future? Nobody knows what the future will bring," Bunzy cautions him.

"I do.," Rinpoche asserts. "Allow me to explain to you how I can do this."

"Go ahead. Knock yourself out," Bunzy says smiling at Isabel.

Isabel doesn't return the smile.

Rinpoche begins, "I am an American now, but I was born a long time ago in Tibet. When the Chinese invaded, I was young, but already the assistant to the Supreme Abbot of the venerable Yungdrung Monastery where the masters of dream yoga reincarnated generation after generation. The Abbot and I fled along with two hundred fellow monks towards India on foot and horseback. We trekked for almost a year before we crossed the border because we had to stay hidden in the wilderness and constantly keep moving around to avoid the Chinese troops. By the time that we crossed into India only twelve of us, plus our master, remained. The others had died or been captured by Chinese soldiers. When we reached Dharamsala, the Abbot gave me the teaching of the Dream Key, then entered the rainbow body and departed."

"The Dream Key, rainbow body? What is a dream key?" Bunzy asks.

"There are may worlds around us, but we don't ordinarily see them because they vibrate at different frequencies than that which we perceive in our normal lives. You may find this hard to understand and even harder to believe."

"I do," Bunzy says, looking straight ahead.

"Let me explain it this way, you know that there are television signals filling this room we're sitting in, but because we don't have a receiver, we can't experience the shows playing on those signals. If we had a receiver, we could see many different shows by changing the channels on the television set. If we were in a television studio, we could even be in a show. When we go to sleep, we naturally slip from this waking world frequency into a dream land frequency. The Dream Key is a receiving/transmitting device which connects the possessor of the key to other realms while he is still conscious of this world frequency. It is possible for the possessor of the Dream Key to do things that are miraculous to those who have never heard of it."

"That seems plausible, even possible. Will you show me this Dream Key and let me try it out?" Bunzy asks.

"Maybe, but before we worry about things to do, let's consider motives. What is your interest in dreams? What are your intentions?" Rinpoche wants to know.

Bunzy tells him, "I recently had a dream which interests me very much because I believe I heard a message that could help us live better lives. So, my intention is to understand dreams to empower our waking lives."

"What do you mean by power?" Rinpoche asks.

"By power I mean control over our health, wealth, and relationships. That sort of thing."

"So, you want to learn to dream so that you can get control over the things which you perceive as being real in your life?"

"Sounds a little crass when you say it that way, but yes, that's the reason. I want to control my dreams so I can control my waking life."

"Why don't you short circuit that whole process and learn to control your waking life?"

"Okay. Can we do that? I haven't been very good at getting my life to turn out the way I want it to so far, but I didn't have a Dream Key or your help. Things could be different now if you help me. Will you help?"

"Maybe."

"Where should we start?" Bunzy asks.

"Let's continue our conversation about your desires."

"I just want everyone to be happy," Bunzy declares.

"So, your reason for dreaming is so there will be more happiness?"

"Yes, that's what I want." Bunzy says.

"What do you mean by happy?" Rinpoche asks.

"Happiness is when someone has everything they need and they find themselves in a beautiful, friendly, comfortable environment with friendly supportive companions. Everyone has the time to enjoy all of this goodness and at the same time they have meaningful tasks to perform which support and uplift them and all of those around them," Bunzy describes.

Rinpoche says, "Notice that your definition of happiness is the definition of a being who has suffered powerlessness and lack. What if everything that you imagined, happened? What would your definition of happiness be in that case?"

"I have a hard time imagining a situation in which my thoughts affect our world in that powerful of a way."

"Yes, I know. We're just pretending. Imagine your thoughts affect what happens in such a forceful way that your thoughts and what happens are the same."

"I guess that is what I'm imagining a dream master's existence is like."

"I know. That is why we are contemplating this. Instead of denying yourself anything, go the other way. Indulge yourself in every way."

"I can't. I don't have the power or the resources."

"Well imagine you do. In fact, imagine having more than enough of everything, including safety and security. What are you going to do? Imagine that anything is possible."

A vision fills Bunzy's whole being with white light and warmth.

He announces, "I am a shining star of perfection manifesting in a physical body. I am capable of anything I can imagine," and in this moment he really feels this way.

Rinpoche observes, "Yes, I can see that you are. I'm going to tell you a story. Ready?"

"Yes. I'm ready for whatever you want to do."

"Okay. You don't need to understand the story that I'm going to tell you as I'm telling it to you. You don't even need to believe it is true. You just need to listen and to understand that a different explanation for how things are, than the way you have been believing they are, is possible. The big picture is so much bigger, it is so much more profound and so much more complex than your current understanding if you stop and contemplate the details as they are presented, you won't live long enough to get to a full transformative comprehension of this story. Just listen and somewhere along the way, you will step up to a higher realization which will be a way to look at things that is more conducive to harmony, happiness and prosperity."

"Alright, I can do that," Bunzy says.

"Are you ready to run through this story, front to back, and burst into a new world?" Rinpoche asks Bunzy and Isabel.

"Sounds exciting," Bunzy says. "I can't wait. I'm already filled with questions, but okay, let's go."

Isabel adds, "Yes. Me too. Let're rip Tilopa. I can't wait to hear this story after your mighty buildup."

Rinpoche begins, "The Dream Key was last seen by humans thousands of years ago in the area of the Tigris and Euphrates Rivers in the Middle East."

"Wait! You mean you don't have a dream key in your pocket?" Bunzy asks.

Rinpoche stops. He stares hard at Bunzy. Then he asks, "Are you going to listen or are you going to keep interrupting me?"

"Sorry. I'm just so excited, I forgot myself. Go on with your story. Please."

Rinpoche continues, "The Dream Key was administered by a dedicated group of saints known as the Masters of Dream. This waking world where we live is an amazing opportunity because it allows spirits to have material experiences such as eating chocolate, swimming in tropical seas, or making sweet love. Billions of ethereal beings want to come here, but there is a problem. The experience of living in this place is exhausting. After being here for a few hours, we must go back to Source and be re-energized and re-harmonized. You call this process sleep. The Dream Key allowed people to enter the dream realms and become re-balanced and re-energized whenever they needed. They didn't have to wait to go to sleep. They could be fully re-connected, re-built and re-charged anytime, at will. In the dream realm we are closer to Source and we can manifest anything that we can imagine whenever we imagine it."

"Wow!" Bunzy exclaims. "Anything, anytime!"

"When the Masters of Dream possessed the Dream Key, Earth was a place of peace and prosperity, even the climate was mild. People were happy and productive. They lived meaningful lives of equality and respect. They knew that everything was alive, connected and sacred. Everything was treated with devotion. Whatever was done was done with the intention that it would benefit all. This was true not just for the waking world, but for all of the realms. People knew they were spirits having a material experience because they consciously spent much time in the dream lands and in other realms. Most in the known dimensions were in harmony.

"Then thousands of years ago a group of Archon Lords appeared in this world. They came from a place where beings were technologically very advanced, but they had lost their soul connection to communicate with the Divine. They were moved by a desire for gold and a lust to have their material wants satisfied immediately. The problems which you and I are contemplating arose because these Archons could only achieve their goals by controlling and manipulating the things which they could see with their limited understanding. They destroyed the Masters of Dream and stole the Dream Key. When they alone possessed the Dream Key so that only they could knowingly, easily cross over into the Dreamlands, they took control of peoples' minds and bodies. They restricted humans' thoughts to only those which the Archon lords can control. They shrunk peoples' perceptions to only five senses and limited those. They confined human creativity to producing what the Archons and their servants desire. People no longer know who they were or what they were or how to live independent of the Archons' thoughts.

"This first group of Archon pioneers brought their brothers and sisters and cousins and friends and associates to this world and taught their method of mind control to them. These early Archons became the great kings and lords who created the Serpent's Empire and humans became their servants.

"Darkness fell across the realms. Where there had once been peace and harmony, now there is a terrible struggle for survival. Only the Archon Lords prosper. Their technology and the Dream Key are the sources of their power. They have become very powerful and live long lives because they can constantly go to Source and renew their life force. They have made the rest of us slaves, with most of us confined to the stockyards which we call cities. There aren't many free-ranging humans left. With the Dream Key, the Archons hold the Dreamlands open in such a way they can go into the mind of anyone and create an idea which binds that person's concept of reality, so that, that person can only perceive what the Archon Lords want them to perceive. In fact, the majority of what we call our minds are actually receiving gadgets over which we receive their thoughts. Our real personal thoughts have been buried in a small still voice way in under endless mind chatter. They have given us their minds and deceived us into thinking that our minds are our minds. People's understanding is no greater than that which they are allowed to understand and that is only enough to allow them to be the servants of the Archon Lords.

"Think about that kind of power for a moment. Imagine that you are an employer and everything that you want your employees to do, they believe that they have decided to do themselves, or imagine you are a politician and the voters decide that they have made up their minds to support you, no matter how awfully you treat them, or think about what is possible if you are in a romantic relationship and the person you are interested in is someone who imagines you in every way that you want them to.

"The people receiving these ideas don't even think about where their ideas come from. They just accept them as their own. Not much creativity is left for people. You are allowed to know only enough to carry out your designated tasks, without ever seeing your restraints or knowing your true potential.

"Through this clever use of the Key, the Archon Lords also give people amnesia so you can't remember anything outside of the narrow band of consciousness in which you labor.

"But because all beings are small pieces of Source, they must go back to the Great All constantly to renew themselves. So, the Archon Lords can't entirely stop people from returning to the dream realms. If we don't return periodically, we go insane and die. So, the Archons have developed this clever ruse called sleep. In sleep people go back to Source and renew themselves, but when we wake up, most people can't remember where they have been or what they have been doing. This amnesia prevents people from understanding what is being done to us and rebelling.

"The Archon Lords have hidden the Dream Key from us. Even the Key's precious memory has been lost to most people and without this memory, how can harmony be re-established and how can we ever be free again? The Archons though can't control the Dreamlands. They are only controlling people's access to them and thus people's lives. This is the most important story that I could tell you and its truth offers a way to happiness. The Dream Key opens the door that leads to happiness. This was the secret that the Supreme Abbot passed on to me before he departed into the Bardo, and that is why Bunzy's quest is so important."

"If your story is true, then it is not only the most important story that you could tell us. It is also the most depressing one too," Isabel observes. "Bunzy would be trying to do something really important, but like I told him, something impossible."

"That is only the beginning of the story," Rinpoche says, "There is much more I want to tell you. The last ten thousand years have indeed been harsh and the tens of thousands of years before that were bad, but there is hope. The Supreme Abbot told me that someday a master will arise who will recover the Dream Key, return the people's memory, and re-establish harmony in the realms. He said that I should teach the way so others might know happiness may again be the birthright of all beings, not just of a few. The next part of the story is the interesting part. It is why I called Bunzy important. I believe he is the one spoke of by the Supreme Abbot."

"I can't wait to hear it," the pretty blond woman sitting beside Isabel says.

The audience's attention is suddenly captured by a tall, thin, white man running out onto the stage. He is wearing a flashy yellow suit. He has bleached blond hair. His hair dyeing job was done weirdly. The color is an unnatural platinum yellow. Black hair is showing all around the edges. In fact, his natural black hair appears as if it were cut with a dull hatchet and then partially sprayed with yellow chrome paint. He is wearing bright red running shoes that are about six sizes too big for him. While Rinpoche, Bunzy and Isabel have been talking the auditorium has filled. People start cheering when they see the clown-looking man. They cheer too.

The man shouts, "Ladies and gentlemen, welcome to the Dream Jam, a dramatic event which will take you beyond sound to the very deepest place of all. You are blessed to be here tonight. You will never be the same ever again. There is no way back from where we are about to go. Flee now or grab your seat and get ready to be amazed." Then more quietly, almost personally, he leans forward and says, "Ask yourself, 'Who is it that looks through my eyes?'" Then he jumps up, thrusting a fist into the air and shouts, "Get ready to know the answer. Get ready to see." More calmly, he explains, "Dream time music is a vibration that you feel. It is different than the music which you have known before tonight because in that other kind of music the musician makes a sound which you hear with your ears. Dream time music you listen to with your feelings, and I don't mean the kind of feeling that you do with your fingers. By feelings, I mean emotions, the feelings that you experience in your gut, in your heart. Hunter Gandhi who will come out here in a moment, will not be playing a traditional musical instrument. He will be playing your feelings with his feelings. We exist in a sea of vibrations and our experiences depend on how we interpret these vibrations. A dream musician influences our interpretations directly. As he uses his feelings to influence our feelings, we envision experiences which evoke strong emotions in us."

"So, prepare for the show! The play that you are about to participate in is not going to unfold on this stage in front of you or on a screen that we are going to roll down. It is going to unfold inside of you. This is going to be a total immersion event starring you. You may become confused. You may think that you are spacing out and attempt to refocus your attention. Don't! That's the event! You will be in it. You will be the main character in the story that is about to burst into your world. Relax. Just flow along with what's happening. Enjoy yourself. Life is about to get more interesting. Get ready to jump the Channel Normal train tracks and head off into the unknown. Put your hands together to welcome Hunter Gandhi who has come all of the way from India for our pleasure."

He throws his hands extravagantly towards the right side of the stage, bows slightly and starts backing slowly toward the left side as he shouts, "Action! Roll'em Hunter!"

As people cheer enthusiastically, a handsome, slender, dark-skinned, young man wearing traditional white cotton peasant clothes walks bare foot out onto the stage. He is carrying two polished, dark wooden chests with glowing brass hinges and locks. He sets the boxes down on the stage in front of a prayer mat that has already been rolled out onto the stage. The mat is colorful with intricate ancient magical symbols woven into it. He smiles, bows with his hands in a prayer position in front of his chest which calms the audience, and then sits down cross-legged on the mat behind the wooden chests. The bottom box is about three feet long and a foot tall and a foot wide. It has an array of switches, knobs, and dials which Ghandi adjusts then pushes a button. He sets the smaller, darker box on the stage to his right, opens it and from it he takes two crystal balls which glow and pulse. Holding a ball in each hand, he gazes out into the audience and announces, "Showtime."

He starts by asking, "Remember that movie that we're making, the one about the giant spiders that are taking over the world?"

As he talks, Bunzy feels as if he's sinking away from his forehead into the back of his head. His eyes roll upwards. His awareness falls down behind him.

He's walking on a street in a movie set in sunny California with his co-star Robert. The scene is a shabby neighborhood street in England in 1887. The houses are worn old brownstone three story walk-ups. It is a foggy dreary grey afternoon. Robert and Bunzy are dressed like gentlemen. Robert wears a dark topcoat and bowler. Bunzy has on a black cape. There aren't any other people on the street. A spider trap crosses the sidewalks and cobblestone street ahead of them. The trap is about forty feet tall with two round black metal legs which are thicker than a man. It's shaped like a square upside-down U. The spider smashing foot which is hanging in the center of the top of it, is ten feet tall and thirty feet wide and shaped like a gum drop, round at the top and flat on the bottom. This stomper is poised like the arm on a set giant mousetrap, ready to smash any marauding spiders.

"That thing certainly looks deadly," Bunzy observes. "I don't think that I want to have anything to do with it. How can we get around to the other side of that trap without walking through its stomper?"

"You know Bunzy, these traps only smash killer spiders. They don't crush people. They are perfectly safe."

"I don't believe that, that gadget, can tell the difference between people, spiders, or dogs. It looks like a nasty killing machine that stomps everything that passes under it including the neighborhood kids. I don't like it. There must be a better way to deal with those monstrous spiders that are causing so much trouble. How can that machine tell a spider from anything else?"

"Those machines have spider sensing receptors built right into them."

"Robert, I don't know if I can trust you to know what you're talking about," Bunzy says. "You've been acting pretty weird lately and drinking a lot."

"I'm under a lot of pressure," Robert tells Bunzy. "I put all of my family's money in that mill in the East End and it failed. These spider traps are my last hope. My wife emptied our bank accounts, took the kids, and left me. I don't feel very good about myself. Things haven't been working out very well lately. I just don't see any good options for me, and I've looked. I've really, really tried hard, but I just can't get things to work. I'm a failure. There's no hope. There's nothing that I can do about it. These traps are my last hope. I've invested the last little bit of money that I could scrape up into the company that makes them, and I think that you should invest in them too. Go ahead. Give it a try. After you've tried it, you'll want in on the company's stock too."

"Why don't you walk through it if you believe in it so strongly?" Bunzy asks.

"Don't be frightened. These things are foolproof. They are going to save the world. You'll see."

"Okay. I'll tell you what. I'll walk through the darn contraption, if you'll walk through it with me. I believe in you."

Bunzy and Robert walk into the device. SNAP! The big metal gum drop plunges down and smashes Bunzy flat.

The technical crew rushes over, disarms the trap, and rolls the heavy metal plunger over. Bunzy's body is on the bottom of it crushed like a bug on the bottom of a size thirteen boot.

Bunzy stands a few feet away from the crew, beside Robert, watching therm work. When Bunzy sees his destroyed body, he screams at Robert, "You're wrong! You just got me killed! And where's your body?"

"I'm sorry man," Robert tells him, and seems to be sincerely sad.

The two of them start drifting upwards.

Pondering what just happened, Bunzy says, "I don't remember this in the script."

"No. This isn't part of the movie. You really did just get killed," Robert informs him.

"What are you talking about?" Bunzy shouts. "I didn't see your mutilated body under that ugly piece of iron, but you're floating along with me. How can this not be part of the movie? You're an actor right along with me and you're floating right beside me."

"Yes, I know. I was already dead. It took a lot of energy for me to act like who I used to be, but I was lonely. I need you. Sorry. I got drunk and shot myself three days ago.

Bunzy panics. He's confused. He starts slipping into shock.

By this time, they're a couple of thousand feet in the air. They come to a big stump with roots sticking out from the side of a cliff. Stump and cliffs drift in the sky. Bunzy and Robert land on a knarly root platform. Bunzy immediately scampers away from the edge of the platform and puts his back against the rock bluff.

"This can't be real. It's all part of the movie," Bunzy guesses.

"I don't know how this is being done, but we're not up in the air," Bunzy concludes.

Then Bunzy shouts at Robert, "And I'm not dead."

"Yes, we are," Robert assures Bunzy. "We are in the sky, and we are dead."

There are an apple and a screwdriver lying on this platform. Robert picks them up, stands, steps out onto the edge of the platform, and drops them over the side.

Bunzy quickly leans out, not clear to the edge, but there's a hole through the roots and he looks down through it. By this time the screwdriver and apple are hundreds of feet below them and falling away fast. He suddenly has a tremendous sense of vertigo. He leans back when he realizes this is real.

Those things just fell a long ways, really fast. This isn't some 3-D movie effect. This is real, he thinks. Then he wonders, but how did I get up here? I have the belief that I floated up here and yet I have an equally strong belief that if I fall over the side, I will fall to a sudden painful death.

Robert is standing on a root right on the edge of the bluff. If he leans out, he could fall, but he has no fear of falling, because he believes that he can't fall. Bunzy believes he can fall and yet he knows he can't. Nothing is as it seems. Bunzy can't reconcile his beliefs with what is happening. Something is wrong. Something is really very wrong with his idea of what is real. He can't square his beliefs about the nature of reality with what is happening.

Someone who is sitting beside him is shaking his arm. Looking to his right, Bunzy stares into the face of Rinpoche. Rinpoche asks, "Are you here Bunzy? The Dream Jam is over."

Bunzy is soaked in sweat. He shakes. He grinds his teeth. White foam accumulates at the corners of his mouth. Rinpoche drops his arm.

"That was intense," Bunzy says and attempts a weak smile at Isabel.

Rinpoche adds, "Life is a dream."

"Yeah, but your trite little saying doesn't mean anything," Bunzy says in a combative manner. He suddenly feels very attached to his body. "Life's real when you are here in a real body." He thumps his chest. "This is a real body, not a dream body."

"What's the difference?" Rinpoche asks.

"A real body isn't a fantasy body. When a dream body is hurt, it doesn't really matter because you wake up and forget about it. The next night you get a new body. If you get a finger cut off of this waking body, that finger is gone forever."

"How do you know that, that isn't true also for the dream body?"

"I just had a dream in which my dream body got smashed and I'm still here in my waking body and when I go to sleep tonight I'll be in another dream body in a completely different dream world. Whereas if I were killed in a car wreck in this waking world body, I would never ever again be in this world in this body."

"You're never going to be in that dream body that you died in, in that other world either."

"Yes, but that doesn't matter because that's not the point from which everything is being generated. I'm generating everything from this body, in this world. This is the central world, the one from which all of the dreams emanate. So, as long as I have this body, dreams will continue to come from here. Whereas if I lose this body, all emanations will cease. That makes this the most essential moment of beingness and the most important point of consciousness. This is the center of everything."

"Well then, the important thing is to determine where this central point of consciousness is and what the nature of this situation is. Right?"

"Yes."

"You're assuming that the waking world is the central world and that existence is temporal. Right?" Rinpoche asks.

"Yes. That's right," Bunzy tells him.

"Well then we really need to examine the waking world and understand it," Rinpoche concludes.

"Yes, I agree," Bunzy says.

As they rise to leave, Rinpoche asks, "Why don't you come visit me at the Naropa Yoga Center overlooking the Umpqua River in the beautiful Oregon Coast Range. It's not far from here. I'm sure that you would have a wonderful experience there. And Isabel won't you come too?"

"Thank you for the invitation," Bunzy responds. "I think I will come for a visit."

"I don't think that you understood the deep implications of the story that I told you," He looks Bunzy searchingly in the eyes and says seriously, "You didn't react with the large amount of outrage and shock that you should have if you grasped what I have revealed to you."

Isabel smiles at Rinpoche and says, "Master Rinpoche, I take very seriously what you have said, and I think that a visit to your Yoga Center would be lovely."

Rinpoche smiles and bows slightly to her, then he hands Bunzy a pamphlet with directions to the Center and a small pretty bag which has been hand woven from bright yellow, pink and sky-blue yarn.

Bunzy pulls the drawstrings open at the top of the bag and shakes an ancient jade jaguar's face into his palm.

Rinpoche says, "I am giving you this very precious gift. It is a vehicle which will get you safely to the Naropa Yoga Center. When you wish to journey to me or when you think about me, do this ritual which I am going to describe. Get a drum such as is used in shamanic drumming ceremonies. Hang the jade jaguar around your neck so that it falls against your breast. Begin drumming and chanting. Chant for at least twenty minutes. If you are traveling towards me, don't journey for more than two hours without stopping and doing this ceremony again for at least twenty more minutes. Repeat this ceremony every two hours. If you are in a place where you can and if you feel like it, you can dance around in a circle doing a simple toe/heel step. This ritual will place you in dream-time space. This is necessary to keep you from being observed by the Archons. It will also block their mind sendings. If you don't do it, you will be led astray."

Bunzy is speechless. The carving that he's holding in his hand is obviously a priceless ancient artifact. He just says, "Thank you."

Rinpoche smiles and bows slightly to Bunzy.

He shakes Isabel's hand and they smile at each other like old friends who have just had the best time ever. Then he turns and leaves.

Isabel hugs Bunzy. She takes his arm. They leave too following Rinpoche out of the Hope Center.

CHAPTER 2
BUNZY'S BAD CHOICES

"The eyes are useless when the mind is blind."

Terence McKenna

On Sunday morning as she sips her morning Americano coffee in their breakfast nook, Isabel asks Bunzy, "Are you going to go to the Naropa Yoga Center and visit Tilopa?"

"Nah, I don't want to go see that crazy old, touchy feely, Chinese dude. I like stuff that's real."

"I would kind of like to go see Rinpoche and his place. And he's not Chinese. He's Tibetan. Quit being such a racist fool."

"Well, whatever he is, he's creepy and weird and I don't want to have anything to do with him. I don't believe his story and I don't believe in whatever strange techniques he wants to teach us."

"Bunzy, you are even stupider than I thought. No Archon worth two grains of salt and a raven would ever consider you to be a threat. So, what are you going to do?"

"I'm going to do things right. I'm going to do them the American way."

"Oh God, I think I'm going to be sick. Rinpoche gave you a valuable object and you said you'd go visit him."

"Yeah well, thanks but no thanks. I want to do things based on real hard American facts. I want to do things that scientifically make sense, none of that hippy flippy bullshit. I'm not going to get all paranoid and start imagining that some extra-dimensional Aliens are out to get me because I'm the One. Besides, some important games are being broadcast today, and I want to watch them."

"Bunzy, if you got any more normal, you'd turn into dirt, and I could plant my vegetable garden in you

"Uhhhh, thanks, I think. What do you believe we should do?"

"I think that what Tilopa said makes sense and his story about the Dream Key and Archons was intriguing. He is a genuinely good person, and we should go visit him."

"Alright, we'll go see him if everything I try fails. Otherwise, it's sayonara Bozo."

"People like you are mad with technology. You're just going to go into the library and stare at your big screen, two hundred channel demon box and fill yourself with mind parasites and beer. People don't talk directly to other people anymore, much less go for a walk and commune with nature. Dreaming is simple. It's like slipping beneath the waves while swimming."

"Maybe. What are you going to do?"

"I'm going to lay out my shoes in the front room and take pictures of them with that SLR camera you bought me."

"Take pictures of shoes?"

"Yes. Is there something wrong with that?"

"No. It's just something that had never occurred to me. I think it's a great idea. I can't wait to see what you do with that concept. You constantly surprise me. I guess that is one of the reasons I love you so much. Jazz says that we should try to surprise ourselves. I don't need to surprise myself when I'm around you. You'll do it for me."

"Jazz should mind his own business. Have fun with your dream research. Remember, a dream is only as good as what you do with it."

"I'm not sure what that means, but thanks. I'm going to start on my studies right now. See you later."

Bunzy leaves the table and goes into their library.

It doesn't take long for the books about dreaming to bore him. He checks his email. There's a message from his old college buddy Huey Gwyther. Their friend Fred Ackley was killed yesterday in a freak automobile accident. Fred was their political activist friend. In college he went to all of the anti-war events. He belonged to a bunch of political organizations and a couple of political parties. Lately he had been working against the new free trade agreement between the United States and several Asian nations the transnational corporations were trying to get the government to enact. He informed Huey and Bunzy that every free trade agreement lowered American working peoples' standard of living while making the rich few even richer. Fred was also actively trying to get the immigration quotas for the United States reduced to zero. He told them the US is now the third most populous nation in the world, behind only China and India. He argued that big immigration quotas were leading to low wages, poverty, and environmental degradation in America.

"We have enough people!" Fred once shouted at Bunzy.

It seems that Fred had been at a conference on trade agreements in Central Oregon. On his way home driving through the Cascade mountains, his car, for some reason, went straight ahead on a sharp curve. It plunged over a cliff into a deep ravine. Fred was killed instantly. The accident was especially odd because he was a very careful, sober man and always drove new well-maintained vehicles. Fred was happily married with two wonderful children and he had a good job. He was quite successful and well respected.

Bunzy emails Huey, "Sorry to hear about Fred's accident. He was a good man."

Then Bunzy watches some television, but even with a whole lot of channels he can't find anything interesting to watch. So, he downloads the newest, just released action thriller movie. He watches it for a while. It's pretty good, but he loses interest. Some important games are being televised, but nothing is happening in any of them that he finds worth watching. He goes over to the news and checks it out. There is the threat of another war, and the US needs some financial reforms or else there is going to be some kind of terrible economic disaster. It's the same old news. A lot of robberies, violence, rapes, disasters and bad weather splash across the screen. Some movie stars and sports idols are doing rotten things. Bunzy thinks it's all kind of interesting for a little while. Finally, he drinks and plays video games for a couple of hours. Then he remembers his interest in dreaming. It's hard to pull out of game world virtual reality, but he does and goes shopping online. He buys a sleepwalking mat. According to the advertisement, the way to consciously get into a dream is to stay aware while falling asleep. The conscious sleepwalker will then be aware that they are dreaming and can go wherever they want to go.

While Bunzy is waiting for the sleepwalking mat to be delivered, he starts following the adventures of A.E. VanWatt. In an article in Scientific World Magazine, A.E. explains the theory of the dream barrier. According to VanWatt, there is a membrane between the waking world and the dream world. If a person goes fast enough, they will break through the dream barrier, much like an airplane breaks through the sound barrier. He explains that all things are being expressed as a particular frequency which he says is another way of saying speed. Light shines at a specific speed and in light we experience this reality. If one wishes to experience a different world then they need to be vibrating at the frequency at which the things in that reality vibrate. So, one only has to increase or decrease the frequency at which their body is vibrating to match the frequency of the world that they wish to experience then they'll be there. One can do that by speeding up or slowing down the speed at which their body is oscillating. When you do this, A.E. says, you'll move through the veil between the worlds and start experiencing what is being expressed in that other world at that other frequency. A.E. claims this is what you do with your mind when you go sleep, but your sleeping body continues to vibrate at this world frequency, so it stays here. A.E. is building a capsule which will change the frequency of anything that is in it. He has a stock company called AWAKE which is building this machine. The module is close to being ready to operate. A.E. VanWatt is set to become the world's first physical oneironaut. There are lots of AWAKE videos of VanWatt and other scientists explaining how the dream capsule works and showing off the chamber and the launch site which is on an island in the Caribbean.

Bunzy thinks, *what a great idea! I can't wait to buy a ticket on the Dream Line Express and then to shoot across to the dream of my choice. I'll buy some stock in the company and sign up for the AWAKE newsletter.*

Bunzy's busy all week trying to make enough money to help pay their bills, but on Thursday night, he realizes that the dream mat hasn't arrived yet and the weekend is almost here. He wants to do something on his dream project this weekend, so he books a ride on the dream boat on Sunday night.

It turns out that the dream boat isn't a boat at all. It's a bed in a sleep center research facility at the Sisters of Mercy Medical Center.

As he lies on a narrow, high bed on a cold Sunday night with nurses smearing gel on the ends of electrodes and then taping them to his head and chest, Dr. McManus explains, "There are only four different states of consciousness which a human can be in at any one time. When you go to sleep, you sink down into one of those states of mind. In that state you can slip through a portal into a dream world. This happens several times each night. You normally don't have any control over where you go or how long you're there. You don't even control how many trips that you take each night and you don't remember any of this. The entrance to the dream worlds is through your waking body. All that you have to do to activate the opening is to relax your grip on the waking world and you'll slip out of this world and into a dream world. Imagine that you are a shipwrecked sailor who is holding onto a piece of driftwood with all of your strength. When your strength runs out, you lose your grip on the piece of wood and slip beneath the waves, but instead of drowning, you slip into a whole new world. You don't die. You enter a wonderful adventure in a beautiful place, or you have a nightmare. After your adventure, you resurface rested and ready to go in this reality. You are staying up here in this waking world which you perceive as a solid, secure, and known world only through great effort. As soon as your concentration wanders, you slide out of this world and into another. We here in the Sleep Center are going to control that process for you. We have developed a way to take you where you want to go. When you are relaxed enough and ready to cross over, we will know by watching our computer screen and reading our printouts in an adjoining control room. You see, in only one of those four states of consciousness which I told you about, will you be ready to dream. We are going to monitor your state of mind with that machinery over there," he gestures towards a big array of electronic equipment along the wall. "When we see that you are in dream readiness, we will stimulate the place in your brain where your dream memories are stored with a mild electric shock. This will jolt your dream memory. At the same time that we stimulate your dream memory, we are going to start flashing red lights in your eyes under the dream mask which my assistants are putting on you now. The flashing red lights are to alert your conscious mind that you are dreaming."

Bunzy looks like the Lone Ranger in a hospital gown on Dr. Frankenstein's laboratory table.

Dr. McManus continues, "When you perceive flashing red lights, you will have to go into your dream memory and strongly visualize that brightly lit tent in that hay field. This is the backdoor to re-entering a dream. From the dream memory you will find yourself back in your dream body in that dream tent. When your consciousness starts to change out of the dream state, we will know that you are slipping out of the dream and we will immediately wake you up and record your memory of what just happened to you. That way the memory of the dream won't disappear as you wake up. Are you ready?"

"Let's do it," Bunzy responds.

"Relax and go to sleep then," McManus tells him.

The Doctor and his assistants turn the lights down and leave the room.

Bunzy finds it difficult at first to relax in this strange room on this hard bed and he can't move much with all of these wires hooked to him, but after a while he gets bored and drifts away.

Bunzy is sitting at his and Isabel's dining room table talking to his buddy, Johnny Jones. It's a big twelve-person table. There is a big screen television set across the room from them with a documentary on the aurora borealis flashing red lights across the screen. Bunzy thinks, *that's odd. I thought that the Northern Lights were more fluorescent greens and blues rather than reds, but this show is all reds.*

Johnny and Bunzy ignore the show. They are sitting at the end of the table near a sliding glass patio door. It's noon on a sunny day. Johnny sits in a captain's chair at the end of the table. Bunzy sits in a guest chair at the side of the table with his back to a large window adjoining the glass doors. He's barefooted wearing blue jeans and a navy-blue pullover. They're discussing envisioning things like when one is meditating and their teacher instructs them to imagine a beautiful dakini of clear light in front of them.

Bunzy says, "I can't do that. I just don't have the ability to visualize something really well."

"I can," Johnny responds. "I can create a hologram of you in my mind right here, right now and make it so real that I can introduce it to yourself."

"I just don't have that ability. That is a real gift being able to see things that powerfully. I wish that I could do it too. Can you show me how to do it?" Bunzy wants to know.

"Sure," Johnny says, "I'll create a hologram of you right here," he gestures at an empty space on his left and to Bunzy's right, "and introduce the vision of you to you right now. Ready?" Johnny smiles.

"Sure," Bunzy returns his smile. "Go for it," Bunzy tells him.

Johnny turns to his left and concentrates. There is a shimmer in the air in front of him. In the flickering light an image of Bunzy stands looking at Johnny. The image stabilizes and becomes solid. It is wearing a blue plaid shirt, khaki pants, and sandals; but it's Bunzy, for sure. Johnny says to the essence that is standing between them, "Let me introduce you to yourself," and he points at Bunzy.

Bunzy stares up at the hologram with his mouth open. When Johnny said he could realistically envision something, Bunzy didn't expect to be able to see Johnny's imagining.

Bunzy's other glances over at him, does a double-take, and stares hard at him. The hologram slowly feels his body, then looks back at Johnny and asks him while pointing at Bunzy, "That's me?" Bunzy and Johnny can see that the hologram is astonished. It was surprised to be here, but it is astounded even more to be looking at itself sitting there staring back in wonder.

Johnny answers, "That's you buddy."

The vision reaches down with his left hand and picks up an antique ornate metal hand mirror from a lamp stand that is between Bunzy and the hologram, but to Bunzy's right and the hologram's left.

Johnny flinches and seriously stares at the figure. Bunzy can clearly see by Johnny's facial expressions that they both thought they were imagining this image. They both imagined this vision was a hypnotic creation of Johnny's mind. But no, this thing has a mind, a body, and a separate world of its own. It's independent of them. Bunzy knows

Johnny didn't intend for the creation to pick up that mirror, but it just did. It has a mind of its own, or some type of consciousness. The vision looks in the mirror. Johnny looks past it into the mirror too.

Johnny's creation says, "I'm not here."

"Wait!" Johnny shouts and picks up a camera from the end of the table between Bunzy and Johnny.

"Let me take your picture," he commands.

The apparition's hand with the mirror falls to the image's side. He slowly turns to Johnny and says, "Pictures, mirrors, they all do the same thing. I know now. You've showed me a lot. I don't want to be a dream anymore." It disappears.

Standing there holding the camera, Johnny looks at Bunzy.

He says, "I was looking in that mirror too. There was no reflection of him in the mirror. I was there, but he wasn't. When he didn't see his image in the mirror, he woke up. He knew that he was a spirit out of body."

"What are you saying? What do pictures and mirrors do? What did he mean?" Bunzy asks Johnny.

"Did you make it Bunzy?" Dr. McManus asks.

"What?" Bunzy responds.

A nurse is removing the sleep mask from Bunzy's eyes. Dr. McManus is speaking to him.

"No, Doctor. I was just in my dining room talking to my friend, Johnny Jones. I guess I got lost. I can remember it all though."

"Sorry. This dream work we're doing is experimental. If you would like, we can try again."

"No," Bunzy tells him. "I'm exhausted and confused. I have to go to work in the morning. Thanks though. I have enough to think about. You were great. This whole experience was great. I sincerely appreciate your help, but I need to go home now."

They unwire Bunzy, unstrap him, record his dream, and he leaves.

After a night's sleep from which he remembers nothing, the dream mat finally arrives. It's bigger than Bunzy expected. It's a combination of a Persian carpet mounted on a tread mill with a clock and a computer in an impressive control panel.

Bunzy and Isabel set it up next to his bed.

While they are constructing it, Isabel asks, "Hey, did you hear that the Green Party President in Bolivia was killed in an airplane accident?"

"Who?" Bunzy inquires.

Raising her voice, Isabel tells him, "You know, the guy who was battling the multinational mining companies for better working conditions and wages for their employees."

"No, I didn't hear about that," Bunzy says. "That's too bad. He seemed like a genuinely courageous and decent man who was trying to help his people. What happened?"

"He was flying to a conference on species extinction in Brazil where he was going to make the keynote address. It was rumored that he was going to deliver some new information that was going to be a real bombshell. His plane exploded, then crashed into some rugged mountainous terrain. Authorities say they think there was a problem with the fuel system. Did you know we are in the biggest die off of species on this planet since the dinosaurs disappeared?"

"Yes, I've heard. It's too bad the guy didn't get to deliver his speech. I'm going to bed. See you in the morning."

"Later."

It's about ten o'clock at night when Bunzy steps onto the carpet. The rug has all kinds of occult designs sewn into it, mythical creatures and mystical Eastern symbols coming out of and returning back into each other. The carpet creates a vortex of magic as it goes around. The computer starts softly playing nature sounds: water, birds, the wind. Every fifteen minutes a husky woman's voice announces, "This is a dream."

Bunzy begins walking. He walks and walks, on and on, lost in his thoughts. The carpet rolls on through a jungle by the sea, over mountains, through deserts and back to the sea.

Bunzy is startled awake by the Sun shining in his face through the glass doors in his bedroom.

He thinks, *I must have tumbled into bed and fallen into a deep unconscious sleep. I don't remember anything after walking on the carpet for a while. This didn't work at all. None of these sure-fire, high tech, new-fangled things are working. I'm just getting more confused.*

Wandering into the breakfast nook, Isabel greets him, "I don't think that AWAKE stock you bought is going to pay off very well. Maybe you should dump it."

She is reading the business section in the paper. Bunzy thinks she appears to be enjoying herself far more than she usually does when she looks in a newspaper, especially in the business section.

"Why?" Bunzy asks.

"A. E. and AWAKE's money have evaporated," she tells him.

Bunzy looks like a buffalo that's just discovered a pack of wolves in a thicket by the herd. He feels out the situation asking Isabel, "What do you mean by evaporated?"

"Poof! Gone." Isabel claps her hands together, opens her eyes wide, and looks at him.

"What does that article say?" Bunzy growls.

"A. E. got into the dream capsule yesterday. The technicians fired up the launch machinery. A green fog appeared in the room. It was especially dense around the module which was shaking and vibrating violently. A film of electronic fire started dancing on the metal which covers the module. Lightening flashed from the metal skin of the capsule to other metal objects in the control room which caused various electronic machines along the walls to start smoking. Then there was a blinding flash and the capsule and A.E. were gone, leaving behind some trailing smoke and a strong ozone odor. Other machines in the room exploded and burst into flames. After the technicians got the fires out, they started frantically trying to get more machinery to replace the blown-up electronics so they could begin searching for A.E. They discovered the company is out of cash and its credit is exhausted. A.E. is gone and the money is gone too. They both vanished into thin air."

Bunzy sits down heavily and numbly stares at her.

"My life just isn't working out at all," he states. "I have a sense that what I am doing is like watching the news. It's always the same bad news over and over, keeping us viewers upset about things we can't or at least we aren't going to do anything about. I'm just spinning around in circles like a puppet on a string wasting time on imbecilic dramas. None of these modern technological methods I've been trying out, are working. The best educated minds in this world fall far short of a useful explanation. None of the videos, podcasts, television shows, or movies that I've watched have helped me. I don't understand what's happening. This isn't over though. We're not done. I'm going to go see Tilopa. Would you like to come?"

"Good decision," Isabel answers. "I'm behind you one hundred and ten percent. Yes. I'm coming with you. But I thought you didn't believe Rinpoche's story."

"I don't. I still think he's delusional or running some kind of con game on us, but he's making the best offer we've got."

"Plus, he's a nice guy living in a fun place," Isabel adds.

"Yeah, that too," Bunzy admits.

CHAPTER 3
MAYBE IT ISN'T AS IT SEEMS

"To understand is to transform what is."

Jedu Krishnamurti

"It's late and we've gotta get going if we are going to get there before dark," Isabel warns.

"I'm ready. Let's go." Bunzy grabs his bags and heads for the car. They have a long journey ahead of them.

As they walk towards the Jeep, Bunzy starts seeing glowing caterpillar-like lights crawling across his vision. When he tries to read the logo on the Jeep, he can only see the J and the P. The center of his vision has disappeared. He's dazed and wandering.

Isabel notices that something's wrong with him and asks, "Are you alright?"

"No," Bunzy tells her. "I won't be able to drive. When I look directly at something, all that I see is a dark, blank spot. I can see by looking sideways at things, but I can't see by looking directly at them. My mind isn't working very well either. I can't think straight. I definitely shouldn't drive. There is a loud ringing in my ears and I've become disoriented and nauseous."

As they discuss Bunzy's strange sudden illness and whether or not they should continue on their trip, or go to an urgent care clinic, or if Bunzy should maybe just go in the house and lie down, Isabel's cell phone rings.

After she hangs up, she says, "That was Julie from work. Laurie was suddenly attacked by a terrible pain in her abdomen. Her husband has come and gotten her, and they have gone to an urgent care clinic. The store is going to be closed if I don't come in right away. I have to go now. Are you going to be alright?"

Bunzy says, "Uhmmm, I think so. It's just some kind of bad headache. I have to go lie down for a while."

He dazedly wanders back to the house. He can't think clearly enough anymore to even discuss his pain with her. She leaves.

When she comes home after work, they cancel their trip.

After working for a few weeks and not discussing anything that happened to them when they tried to go to Rinpoche's place, there is a long holiday. On Thursday morning, the first day of their vacations, they look at each other and without saying anything, Bunzy puts on the jade jaguar. Isabel gets the drum and they start drumming and chanting.

After chanting for half an hour, Isabel asks, "So, we've decided to go see Rinpoche?"

Bunzy answers, "Yes."

They haven't unpacked their bags from their earlier attempt to visit Rinpoche. They throw them in the car and quickly leave.

First, they drive on the Freeway for a couple of hours. Then they head west through the mountains driving towards the Pacific Ocean. After another half hour of turning through tight rocky canyons with fir trees surging upwards and water tumbling down through smooth round grey boulders, the glowing worms start crawling across Bunzy's vision again. He can't concentrate or drive any further. He pulls over on a wide spot beside the Umpqua River. Isabel quickly gets out the drum and starts drumming and chanting. Bunzy does his best to chant along with her. After ten or fifteen minutes, his vision begins to get better, and his mind starts to clear. They drum and chant together for another half hour. They have two quarts of freshly squeezed green vegetable juice with them. Isabel pours Bunzy a cup. He drinks it. That helps too. Then they hurry on to Rinpoche's ashram.

They both now believe there is a connection between trying to see Rinpoche and the attacks against their health. It's mysterious and frightening, but it's happening, and they don't dare discuss it for fear they will cause another attack.

When they reach the Yoga Center, a dozen brightly painted ten-foot-tall prayer wheels which are rotating slowly and being spotlighted in the evening twilight, greet them.

Barely seen, a statue of Padmasambhava meditates among a field of twenty-foot-tall stupas. Rinpoche's reception hall glows in the dark beside a pond filled with singing frogs. A light rain falls.

In the great hall a hundred initiates are droning hypnotic prayers in a ceremony. "TSOG ZHING NAM RANG LA T'HIM PAR MO."

Bunzy and Isabel's souls soar on the mystical vibrations. They stop at the Treasure Warehouse, the Center's store, to get oriented.

"Hello. Welcome to the Naropa Yoga Center. How may I assist you?" a short, dark, pretty, young woman in blue jeans and a colorful shirt greets them from behind a counter stacked almost to her chin with books, jewelry, art, and prayer flags. "My name is Robin."

"Hi Robin. We want to join the practice in the great hall. What do we need?" Isabel asks.

"The only thing that you really need is a copy of the prayers which are being chanted, but even those aren't really necessary at first because everything is hard to follow when you are new to Tibetan Buddhist practices, but the place to start is with booklets of the prayers and practices which are currently being chanted, plus a chuba, zen, and katak."

"Chuba, zen, and katak?" Isabel wonders.

"RANG NYID KAD CHIG GIY PAL CHEN DOR JE ZHON NU YUM."

"The chubas are on those shelves behind you. The zens are over there under the window and these are kataks," she points to packets of white clothes in various lengths in a big basket on the far-right side of the counter.

Isabel and Bunzy turn towards the shelves behind them. They stare at stacks of maroon cotton and silk cloth. Their confusion is obvious.

Robin explains, "Chubas are long wrap around skirts and zens are large shawls which are worn over the shoulder."

Bunzy is still confused. He asks, "Do men wear them?"

"Yes. Men and women both wear them," Robin informs him.

"Why?" He questions.

She politely explains, "When you enter sacred space it is good to dress differently than you normally do. Then your consciousness knows that it is going to do something different than it normally does. The chuba and the zen are worn over your ordinary clothes creating a new you from the old you. The katak is used to make offerings."

She takes a silk cloth about a foot wide and five feet long with sacred designs woven into it. She holds the cloth draped over her hands palms up shoulder width. The tasseled ends of the cloth fall down towards her knees.

"When you hold the katak like this you are making your intention clear to be of benefit to whomever or whatever you are making the offering to."

"I'm not comfortable with wearing a skirt," Bunzy says.

"I like the idea," Isabel contradicts him. "I think the zens are beautiful. We'll take two sets of all three plus prayer booklets."

Dressed in chubas and zens they enter the main hall and sit down on the floor in the lotus position placing their prayer booklets on little platforms on the floor in front of them. The prayer booklets are stacks of four inch by eight inch flip cards with writing on both sides. One just flips the cards to follow the chant. The words are written in Tibetan and then in English.

"DANG CHAY PA RAB TU BAR WAI GAR BYI TRIN MI ZAD PAR T'HRO WAI KUR GYUR."

"Listen, you forces of hindrance who lead us astray. Do not go against my command! Whatever dark forces go against this secret vajra command, the powerful great wrathful ones will burst the very source of your intellect into a hundred fragments. So, leave now! Flee!"

"HUNG HUNG HUNG SARWA BIGHANAN UTZ TSIK TRAYA P'HAT."

Two large drums hanging from frames are being beaten. Horns from one foot to eight feet long are blown periodically. The initiates have small double drums with stones in them held in one hand which they shake like rattles to punctuate certain statements and brass bells which they chime at other times in their other hand. Rinpoche is seated cross-legged on a raised platform in the middle of a side hall on the left leading the prayers. A tall thin young man wearing a chuba and an ornate zen walks back and forth with various sacred objects between Rinpoche on the left side and a colorful altar in a side hallway on the right side of the main hall. He is currently carrying a pot of sacred water with a feather plume in it with which he sprinkles blessings around the room. After the blessing, he takes an arrow with colored ribbons tied to it to Rinpoche on a katak. Rinpoche accepts the arrow, unrolls the ribbons, waves the arrow around in circles, then gives it back to the young man who takes it back to the altar. Next, he brings food offerings from the altar to Rinpoche who blesses them, then the young man takes them outside. Meanwhile colorfully costumed men and women dance slowly in a clockwise direction around the altar, which is in the smaller right side hall, pausing at the four cardinal points. All of the time, the chanting continues.

"SARWA TIKSHAN VAJRA DZOLA MAHA KRODHA RAKCHA RAKCHA HUNG HUNG HUNG."

Bunzy can't follow the Tibetan. So, he drifts along on the sound and reads the English verses. For him, the modern world melts away. His reasoning disintegrates. Thoughts disappear. Knowing something previously unknown fills his being. A powerful happiness surrounds Bunzy.

Isabel smiles at him.

When the chanting ends, everyone files slowly past Rinpoche for blessings and advice. Isabel and Bunzy join the end of the line. The room is hot. The line moves slowly. Everyone wants to speak to Rinpoche. He patiently advises and encourages each person who speaks to him.

When Bunzy and Isabel reach his seat, he looks both of them in the eyes, smiles, bows to them, then says, "Bunzy, Isabel, I am most pleased to see you again. Bunzy, I have been wanting to ask you, who benefits by your beliefs?"

"I don't know," Bunzy replies. "I haven't given that question any thought."

"Haven't you ever wondered about where the ideas that you believe, came from and how you acquired them?"

"The world as I know it was here when I was born. I have just chosen what I believe are the best explanations for what is happening and lived with those concepts."

"Bunzy, why do you think that butterflies exist? What is the meaning of the life of a butterfly? What can be expected of a butterfly that you could judge whether a butterfly's life was a success or a failure? Where do butterflies go when they die? Where does a butterfly's life come from? Where did that spark of butterfly consciousness originate? Do you think that butterflies stand around on flowers much of the day waving their wings and antennas, and discussing the purpose, meaning and importance of their lives? Do you think that butterflies want to become enlightened and get into Heaven or do you think they feel they are perfect the way they are? Answer me these questions and then tell me about humans and then about yourself."

"That's a strange tack that you are taking to ask me what I think is important," Bunzy says.

"Why do you want me to think of myself as an insect?" He asks.

"Because it is going to be hard to have a meaningful discussion with you when you are wrapped up in your self-importance. Therefore, I'm asking you to think of yourself as a bug to help us have perspective," Rinpoche explains.

"You're saying that I'm insignificant?" Bunzy asks.

"I am saying that you are like a precious, beautiful butterfly in a vast jungle. Remember chaos theory where because a butterfly flapped its wings in the jungle a tornado hit the prairies. A seemingly minor event can have large unforeseen consequences. Nothing is insignificant. Everyone and everything matters. Every thought is important. Stay with us awhile. Let's share some time enjoying each other's company."

"Alright," Bunzy agrees.

Rinpoche gestures to the tall young man on his left who is wearing the chuba and ornate zen. "This is John. He will explain how things work in our community and get you and Isabel a room. What do you say Isabel?"

"I think that this is a beautiful place. The feeling here is wonderful. I would very much enjoy visiting with you. Thank you for inviting us." She puts her hands together on her chest below her chin and bows to Rinpoche.

He smiles back at her, returns the gesture, says, "Namaste," stands and walks to an exit in the back of the room. Everyone who is still in the room stands and waits reverently until he departs the great hall.

"Okay, Bunzy, Isabel, let's get you two situated in a guest room. Follow me," John says after Rinpoche is gone.

As they leave the temple, they pass a room with several people sitting in front of a flame chanting.

"What are they doing?" Bunzy asks pointing at the chanting people.

"That is the sacred center of our community. There is at least one person chanting day and night before the eternal flame. They are holding this holy space open at all times."

The three of them walk on in silence.

John has a flashlight and leads them down a pathway through flower gardens, over a bridge, past the pond with the frogs and into the woods to a large natural wood building. Inside it there is a great room with a fireplace, bookcases full of books, and comfortable chairs and couches arranged in a semi-circle facing the wall with the fireplace built into it. The door to Bunzy and Isabel's room is in the wall behind the furniture. There are maybe ten rooms along this wall. Their room is a clean cozy, homey room with two beds, a chair, and a cupboard with dresser drawers. There is a window, but they pull the curtains closed.

"The men's bathroom and the women's bathroom are further down the hallway on your left," John tells them.

He points.

Then he continues, "Breakfast is from 7 to 8:30. At 8:30 we have a short meeting concerning community affairs and at that time you can decide how you want to fit into our community. The place where we gather to eat is in the building by where you parked your car. We call it the Dining Hall. Do you have any questions?"

Isabel replies, "No. This is all very nice John. You are a great host."

He smiles at her and leaves.

Bunzy and Isabel go get their bags and go to bed.

In the morning when it gets light, Bunzy gets up and opens the curtains. Isabel closed them the night before because she didn't know what was out there in the dark. They didn't want someone watching them while they were going to bed. That fear was totally unnecessary. Isabel and Bunzy are high in the air on the second floor of this big structure with the ground sloping steeply away from the building. Although they entered this hall on the uphill side of the building at ground level, their room is on the second floor on the downhill side. The mountains drop away from their room to a river that is half a dozen miles away. The shores of the river and the mountains are covered by a fir forest. There are no houses or roads to be seen. They are comfortably secluded in a wilderness. The mist coming off the river looks like a white Chinese dragon rising into Heaven. Isabel has gotten up and is standing beside Bunzy.

"It's beautiful," she says. "We are very lucky to be here."

"Yes," he agrees.

Breakfast is a lovely vegetarian buffet. Bunzy has a bowl of warm cereal with almond milk sweetened with organic raw pure cane sugar. He could use stevia or honey, but he chooses sugar. He also has a slice of fresh community baked bread with quince jam from the community orchard which they can see from their bedroom window. Then for a real treat Bunzy adds a slice of bread with peanut butter. He also has a couple slices of cheese and a cup of yerbe mate tea sweetened with honey from the community bee hives.

After breakfast there is a short meeting led by Sean, a senior community member, who discusses some issues that are of importance to the community for the day. Then he reads some inspirational verses from Rumi and closes the meeting.

Bunzy is introduced to Paul, the head gardener, and assigned to do service during the day as a gardener in the green houses. Isabel is given the service of helping Robin in the Treasure Warehouse. Bunzy doesn't know how this was decided, but both of these ways of giving service are matched perfectly to their individual inclinations.

On Bunzy and Paul's walk to the garden, Paul explains, "Members of our community arise early around five in the morning and either do a light and sound meditation or go to the Sacred Hall and chant before breakfast. We then do service until eleven when we again either chant in the Sacred Hall or meditate until lunch which is from twelve to one. At one o'clock we do service again until four when there is a rest period until dinner at six. At eight we have our major gathering of the day in which we gather together in the Sacred Hall and perform a ceremony like the one you attended last night."

Bunzy enjoys his service in the green houses. There are two of them, a big one and a small one. The big one is very large, maybe ninety feet wide and a hundred and fifty feet long. It is built of metal hoops with a double layer of clear plastic spread over the hoops. Air is pumped between these layers of plastic. This inch of insulating air keeps the temperature in each of the green houses comfortably warm. The front and back of the greenhouses are made of solid see through plastic. A sliding door in the big greenhouse is big enough to drive a garden tractor through. Plants are being started in the big greenhouse but there are also row after row of plants growing in the soil in the greenhouses. The community has a steady supply of fresh, organic, vegetarian food all year round.

Bunzy is given the task of mixing potting soil for sprouting seeds into small plants. Next, he takes spinach starts from starting trays in the big greenhouse and plants them in the ground in the small greenhouse. This is mostly social service. The workers work hard but they visit and discuss everything that interests them as they garden. Bunzy works with a crew of a dozen men and women. During the morning break when the others go off to chant and meditate, he goes back to his and Isabel's room, takes a short nap and then reads passages in a book from the community library called "Enlightenment Without Meditation". Then Isabel and Bunzy go to lunch which is another vegetarian feast. Isabel and Bunzy have fun visiting with the thirty or forty other people in the Dining Hall. Before going back to their jobs, Isabel and Bunzy help wash the dishes. Isabel is having a wonderful time in the store.

After the dishes are put away, Bunzy goes back to transplanting plants. During the afternoon, mostly he works by himself in the small greenhouse. His two co-planters have gone off to split wood for the fireplaces and stoves that heat all of the halls. The other gardeners stay in the big greenhouse.

During the afternoon break Bunzy continues reading the meditation book while sitting in the Sun on the hillside by the bee hives. Isabel comes by and they go for a stroll in the forest. Then they go to dinner and the evening service.

At the end of the service, Rinpoche suggests, "Let's go over to the Common Hall where your room is and sit by the fireplace. We can have a discussion."

They are both delighted by his suggestion because they have been wanting to talk with him. Bunzy and Isabel wait outside the Sacred Hall until Rinpoche has spoken with those who wish to speak with him and then the three of them walk together over to the Common Hall where they sit down in big overstuffed comfortable chairs by the fireplace. At first their conversation is very casual. Rinpoche discusses his early life in Tibet. Isabel talks about her life growing up on a farm in Garden Valley. Her father was a logger working long hours and her mother stayed at home and took care of their children. Isabel very much admired her grandfather who adored her and her brother and sister. She loved her mother and spent as much time with her as she could cooking, gardening, cleaning house, sewing, and taking care of the chickens.

Suddenly Rinpoche turns to Bunzy and asks, "Bunzy have you ever had an original thought?"

Bunzy considers the question and answers, "No. I don't think I have."

"Then that means that every thought you have ever had, has been planted in your mind. Who put those ideas there and where did the ones who put the ideas in you get those thoughts and why did they embed them in you?"

"I don't know either who or why. I don't think that anyone has ever asked me those questions before."

"Well, there you go. Something to think about, eh?"

"What should I consider?"

"Humans don't think. They aren't thinking creatures. They accept what they are told and act on the information without reflecting on it. This is important because what you believe that you see, you do see. Have you ever been to a hypnotist's show?"

"No."

"I have," Isabel says. "This hypnotist got people to eat onions and believe they were eating apples. He even got a man and his daughter to come up on the stage and then convinced the man that his daughter wasn't there. The man couldn't see his own little girl even though she was standing right in front of him. The hypnotist even held a watch behind the girl's back and the man read the time right through the little girl. It was amazing."

"Well, there you go," Rinpoche says. "Like that hypnotist, I am going to convince you that you are not seeing the world as it is. That is important for you Bunzy, because if you are going to succeed in your quest to find happiness, then we are going to have to change your understanding of this reality. You are going to have to change your beliefs and because we are all one, when you change your beliefs, the world will change."

"Okay. Where should I start?" Bunzy asks.

"This language that we are speaking is the material from which our prison walls are constructed. Each word represents a concept and each concept is a misguided message. Anyone who uses that thought will use it to construct a world view which is wrong. Then they will believe this wrong world view they have constructed and live trapped within it. They will be unable to have any other understanding because they live within their words and there are no longer words in this language for the correct world view. The words for the way out of the trap have already been eliminated from the slave languages by our masters. Without help, there are no ways to even think or conceptualize a free thought within the slave languages. English is the main prison language, but most of the still surviving languages are also captive people languages. So, we are doomed to thinking trivial thoughts. We can't confront our problems because we don't know what they are. It's time for you to make a change Bunzy. That is what this conversation is about."

"Hunh? What's it about?" Bunzy asks.

"The big picture," Rinpoche replies.

"The big picture?" Bunzy repeats.

"Yes. That's right," Rinpoche tells him. "When you hear someone speak, you are actually hearing a description of our prison walls from the inside. So, take a look around and describe our world and realize that every word that you write or speak, every thought that you think with a word, was put there as a brick in the wall of your prison. Every word that you were given in your education or in the media, whether it is of science, religion, or art, no matter how complex, high and transcendental it seems, is a brick in the wall. People are deluded and living in an illusion and that illusion is constructed of false concepts which are carried within the words of our languages. To get free we have to understand we're trapped in a limited way of perceiving. We're deluded and living in a delusion and this illusion is constructed of false concepts which are carried within the words of our languages. Have you ever thought up a new word?" Rinpoche asks Bunzy.

"No," Bunzy replies.

"So, every thought that you have ever had was already thought before you had it and that thought was put into your consciousness by some means outside of you, isn't that, right?" Rinpoche asks.

"It would have to have been," Bunzy answers. "I haven't thought up any new words. I haven't thought of any thoughts as the first person with that unique thought. Every word I know has been taught to me by somebody at some time."

Bunzy pauses. He watches the flames in the fireplace for a moment. Then he asks, "So, what do I have to do to achieve a more powerful consciousness and then once I gain this new understanding, how do I get some new communication techniques with which you and I and Isabel and others like us can share these new thoughts that are outside of the words which have been given to us?"

Rinpoche answers, "First, I want you to describe your prison cell. Only when you truly understand and loathe your current situation will you have the motivation to transcend it."

Bunzy says to Rinpoche, "I'm confused. Of what use to understanding is using confusing words to describe things?"

Rinpoche explains, "By consciously describing the walls, you will more clearly see your prison. When you see the barriers, you will be able to see and describe the cracks, the windows, and the doors that lead out of our confinement. The fences which confine us are really very weak and only exist as long as we don't see them and act."

Bunzy says, "But you just explained that we are constrained in our conceptualizations. We can only go as far as we have words to go and we don't have the words to transcend the limitations that constrain us. I can't see any doorway to describe for you. How does one access this new knowledge?"

Rinpoche answers, "That is a problem alright. I am going to give you a mantra. This mantra will be for you and Isabel. Chant it either silently or out loud as often as you can, in as calm a mood, in as quiet a place as possible. Do it with your eyes closed and watch and listen. Do not write it down or share it with others. This is for your personal use only. Ready?"

"Yes," Bunzy says.

"Relax and close your eyes," Rinpoche tells him.

Bunzy puts his hands in his lap, takes a few deep breaths, relaxes his body from the top of his head down to his feet and closes his eyes.

Rinpoche touches Bunzy's forehead and says a few short syllables. Then Rinpoche commands Bunzy to, "Repeat what I just said."

Bunzy tries, but even though the phrase is a very short one, the words aren't expressions he has ever heard. He can't get them right. He can't even remember them.

Rinpoche repeats the phrase again. Then Bunzy follows his lead saying the sounds as close to the way Rinpoche says them as he can.

They do this over and over until Bunzy can follow Rinpoche's lead.

Rinpoche then does the same procedure with Isabel.

When they are done, Bunzy asks, "What do those phrases mean?"

"It isn't what they mean that matters. What matters is what they do. By making those sounds, you are creating a vibration that opens a door."

"Alright, but this mantra thing doesn't seem like that much of a big deal to me. Isn't there more we can do?"

"Say the mantra as often as you can, for as long as you can. Dream, meditate, walk in the woods, travel, communicate with the plants and animals and spirits around you, realize that all of creation is vibrating together and that this vibration is communication. Start journaling about all of this."

Bunzy wonders, "Journaling? Why? You just explained that if I can think it, if I have words for my thoughts, then they are slave thoughts. Words are the bricks in the prison walls. How can journaling help?"

Rinpoche explains, "Imagine we are approaching our problems from many directions. You must clearly understand your limitations. Play with words. Imagine building a doorway in our prison wall with the words you have. Meanwhile you are going to do mantra and think thoughts that are not describable with your current words. You are going to see things that were not previously conceivable to you. You are going to feel emotions bigger than any you have ever felt before. Chant and quietly watch."

Bunzy tells Rinpoche, "I can't even imagine what those big transcendental thoughts would be like."

Rinpoche says, "Well, to get to those thoughts which surpass all others, shut the rational mind down and just watch. Your mind is the mortar that holds the bricks together. The bricks are the words, and the mortar is the mind. Go beyond words and mind. But to begin with, I just want you to expand your world by describing it in bigger and bigger ways and at the same time record your dreams, meditate, do mantra and walk in the woods. Carefully watch everything and everyone. It's nearly eleven. Shall we call it a day?"

Isabel and Bunzy look at each other. They suddenly realize they're quite tired.

Isabel says, "Thank you for allowing us to have this wonderful visit."

"Really the pleasure is mine," Rinpoche responds.

"I'll do as you advise," Bunzy says. "This is all very interesting."

They all stand. Rinpoche warmly hugs Isabel. He shakes Bunzy's hand. Rinpoche goes one way. Bunzy and Isabel go another.

During the afternoon break the following day, Isabel and Bunzy decide to walk down to the highway where they can explore along the river. But as soon as they get away from the Yoga Center and start walking through a large multinational corporation's timber farm, Bunzy starts getting sick. Isabel gets anxious and worried. They turn around and return to their room to rest until dinner.

After the evening service on Saturday night, Rinpoche asks them, "Would you two like to see what is in the Wonderful Warehouse of Amazing Things?"

They both immediately agree. Bunzy and Isabel meet Rinpoche outside the Sacred Hall when he finishes with his responsibilities, and they walk down to the Wonderful Warehouse.

It's a big old green metal building with huge double sliding doors like those on airplane hangars. This building is huge. It reminds Bunzy of the ones that the American Air Force kept their dirigibles in between the World Wars. There is an ordinary walk-through door to the right of the large sliding doors. A big old battered and rusty yellow, metal track-type, crawler tractor with a big steel push blade on the front of it is parked outside at the far-right corner of the building. From the outside, the Wonderful Warehouse of Amazing Things looks like a combination repair shop and storage shed.

The three of them walk through the little door. Rinpoche flips on some lights. Bunzy realizes he has never been in a warehouse this big before. There are row upon row of machines, gadgets, and clothes. They have entered a beautiful, clean building in an area with racks of costumes. Beside them are hangers with tuxedos and gowns hanging on them. Rinpoche walks up some steps onto a brightly lit stage. There is a big couch on the right side of the stage. Hanging in front of the couch is an ancient silk Chinese robe embroidered with bright fire breathing dragons soaring over mountains and valleys. To the left of the robe is a sewing machine and a table covered with seamstress tools. Rinpoche takes the robe over to the seamstress table and starts making some adjustments to it. Isabel and Bunzy walk up onto the stage. Isabel stands alone off to the left while Bunzy walks over and flops on the sofa, then sits up on the cushion closest to Rinpoche and watches him.

Boring quickly, Bunzy looks past where Isabel stands watching them. Over in a darker part of the warehouse where he hadn't looked previously because of the bright lights shining on the stage, are three brand-new very large crawler tractors inside an eight foot tall wire fence. Nobody can get to them or harm them. Each of them is twenty-five feet long, fourteen feet wide, and twelve feet tall.

Rinpoche notices that Bunzy's looking at the tractors. He asks, "Would you like to examine those machines?"

"You bet I would," Bunzy says.

All three of them walk bacl down the steps and over to the fence. Bunzy can tell by Isabel's lingering look at the costumes and especially the shoes as they pass through them that there are other things that she would rather do than look at big bright yellow heavy steel machines.

The tractors have substantial metal blades on the front of them which are at least five feet tall. Instead of tires, they have metal tracks with three-inch-tall steel cleats running across them. On the backs of the machines are different types of attachments. One has a big winch with wire rope spooled on it for pulling logs out of the woods. Another has two metal arms with hardened sharp tips at the end of each arm for ripping rock into smaller pieces. The third machine has a tow bar for pulling farm machinery such as plows and fertilizer spreaders.

They start walking up and down the rows of machinery outside of the fence. Much of it is one-of-a-kind equipment that never made it to mass production.

Rinpoche interrupts his description of the machinery and casually asks Bunzy, "How is your journaling going? Do you have any questions?"

As they pass by an old 1930's style flatbed truck with tall wide steel wheels which are equipped with six-inch shovel blades all around each wheel for traction in the sand, Bunzy says, "Yes", and then asks, "Why can't everything be peaceful, pleasant, and happy? Why is there evil in the world?"

Rinpoche explains, "It's important for you to understand humans aren't running the show on this planet like we think we are. This planet is in the grips of the Archon Lords. They took possession of it and of humanity thousands of years ago and they have been tightening their control ever since. Now Earth has become a combination pleasure palace, feedlot and resource mining operation for these Archon Lords."

Rinpoche says, "What I want to know is how much longer will people trade the use of their spirits for fancy red sports cars, big entertainment centers, thoughtless sexual pleasure, and mind-numbing drugs?"

"I don't know," Bunzy answers. "But tell me something before you go any further. Why haven't I ever seen an Archon or heard about them in school or on TV or in a newspaper?"

"That's easy," Rinpoche says. "The Archons control the schools and the media. All of the ancient texts discuss the capture, alteration and subjugation of humans. For example, your Bible discusses how people were created by a god in his image, then held in ignorance in a walled and guarded garden until a disagreement amongst the rulers of the garden got the humans thrown out and put to work doing ugly manual labor and reproducing more laborers."

"Okay. That seems reasonable alright. What about that Dream Key thing-a-ma-jig?"

"The Archons have used the Dream Key and sophisticated technologies to deceive humans and to get the power over us to make us their slaves. By giving us their minds and making us like them, they have made people forget that we are white light beings who are more creative than dark light beings such as them. That is the great secret they don't want people to learn. If we had access to the Dream Key, or if we just understood the concepts behind the Dream Key, we could return to paradise."

"You say that we are powerful spiritual beings of white light, do you mean that literally?"

"Yes."

"What is the highest and best source of that light around here?"

"In our situation, the Sun is. In the morning when it rises, face it, greet it, expose yourself to it, and absorb it."

"I thought that the Sun was a big dangerous and toxic nuclear explosion."

"The Sun is the heart chakra of this solar body. It is not a nuclear explosion. That is an Archon deception. They want you to see the Sun as your enemy. The best way for you to understand what the Sun is, is to think of it as being electrical, like a grow light. The Sun is a place where powerful meridians of energy from the cosmos intersect. Then meridians from the Sun come to Earth and to each of us. These lines of force energize us."

"Energize us how? How can I intentionally absorb this energy?"

"You don't need to know that. Your body knows. Just do it."

"I don't think that I'm understanding what light is."

"This is one of those concepts that has been disappeared from your consciousness. Light is information. Light isn't what you are thinking that it is. It does shine and make it possible for you to see things. That is because it is a burst of information from Source and you need this information to assemble your awareness. If you get too much information, you burn up. If you get too little, you burn out. If you get just enough, you gain more coherence and get brighter and brighter. Thus, people say that a person who is smart is bright. Bright people have more information. They're smarter and they actually are brighter."

"I want to get brighter. How can I do that?"

"Expose yourself to the Sun and eat raw plants."

"Eat raw plants? I still don't understand what light is."

"Well, I'll say it again, light is information. It isn't the way that you visualize it. It doesn't light up the world by shining on it. It lights up your understanding by describing it. Plants know this and can convert light into life. By consuming raw plants, you are consuming the plants knowledge. You are absorbing information from them. You become brighter. You become a life force."

"How can I become a powerful life force?"

"That is going to take a big effort and some time. We are going to need help from powerful spiritual forces to light up your awareness. Do the things that I've been telling you to do. You need to have a garden. In a garden you can co-exist with other white light forces without destroying them. Together in the garden you can gather more white light force, and you get to spend a lot of time in the Sun doing mantra."

"I don't think that that is going to be enough."

"No, but if you'll do it, you will grow and be attracted to other white light sources. It's a beginning and you have to stop taking in the dark light. This will start the struggle and get the show on the road."

"Can you give me an example of how at my level of consciousness I could use some of this light information?"

"Not really. You have to absorb a great deal of light before you can manipulate light."

"There must be a small way that I could do something. For example, healing my painful hip or getting some money. I'm trying to grasp this. Give me an idea."

"Money isn't the issue which should concern you. Money is an organizing principal of the Archonic dark light. The issues which should concern you are consciousness, clarity, impeccability, and intentions. If you are going to reach your goal, you need to understand those issues. Without lighting up your awareness in those areas, you will cause greater harm than good with money. If you absorb more light, your hip will heal."

Isabel interrupts, "Bunzy, please no more. You've been over this like five times. Leave the poor man alone."

Rinpoche laughs.

"Wow! It must be really late," Bunzy exclaims. "I had been so focused that I wasn't paying any attention to anything else except my thoughts. Sorry, I didn't realize how much time has passed. This is all so interesting."

"Don't be sorry for seeking light," Rinpoche says. "With clarity comes power, the power to re-establish harmony. Allow me to show you what I mean. You perceive that you are in a huge open space called the cosmos, but I say that you are in a tiny little coop, like a chicken coop, which I'll call a human coop. When you know where the door to the human coop is, you can just walk out. Watch."

Bunzy and Isabel stand with their backs to the wall by the walk-through door in the Wonderful Warehouse of Amazing Things. They face Rinpoche. He walks past them continuing on through the wall behind them and disappears. Bunzy and Isabel run over to where he vanished. Bunzy reaches out with his right hand and pats the wall. It's solid. Isabel feels the wall with both of her hands. Then they both step back and stare at it. At that moment Rinpoche walks back through the wall and stands in front of them smiling.

Bunzy thinks, *this is some kind of trick.*

He asks Rinpoche, "Can you do that again?"

He's thinking, *if I watch him very closely, I will see how he does it.*

Rinpoche answers, "Sure," and turns around and walks back through the wall as Bunzy and Isabel carefully watch. They cannot grasp what they're seeing. Rinpoche returns back through the wall. They see his right hand and foot appear, then his face and torso, then he's through.

They appear dumbfounded. Rinpoche looks at them and laughs.

He says, "Think about it. Goodnight Bunzy… Isabel."

He opens the front door and walks away.

Bunzy and Isabel are not in the world that they were in this morning, and they know it.

They go to bed.

On Sunday in the evening instead of the usual chanting service there is a musical program and Rinpoche doesn't attend. Monday is the community free day. There is no work and no programs. The community rests. Bunzy and Isabel eat leftovers. Other members of the community fast.

Bunzy and Isabel go to the nearest town to take care of personal matters and to deal with their work-related issues. They want to extend their vacations. There's a lot to do. It takes hours. They discover they need to go home and deal with problems their sudden departure has created, but they both agree what Rinpoche is teaching them is more important than going home and instead they decide to go back to the Yoga Center.

Suddenly, Bunzy is attacked by the most vicious headache he's had yet. It lays him low. Isabel doesn't talk to him about urgent care clinics or medicines. She just starts doing her mantra and encourages him to do his. Bunzy concentrates the best he can and chants. Things slowly change. His headache goes away. Work issues are resolved. Solutions for personal problems are found. They go back to the Center.

After the Tuesday evening service when they come to the place in the audience line where they are standing in front of Rinpoche, Bunzy begs him to come speak to them in the Common Hall again. Rinpoche agrees.

As soon as they are seated, Bunzy blurts out, "I'm deeply disturbed by the idea that my mind is not my own and that we are being controlled by alien monsters. Isabel and I are having some frightening experiences that may be related to what you are teaching. What should we do?"

Rinpoche answers, "We need allies. We need a great spirit, a holy one, to help us. You're the one who can attract spiritual help. Magical power words need to be said to explain things to you and to lead us, but spirit pays attention to actions. You must act. To spirit it's what we do that matters. To attract the attention of Spirit will require grand acts. When great spirits are attracted, they will support the person who makes the gestures. So, it is necessary for you to make some grand gestures. I am going to help you do that."

"Why is that necessary?"

"The Archons have made grand gestures in the past and they continue to make bold gestures and thus they have been continuously supported in their efforts for thousands of years. Now it is time for us to make a grand gesture to gain spiritual support for a way that is different than theirs."

"Alright. Where do I begin?"

"Eat only fruits and grasses which includes everything which you think of as vegetables. Drink only pure water. Spend time in nature in the Sun. Absorb as much sunlight as you can. Learn to energize your spirit with sunlight by taking it in through the eyes. Spend time outside, in peace. Become one with nature and cleanse. Cleanse the body. Juice. Do all of the cleanses, all of the ways that you can think of, such as: colonics, fasting, getting rid of parasites and heavy metals, drinking lots of high mountain spring water, and meditate. Be gentle. Do natural things. Spend time touching Earth, touching it with your hands, with your bare feet, sit on it, sleep on it. Bathe in pure water. Let fresh, clean water run over you. Swim in fresh water. Do breathing exercises in the wilderness. Get lots of charged oxygen into your body along with the sunlight and the water. Practice talking to plants and animals. Communicate with them in any way that you can imagine. Do mantra, drum, chant, and dance. Hold holy rituals of togetherness."

"Stay away from TV, radio, electricity, cell phones, newspapers, magazines, and the internet. No drama. No excitation."

"Now that you know that you can eat light by absorbing it, do it. There are more ways to absorb light than sitting in the Sun, become aware of them. Absorb light constantly. You can absorb energy in all kinds of ways and forms. In fact, you are doing it all of the time but become conscious of doing it. Consciously absorb light. Think of light as packets of information which are your food. Your sustenance will become information in the form of thoughts which are consciousness. Expand your awareness."

"Love is a great source of light. Consciously practice loving all of those around you, even though you may not love them. Be in harmony with all of creation."

"What do you mean by being in harmony?"

"Acting in harmony means to treat everyone as you would want to be treated and encourage others to act in the same manner. Trust that

Divine Consciousness is aware of you, loves you, and will protect and care for you and your loved ones. Staying in the pure and potent white light love of the Divine presence is a good reason for you to love all of creation. Eat less and less and absorb more and more energy through your whole body directly."

"How do I do that absorbing thing?"

"Intentionally expose yourself to Divine Consciousness such as the Sun and other love emanations. Then these love emanations will feed you."

"Could you list some love emanations?"

"You know them by their feel. Seek out situations and beings who make you feel awe and goodness, joy and happiness: great saints, holy trees, magical places, ancient sacred sites, awesome and strange creatures, noble spirits, luscious gardens, high mountains, bodies of water like oceans, but lakes, rivers, ponds, and springs too. Sit silently in the wilderness by water even in the desert and absorb blessings of grace and energetic power. Spend time with friends and family. Celebrate our incredible good fortune to be here in this wonderful place with each other. Be grateful."

"All that I have told you ought to give you enough to do and to think about, to be and to know for a while. And if you go do them, they should attract a great spirit to you. That should get the show going. What do you say?"

"I agree. Everything that you have told me requires some real changes, but I'll start right away."

"What do you think Isabel?" Rinpoche asks.

"Seems awfully complicated to me. Whole lot of words without much being accomplished. I think that it is all a lot simpler, but I can't explain what I feel."

"True. We are already there if we would only realize it. Progress is an illusion. Progress is actually a stumbling block. We are now seeking a holistic realization rather than growth, but we are what we are and it is what it is. For you, I say, do not be afraid. Fear nothing, even death. If you will just love, share, and care for each other in every moment, then everything will be wonderful. All that you have to do is change yourself, change your attitude, and the whole world will change because we are all one. Stop being of this world and you will stop being in this world."

He takes a piece of paper from his shirt pocket. It is white, blank on both sides, stiff like a business card, but about twice as big as a business card. He writes some numbers on one side and signs his name on the flip side. Handing the card to Bunzy, he says, "Please examine this card. Feel it. Look at both sides of it."

Isabel and Bunzy give the card a cursory inspection.

Rinpoche takes it back, strikes a match, and burns it until he is holding just a small piece of paper with some black ash on it between his fingers. As they watch, the paper reconstitutes itself back into the double sized business card with writing on both sides. He hands the card back to Bunzy. Bunzy looks at it and feels it.

The paper feels solid. The writing is still there. Bunzy hands the card back to him. Rinpoche strikes another match and burns the card again.

After the paper rebuilds itself a second time, he hands it back to Bunzy and says, "Keep this as a remembrance. You'll need it."

Bunzy hands the card to Isabel. She examines it and then, smiling quizzically, hands it back to Bunzy who folds it and put it in his wallet.

"So, will you be leaving tomorrow?" Rinpoche asks.

"Yes, I think so. I'm anxious to get started on all of the things which you have told me to do," Bunzy responds.

"What about you Isabel?" Rinpoche asks.

"I'm ready to go home," she says. "I love my home. I always feel safe and comfortable when I'm home, but I've also loved my visit here with all of you. There are some beautiful people here whose friendship I will always cherish. I look forward to visiting you again soon."

"Please come as often as you like," Rinpoche tells her.

"Thank you," Isabel says.

They embrace each other. Rinpoche shakes Bunzy's hand and then hugs him too.

"Rinpoche stares Bunzy in the eyes for a long time and then says, "Brother, be ecstatic. While we are apart there will be joy and sadness, but I will always be happy to see you again. Farewell Bunzy, Isabel. To both of you, I say, expect miracles."

He smiles, nods politely, and leaves.

In the morning Bunzy and Isabel say their goodbyes to everyone at breakfast. Bunzy goes to the Naropa Yoga Center business office and makes a donation to the organization to cover the costs of their visit.

Then they go to their room, gather their things, go to their car, and leave. It is a lovely sunny day. As they drive, they say their mantras.

Bunzy tells Isabel, "I don't know what to think about Rinpoche's Archon story. It doesn't match up with what I've learned, but we've got to be super careful. Someone or something, somewhere is trying to control us."

"Yeah, I agree," Isabel says. "Your friend Fred didn't die in an accident on his way home. He was murdered. We could be next."

CHAPTER 4
PARADISE

"The dragonfly will be the messiah."

Masanobu Fukuoba

B unzy and Isabel move in March to the land which they are going to share with the plants who are going to support them. It has taken over a year to build an off the electrical power grid cottage isolated in an oak forest above a pond at the eastern edge of a large meadow. Below the pond are two, hundred foot by hundred foot, gardens fenced in by nine foot high, woven wire fences to keep the deer out. They intend to build two more garden areas, one for each different type of crop and also so that they can rotate the different types of plants to different areas each year.

Plants mine the soil for nutrients. Humans mine the plants. Plants are like gold miners and like gold miners when the gold is mined out, the miners have to move on to find more gold or get poorer and poorer. Soil is like a gold mine, only with a big difference. This important variation is that with some effort more gold can be produced in the played out garden gold mine and dug up later by the vegetation. Plants can grow and look good when the farmer adds only three elements to the soil: nitrogen, potassium, and phosphorous. However, they need a hundred other things to be healthy, happy, strong, and delicious. People need those other things too. Plants and people need calcium, copper, zinc, iron, magnesium, and sodium. They need boron, chlorine, phosphate, sulfur, chrome, cobalt, iodine, and selenium. Plants also need the soil to be porous enough to let oxygen deep down into the area where their roots are mining and yet not be so porous that all of the water runs away. Health for them and therefore health for people is a delicate balance.

After carefully leveling the two garden areas in the meadow and then fencing them, Bunzy and Isabel get rotted sawdust and horse manure and then spread it over the fields about four inches deep. Then they plow it into the topsoil. After all of those efforts, they get soil tests and balance the minerals in the soil in the top six inches. Then they add organic fertilizers to the dirt for plant food. When all of this is done, they rototill the top eight inches of the gardens, fluffing up the soil again. Finally they install an irrigation system which works on gravity. The water flows naturally down from the pond to the gardens.. From their cabin they can see no other electric lights at night. The commercial power system, roads, and neighbors are far away.

Feeling good about their accomplishments, they decide to go to a meditation retreat in California to relax and enjoy themselves. It hasn't rained much all winter. The pond is about three feet too low. They're not sure if it has enough water to water their gardens through October. Bunzy decides to raise the spillway so that if any rain does fall it will all stay in the pond. They leave a friend who lives nearby in charge of everything.

The retreat in the Coast Range in California is sublime. On the third day in the evening, Molly, the friend in charge of Bunzy and Isabel's farm, calls.

She says, "Bunzy, it has been pouring down rain since you left. The pond has filled and is starting to run over."

Bunzy is incredulous. He observes, "The pond hasn't filled that much in September, October, December, January, and February. Now in just three days you are saying that it has filled and is running over."

He asks, "What do you mean by running over? Do you mean that water is finally running out of the spillway?"

Molly emphatically states, "No, I mean the spillway is full and now water is running over the face of the dam."

Shocked, Bunzy asks, "Is the dam washing away?"

Molly answers, "No, the water is just trickling over through the grass, but the pond is full and looks really big. It looks dangerous."

"Dangerous like wash the downstream neighbors' houses away?" Bunzy asks.

"Yes," Molly tells him.

Bunzy says, "Please get your husband and oldest son to digging with shovels enlarging the spillway. We're on our way home now."

Bunzy and Isabel apologize to the retreat organizers and load their gear in their SUV. They drive through the night, reaching their home in the morning light. The pond is a frightening sight. The spillway isn't deep enough or wide enough. Too much water fell in too short of a time and now their whole project is threatened. They start digging with big machines. Molly and her family have saved everything by enlarging the spillway during the night, but now it is up to Bunzy and Isabel.

Farming is hard, dangerous work. The upside of this disaster is that now they have enough water for their crops all year.

Three weeks later it is dry enough to start planting.

Bunzy has heard that sometimes something goes up that doesn't come down, but in his experience, it is more common that things go down and don't come back up. He believes most gardens are that way. Seeds go in the ground. After a while some of them sprout. They make an effort at life, living in well-manicured straight lines, each staying in their designated area, no pushing or shoving. As long as the farmer feeds them and protects them from hooligan insects, slimy molds, and bully weeds, they grow and produce a few vegetables. This kind of garden is pretty in a controlled, calm, steady way, and there's something to live on in there. The fare might be so thin that the farmer has to seek help from grocery stores to get through the day much less through long, dark, cold winter nights. As far as Bunzy is concerned, this type of farming isn't going up. This is a controlled descent.

Isabel and Bunzy are going for greatness. They want to live on the Plateau of Happiness. They are birthing a garden that is a community of beings who are celebrating joyous lives and sharing those lives with them and their friends. In their gardens, nine foot tall white oak fence posts march around guarding green communities, while tall yellow sunflowers and rows of corn ride herd on strawberries, tomatoes, cabbage, lettuce, broccoli, and cauliflower. A rainforest of squash wanders around tripping over pumpkins, cantaloupe, and watermelon. Everyone is pushing for standing room, for water, for minerals, and space in the Sun. Waist high grasses creep up to the white oak fence post sentries with their wire weaponry. Oak, madrone, fir, and ash trees stand stoically by, hiding deer, coyotes, bobcats, hawks, squirrels, birds and mice. Mice are everywhere. These are not little house mice. Some of these are brush bunny size rodents. They are cute, but they have appetites to match their size.

Silence covers everything along with the sunshine and gentle breezes. This is a happy community. Here there are plants and animals singing. Here there is joy and happiness. There is support and sharing and caring. The plants are bursting with goodness: bright red strawberries, deep purple beets, orange sungold tomatoes, yellow bell peppers, short fat orange carrots, poofy grey-green broccoli, long bright green beans. Big striped white and green watermelons creep, crawl, and push about while bright red peppers stand over them, crowned with bombshell bursts of yellow dill.

Order and control are gone. The multitudes are pushing out onto the dance floor. Honeybees fly here and there with invitations and fulfilling hidden desires. The bees visit yellow flowers on the tomatoes, white and purple shoots on the basil, demure pretty pink blossoms on the pole beans, violet poofs bursting up the stems of the peppermint, and big yellow trumpets on squash and pumpkin vines.

The plants are calling to the bees, "Over here. I've got something good for you."

"No. Come over here. Try this."

"Hey, over here! I've got what you need, what you want. Come to me and you'll be satisfied, really satisfied."

The dance begins with a few sedate fox trots, segues into a wildly flowing waltz, breaks into a tango, a little salsa over here, some twisting over there. Then the whole area bursts into a full-blown, out of control, everyone in, free-style, exuberant rock and roll. Even some heavy metal head banging begins over in a corner here and there.

Just get some baskets and let them fill with the fruits of life and be careful not to be overrun by the avalanche of produce.

There's a riot between these oak posts. A person who gets their life here isn't just eating nutritious, healthy food. They are absorbing joy. This is a dance where everyone gets what they need and even better they are getting what they desire. Happiness happens in every direction. The strawberries are sweeter. The tomatoes ooze scrumptious flavor. The cucumbers are light and juicy. The zucchini are huge but soft and moist with a delicate pasta flavor.

Nobody wants to stay home. Everyone wants to get up and touch each other. These plants have found magic. Underground a symphony of groping amongst Mother Earth's treasures is leading to hugging happiness.

If you are willing to live riotously, this is the place and the time. Here Isabel and Bunzy are living joyously, sharing their essence with the plants and the plants are reciprocating by sharing their happiness and abundance with Bunzy and Isabel. Everyone benefits each other. Life is good.

Isabel and Bunzy are sitting on their front porch gazing out over the pond past the gardens into the forests that roll on to the horizon.

Bunzy says, "This world that we are looking at today is richer and far more beautiful than the one which I have seen all of my life. The colors are more intense and more vibrant and it has the feeling that everything fits together perfectly. That bush over there," he says and points towards a shrub on the left side of the front yard, "is where it belongs and I know that not just from seeing that it fits there aesthetically, but from a heart-felt feeling. This awareness makes that plant and everything else special in a way that makes all of this more precious and beautiful than anything I've ever seen, felt, smelt, heard, or experienced ever before. I am so grateful we made it to this moment so we can experience this place and time. Its preciousness is beyond measure. My pleasure is tactile, but I don't just feel it with my fingers. I feel it with my heart."

"I feel it too," Isabel tells him. "Everything around us is vibrating with energy. Speaking of energy, Bunzy, we need more power to run our lights, juicers, food processor, washing machine, refrigerator, stereo, and all of our other things. We just aren't getting enough power out of the solar collectors and we're too far from a commercial electrical power source to hookup. What can we do to get more gadget power?"

Bunzy says, "Well, look at it this way, we need more energy and for anything to exist and maintain its form requires large amounts of energy. So, there is plenty of energy all around us to operate our machines."

"Yes, but I don't see any plug-in over there," Isabel points off the porch towards some trees, "or over there on that rock." Now she is pointing at a big boulder in the opposite direction.

"That is a problem," Bunzy agrees. "Viktor Schauberger built a flying machine that operated without fuel by balancing gravity and levitational forces. Nikola Tesla developed a coil that can pull electricity out of the air. Wilhelm Reich made orgone boxes which captured life energy forces inside of them. There were ancient civilizations which could move giant stones which we cannot move even today. Even older stone ruins in South Africa seem to be the foundations for power generating plants for some mysterious type of energy. There would seem to be a lot more ways to generate power than the ones which our civilization is using today."

"Like what?" Isabel asks.

Bunzy explains, "Well, if there is gravity, then there has to be levity or else things would be crushed into oblivion. There has to be an anti-gravity force, but if this anti-gravity force is too great then things would float away. There has to be a balance. In the same way if there is death, then there has to be a life force. Tipping those forces back and forth at their balance points could generate a lot of power. Just as a car needs fuel to operate or a computer needs electricity, people need a force to keep them going and planets need a force to support them. The Sun isn't creating energy. It is a flowing force. Everything is being maintained by a force and this force has to be absorbed and balanced.

If we can tap into this power and regulate it, then we can use this energy to run any kind of gadget which we can imagine just as the Universe is using this power to create and maintain everything we see."

"How?" Isabel asks.

"Think of the bodies of all beings as batteries. All that we need is a generator that generates the kind of power we can use when it is connected to the energy in one of those batteries.

"If it's that easy, why don't I have a couple of them helping me out around here?"

"Because I haven't built one yet."

"Time to get busy, Bunsy" Isabel says and pushes him.

When Bunzy regains his balance, he agrees, "Yes, it is."

CHAPTER 5
DARKNESS FALLING

"Our society is run by insane people for insane objectives. I think we're being run by maniacs for maniacal ends and I think I'm liable to be put away as insane for expressing that."

John Lennon

Once Isabel motivates Bunzy and Bunzy understands how every plant, animal, and rock is vibrating with energy much like a battery and how this force is constantly flowing through everything, it isn't difficult for him to build a gadget that captures a small amount of this power. The device operates the way that a lightning rod attracts a small amount of the lightning from the sky. It's difficult to transform the type of energy that this device captures into the 110 volt electricity that human technology uses, but it is possible and on a surprisingly small scale. Reich, Schauberger, and Tesla have already done the hard work and shown the way. Bunsy just follows them.

Because the generator operates like a lightning rod except that it is based on a different form of energy, Bunzy calls it the Attractor. Bunzy and Isabel build Attractor boxes to operate their home and machines. Theses boxes are easy to make and inexpensive so they make some for their friends, but before they give them away, Bunzy patents the technology. This knowledge makes petrochemicals, coal, nuclear power, and hydro-electric generators un-necessary. All that a person needs is an Attractor and with it they can generate all of the power they need to operate their home and transportation and whatever is needed to grow their food and to produce everything they want. If a group of people want a bigger amount of power, they can just build a bigger Attractor.

Soon, everybody wants an Attractor, and a lot of rich and powerful people do not want those people to get Attractors. It was never Bunzy's intention to invent the Attractor to get rich and it certainly was not his intention to do something that would get him killed. So, he decides to develop a website and give the technology away free. He's going to get rid of this hassle.

Johnny Jones and Isabel and Bunzy rent the old Armory building downtown where they start making Attractors and designing an Attractor website. Thomas Calhoun and his friend Harvey Teaguarden come down from Northern Oregon University for the weekend to help Bunsy and Isabel develop the Attractor website. Harvey has an old classic hotrod Chevy pickup with a pumped-up racing engine and a real low geared rear-end. When he jumps on the gas in that pickup, it jumps off the line like a giant frog and gets up to a hundred really quick. With that low geared rear-end though at a hundred this pickup's done.

Harvey is a tall lanky dark-skinned kid who wears coke bottle thick glasses. Without those glasses he's nearly blind. He's a real smart guy and a big help on the computer work, but he's an excitable fellow.

The website is almost complete and ready to activate. The Attractor gang decides to celebrate with a case of wine from a local winery outlet that is only a few blocks away. Harvey's pickup truck is right out front.

Johnny says, "Hey Harvey, let's take that hotrod pickup of yours to the winery."

"Fine with me," Harvey agrees, "but it's only got a bench seat with room three to sit on and I don't know my way around this town."

"We're just going a couple of blocks and come right back," Johnny says. "We can double up. It'll be fun. What can go wrong in that short of a distance?"

They all agree and pile into the pickup.

At the winery they stay longer and drink a few more drinks than they intended to. Then they buy a case of wine and head back to the Armory.

The pickup is really crowded. There's only room for three like Harvey said.

Harvey is driving. Johnny is in the middle with Bunzy on his lap. Thomas is on the outside with Isabel on his lap and the case of wine is on the floorboard between them with their feet on it.

When they stop at the street at the edge of the parking lot for the bar, Johnny says, "Watch out. There's a Sherriff lurking over there in that parking garage across the street."

"Where?" Harvey asks.

"Over there," Bunzy points across Harvey's face to their left.

Harvey rapidly leans forward and jerks his head to his right, knocking his big black plastic glasses off on Bunzy's outstretched hand. They fall on the floor amongst their feet in the dark.

"Damn it. Now I can't see a thing," Harvey says.

"Well act smooth," Isabel suggests. "This is a one-way street. Don't turn left. Just turn right and drive away. There are three undercover black SUV's over there too. Something important is going on that we don't want to get involved in. Don't do anything to attract their attention."

Harvey pulls out and turns left, cruising the wrong way up a one-way street right in front of the Sheriff.

The Sheriff flips on his overhead flashers and pulls out behind them. Harvey punches the gas, flies up the block, screeches around the corner to the right, and pushes his foot all the way to the floor on the gas pedal. They're taking red lights in a twenty-five mile an hour downtown shopping zone on a busy evening at a hundred miles an hour.

Isabel is screaming.

Johnny and Bunzy are yelling, "Slow down Harvey! Slow down! Dead end! Telephone Company offices dead ahead! Put your foot on the brakes!"

Harvey locks the brakes up throwing them into a four-wheel drift around the block while turning left, sliding to the right through the parking area and across the sidewalk up to the telephone office rock wall. Just before they slam into the rocks, the truck suddenly grabs traction and they shoot up the block, screeching around another corner to the left and heading back down a straight stretch back towards where they just came from. There are now three big black SUV's and a Sheriff's car behind them with lights flashing and sirens wailing. Whenever the police gain on the Attractor crew, Harvey turns a corner and punches the gas pulling away from them.

The Attractor bunch are coming back to the Amory which is on a one-way street going in the opposite direction from the way that they're approaching it.

Just before the Attractor pack reaches the street with the Armory on it. Calhoun decides that he has had enough of this craziness. Without saying a word to Isabel who is sitting on his lap, he opens the passenger door and steps out of the pickup at forty miles an hour. When his feet touch the street, he cartwheels across a bank lawn like a cheerleader and piles into the bushes along the front wall of the bank. At the same time Harvey throws the pickup into a left-hand turn sliding to the right around the corner onto the Amory street going the wrong way down the one way street. When Thomas slid out of the pickup Isabel started to fall with him but her right sleeve caught on the door handle and her feet hung on the floor boards. But as the truck picks up G's sliding around the corner, the force rips her sleeve and throws her out the door along with the case of wine. There is a sickening whump and at the same time, she disappears under a parked car in front of the Armory. When the police reach the corner there is only a wet spot where the wine hit the parked car. Isabel is under the car. Thomas is in the bushes and the other three Attractors are a couple of blocks away heading down another straightaway.

Johnny is yelling at Harvey, "Buddy we gotta get this hotrod out of downtown!"

They're now in a straight stretch that goes downhill several blocks then flattens out on old Highway 99 and heads out across the river. Harvey floors it. They hit the bottom of that dip flying with the Sheriff's car and one of the SUV's hot on their tail. All three vehicles bottom out bumper to bumper when they slam into the pavement on 99, sparks and molten metal fly. They're all flat on the pavement grinding shock absorbers off as they slide across the highway. The Sheriff's car spins out of control and smashes into some parked cars in a car sales lot on the left side of the street. The black SUV spins out too, but it gets straightened back around and joins two more SUV's which have caught up with it as the Attractors leave the end of the bridge at a hundred miles an hour. Bunzy knows they're going a hundred because he's looking at the speedometer.

Johnny is kneeling on the seat by the door, hunched over, leaning across Bunzy, looking at the speedometer too, screaming, and "Slow down! Corner! Bad Corner! Get your foot out of it Buddy. There's a bad corner coming up and we can't make it at this speed."

It's too late. They're in the corner and they're not going to make it, but the freeway ramp is straight ahead. There's no choice. They shoot onto the freeway. As soon as those SUV's hit the freeway, they start gaining on the truck.

Bunzy is counting them out the back window, "One, two, three, four, five, six. There's six of them now."

Johnny yells, "Take the next exit. We can't outrun them out here on the freeway."

There's a red stop light on a four lane main street at the bottom of the next off ramp. Harvey takes it at a hundred. They're just a blur. Those cars on Garden Valley Boulevard don't even see the Attractor truck shoot through them. The truck bottoms out here too. To the drivers on the Boulevard, they're a red blur of sparks with a big rooster tail flying behind, that's all.

Now Johnny and Bunzy are both screaming, "Get on the brakes Bud! There's a corner coming up that you can't make at this speed! Coca Cola corners Bud! Get on the brakes now! Coca Cola corners! Slow down!"

As they come around the first corner to the left they just keep on coming around. They slide over the next corner and drop ten or fifteen feet down into the Coca Cola parking lot. Boom! They hit that parking lot so hard they're all three nearly knocked out. They slide backwards across the parking lot into a parking spot between two cars which are parked by the building and slam into the curb so hard that the engine is killed. Harvey turns off the headlights. They're sitting there like stunned frogs as the SUVs fly around the Coca Cola corners and roar away.

Harvey jumps out of the driver's door and runs back to the street smashing into the side of an old Volkswagen bug with a kid in it that was following the chase and is now turning around to go back to town. Harvey jerks the passenger door open on the run and jumps in with the kid who drives away with him.

Johnny leaps out the passenger door of the pickup and crosses the freeway like a champion hurdler and disappears.

Before the men in the SUV's see that they've lost them, double back, and find the pickup, Bunzy follows Johnny out of the passenger door, dashes back along the freeway through a working-class neighborhood, jumping over fences, dodging dogs, and finally re-crosses Garden Valley Boulevard, and sprints down the street intending to lose himself in the activity along this busy street. There is a big carnival ahead on the right. Bunzy doesn't remember there ever having been a carnival here before. In fact, he doesn't even remember there being a big empty lot there where the carnival is.

He thinks, *I just got a lucky break, I guess.*

There's a clown selling tickets at the front gate. He yells at Bunzy, "Hey Buddy, how about a five dollar entrance ticket and a twenty dollar book of coupons for the rides and games? You've never had an experience like this one. I guarantee it. And you look like a guy who likes excitement."

"Sure. Sounds like a good deal," Bunzy says.

He quickly hands the clown two twenties, gets his change, entrance stub and coupons, and walks through the gate, merging with the crowd.

He imagines, *I've escaped. They'll never be able to pick me out amongst all of these people.*

The big rides are straight ahead at the far end of the carnival. Kids' rides are on his right. Fun houses line both sides of the carnival. Here on the fairway are all kinds of games with big prizes. Smash the cushion with a sledgehammer, ring the bell at the top of the pole, and win a thousand dollars' worth of lottery tickets. Become an instant millionaire. Guess the number of Japanese yen in the trunk and get the same size trunk full of silver dollars. The prizes seem too big to be real. The rides are fabulous too. Tumble through space in a rocket ship to Mars. Take a synapse blasting roller coaster ride down the Grand Canyon. Plunge to the bottom of a coral sea in a submarine. For what Bunzy paid to get into the carnival, the quality of these rides is outrageous. This is a really high-quality operation. They could get way more money for these rides. Besides fried bread and cotton candy, there are all kinds of exotic foods such as East Indian curries, Amazonian banana leaves wrapped around jungle casseroles, and mugs covered with ancient hieroglyphs filled with steaming magical brews. These foods are strange. This whole place is strange and really way too fabulous to be in this neighborhood.

Bunzy becomes suspicious. *He begins to think. Something strange is happening. I shouldn't have built the Attractor. We definitely shouldn't have made that wild dash for freedom. The Archons are in my head. They know what's happening. They want the Attractor, and they want me dead. I wonder what this event is all about. I don't have time for philosophizing right now. I've got more important problems that I need to focus on. If I had time, I'd do mantra.*

Trying to blend in with the crowd, Bunzy first attempts to ring the bell, then blasts off on the rocket ship ride, but as he's trying to win a trip to Morocco by pitching rings around multi-colored, custom Plexiglas car floor gear shift knobs, he notices four men in grey suits over by the shooting gallery studying him.

How did they find me? This is all so impossible. I don't understand what is happening. Everything is out of my control and going from bad to worse.

He quickly enters the 21st Century House of Horrors.

What can the 21st Century House of Horrors contain? I can imagine Count Dracula's Castle of Horrors, or the Demonic House of Terror, or the Medieval Creepy Torture Dungeon. But the 21st Century House of Horrors, what can that be?

Before he has a chance to explore much of the 21st Century House of Horrors though, two brutish white men in grey suits appear in a hallway off to his right. These men don't need guns, but they obviously have them.

Maybe they just use the guns to club people with for the fun of it.

He starts to turn to his left to go further down the main hall, but there are two more eye-gouging, bone breakers right there in front of him.

How did these guys surround me so quickly? Where did they come from?

The two men in the small side hallway push him into the main hall where the other two men grab him.

The biggest one, a real monster, announces, "Bunzy Ringer, in the name of the United States of America, we arrest you as a terrorist."

The four of them quickly chain his hands together at the wrists and his legs together at the ankles. Then they chain his wrists to his ankles. With a man in front and a man behind and a man on each arm, they drag him further into the 21st Century House of Horrors, then outside to a street where they put him in the back of a big grey four door sedan with no markings on it. One of them sits on each side of him in the back seat. Two of them sit in the front seat. They speed away to the old County jail in the woods up on the top of Rocky Butte. This prison was built a long time ago and is known as the Rock because it is built out of grey rock and steel, up on top of a rocky butte. Nobody in the car or at the jail explains anything to Bunzy about what is happening. The cells are dark, dirty and overcrowded, soaked in sweat, blood, urine, misery and disinfectants.

The cell that they put him in is ten feet long, twelve feet wide and eight feet tall with two bunks on each side and a toilet in the middle of the floor at the far end of the cell. There are three men already in this dark, dirty cell. Two of them are big men. One of them glares at Bunzy. The other big man looks at the floor. The third man is a small one who even in his prison uniform appears to be a professional of some type.

After the door slams shut, the professional introduces himself, "Hello, my name is Mordecai Smith. I'm a professional killer for a local organization. I won't be here long. This is just a temporary occupational inconvenience. The big guy," he says pointing at the glaring man, "is Jacob Cross. He likes to kill women and mutilate them or maybe he likes to mutilate them and then murder them. I'm not sure which way that goes. Got a bit of an angry attitude as you can see. The unpleasant fellow looking at the floor is Wilhelm Gutt. He likes to kill people too, but I'm not sure why. He just seems to enjoy it."

"Nice to meet you guys," Bunzy says as he shakes hands with Smith and Cross. "I haven't known anybody like you. It sounds as if you guys are having interesting lives."

Three days later when the men in grey come back for Bunzy and find him alive and in one piece, they seem disappointed.

They take Bunzy for trial before Federal Judge William Goering. There is no jury.

Judge Goering informs Bunzy, "Mr. Ringer, you are accused of disrupting the Government of the United States," and then asks, "how do you plead?"

"I didn't know that, that was a crime. What did I do? Don't I get a lawyer and a jury? Don't I have rights?"

"Don't get smart with me punk." Goering shouts. "I don't like your attitude and that can get you hurt in my courtroom. Ignorance is no defense before the law. You are a terrorist not a criminal. You have no rights. Disrupting the government is a very serious crime for which you can get five years in prison for each count with which you have been charged and you have been accused of three counts, two counts of disrupting the government and one count of conspiring to disrupt the government."

"What did I do?"

"Did you not on Friday, November 20[th,] two years ago, while in the United States Social Security office parking lot in this town, not loudly proclaim to your bother-in-law that 9/11 was a criminal conspiracy staged by the United States Government Intelligence Forces and that the Arabs involved in this crime were only working for the United States government, and further that this act was staged to get the Patriot Act passed to suppress people's freedom?"

"I don't know. I don't remember where I was or what I was doing on that day two years ago."

"Ms. Stephens will you please approach the bench?"

A small, mousy woman in a grey woolen business dress rises from amongst the benches in the gallery and approaches the judge.

"Well Mr. Ringer we have a witness that I want to introduce to you. This is Ms. Alice Stephens. She is an employee of the United States Government Social Security Service and was an employee of the Social Security Service on the day in question and furthermore, she was standing in the Social Security Office parking lot smoking a cigarette on said day. Ms. Stephens will you tell the court what happened in the parking lot between the Social Security Office and the Cinema 12 movie theaters at four PM on November 20th two years ago?"

"Yes." She points directly at Bunzy with a shaking hand and in a quavering voice says, "That man accused our government of causing the terrible 9/11 crimes."

"How did that affect you Ms. Stephens?"

"I have been unable to work at the Social Security offices since then."

"Mr. Ringer you have heard the charges. You know the seriousness of the crimes. How do you plead?"

"I don't even remember ever going to the movies with my brother-in-law and I certainly never went to the Social Security office with him. I could have just passed through that parking lot and talked to him though. I don't remember."

"You admit it then Mr. Ringer. You are guilty!" The judge shouts and bangs his gavel down. "Guilty on two counts of disrupting and one count of conspiracy. Your type of dangerous action and reprehensible behavior disturbs the peace of our community and undermines our government. It must be stopped. When I see you Mr. Ringer. I see Gestapo boots marching to destroy freedom. I sentence you to ten years in prison."

Bunzy's legs buckle. A minute ago he had a life. He had importance. He had plans. There were things he wanted to do. That is all over.

"Mr. Ringer, I remand you to the custody of the United States Federal Marshalls. Next case!"

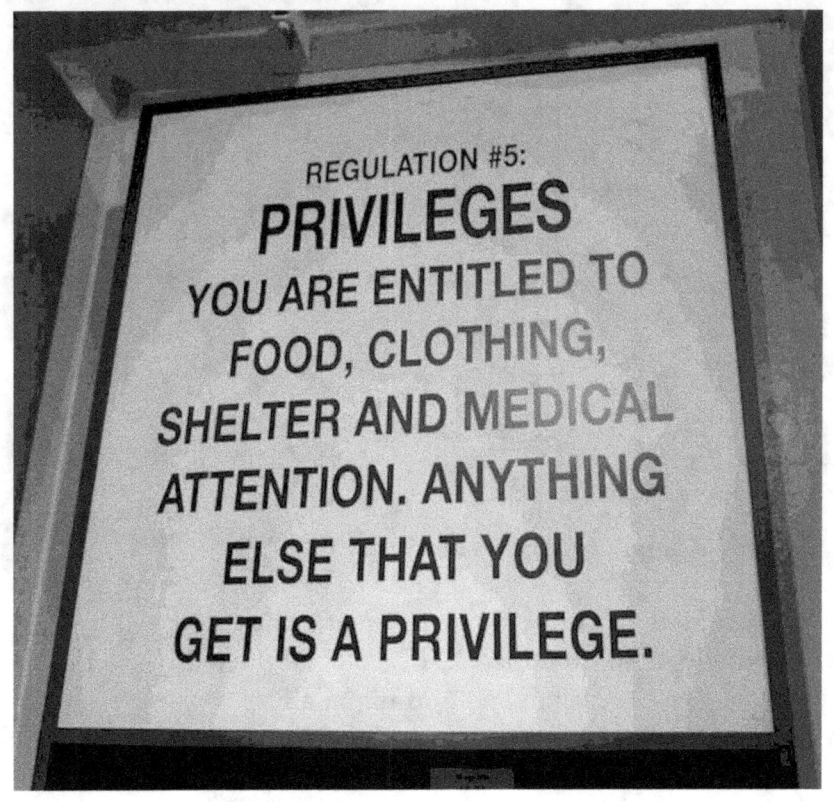

CHAPTER 6
THE ARCHONS

"As soon as you're born they make you feel small by giving you no time instead of it all 'Til the pain is so big you feel nothing at all"

John Lennon
Working Class Hero

Again, Bunzy is chained up, but this time in a bright orange jump suit. With a big man in a grey suit under each arm, he's drug off to another plain grey four door sedan. They drive out through suburbia and then out through the country to a low cream colored cement building surrounded by two nine foot tall razor wire topped fences. The building appears to be mostly underground. They drive down a cement ramp to a small steel basement door and enter the building on foot. This facility seems like a hospital or maybe a mental institution, but it's a prison. There are bars and thick wire screens everywhere. The few men that Bunzy sees are no nonsense guards in black military uniforms.

He's placed in a large clean cement and steel room which is maybe sixty feet by forty feet. There are three smaller cells in this bigger room with only one small iron bed in each one. There is nobody in any of these cells. They seat Bunzy at a large solid plastic picnic table with a plastic bench on each side. These are the only pieces of furniture in this main room. The solid steel door to this area is slammed shut. He's alone in a bright pastel yellow room. The slick enamel floor is yellow. The slick enamel walls are yellow. The slick enamel ceiling is yellow. A row of fluorescent lights shine into every corner of this terrible room. Unlike the cell on the Rock, this room is bright. Everything in the Rock was grey or dark. This room is very bright. The brightness makes Bunzy squint to see. He wants a pair of sunglasses. This place is worse than the Rock in some way that digs in at the back of his skull. There's no place to hide even just his eyes. All of this slick makes him believe this room could be washed down with a high-pressure hose, washed down right into the drain in the middle of the floor without disturbing anything or anyone anywhere. Just take the skinny little mattress pad, two puny white sheets, a pillow and a pillow case, and a thin grey woolen blanket out of the cell on the right and turn on the hose. Blood, guts, gore, and memories would be all gone.

Nothing happens for weeks. It could be days. It could be months. Bunzy doesn't know how much time passes because the room is underground. There are no windows. It's solid everything and the lights are never turned off. Time moves slowly down here. It isn't possible to tell how much time passes when you can't see the Sun come up and go down and the lights don't go on and off. There is no way to measure time in this subterranean vault. He loses track. If Bunzy would have known that he was going to be here for so long, he would have tried to keep track of the time somehow, but the only things that happen in this horrible place are food comes every once in a while and sometimes two men come in and yell at him for not making his bed correctly or for being a worthless person in general and for doing nothing properly, ever. He has the feeling that the food and the abuse don't come at regular intervals though. There is a randomness about the nature of everything in this concrete hell. He never knows when the men are going to come yell at him and push him around. He believes though that he has been in this bright yellow cement box a long time.

He starts wondering about his sanity.

This can't be about a comment that I might have casually made in a parking lot years ago. What is happening? What is this all really about? Is this even real, or am I dreaming?

Finally, four men in grey suits enter Bunzy's cell. One of them informs him, "Your appeal has been decided. Your sentence has been reduced to six years in a federal penal colony in California. We are here to transport you there."

"I didn't know that I was having an appeal," Bunzy says.

"You want to give those four years back to the court?"

"No."

"Then let's go."

He's chained up again and they drive south for a long day. It seems to be summer. In the evening they arrive at a low, modern, very large cement facility inside two ten foot tall chain link fences with manned guard towers at every corner. The last foot of these fences tips back into the prison at a forty-five degree angle and is made of a vicious, sharp, jagged barbed wire. The prison is surrounded by colorful blooming tulip fields and is near a sunny coast.

He's housed in a dormitory and given a battery of IQ, information, and psychiatric tests. After the tests he's placed in a cell on the second tier on a four-floor facility with hundreds of cells on both sides of an open area. This is just one wing in one building in this prison complex. The cells are full. There are two bunks in his cell but he is locked up alone. He's given a job as a clerk in the facility hospital. Time passes slowly in an atmosphere of violence, rape, and murder.

After a few months Bunzy's re-education begins. The classes are led by the Teacher. There are ten men in his class. In an individual session the Teacher tells him, "Mr. Ringer, you are indeed a lucky man. You have the opportunity to repent of your sins and to be forgiven, but if you do not beg for forgiveness, then you are going to be injected with leprosy and slowly your body will rot away. First your fingers and toes will rot off. Then your nose will fall off. And finally your body will rot until you beg for forgiveness or die. What will it be Mr. Ringer?"

"I'm not sure what I'm supposed to repent."

The Teacher shouts, "That attitude will lose you your fingers, toes, and nose, and if you persist, your life."

"I'm sorry, but I'm confused. I'll give this some serious thought."

"That's better. We'll continue our discussion later."

The Teacher leaves Bunzy alone, hope flowing down into the drain in the center of the slick, antiseptically clean, cream-colored enamel floor.

In Bunzy's group there is a tall, slender, handsome, curly golden haired, young man who is from the eastern part of Europe. He calls himself Hans. He is definitely certain that what is happening in this country is evil, damaging the world, and must be stopped. He isn't at all confused like the rest of the group. The Teacher hates him. The guards hate him. Even many of the prisoners hate him. Bunzy likes him. The young man is chosen to be the first one of them to be injected with leprosy.

Within days the skin on his hands and feet starts to flake off. Within a couple of weeks his skin has started to be wrinkly and white all over his body. Large chunks of dead flesh start to come off his toes and his fingers. His face gets scaly particularly around his nose and mouth.

Daily, the Teacher explains to Bunzy's groups the history of America and shows them how their doubts and attitudes are undermining the success and happiness of this great country. They are encouraged to admit their guilt and change their attitude. Bunzy is particularly encouraged in special education sessions with three or four assistant teachers to understand how evil the Attractor Box is. He's shown how much happier and prosperous America would be if there were no Attractor Boxes.

The Teacher tells him, "Mr. Ringer you need to repent of having ever built that box. You need to give the box to the United States government which is much wiser than you are and knows how to use that technology properly."

As Hans rots in front of them and slowly dies, long solitary marathon sessions lasting night and day in individual cells begin. The lights are kept on and obnoxious music plays all of the time. They can't sleep anymore.

The Teacher informs Bunzy, "If you'll volunteer for the United States government space program, you're time will be reduced."

Bunzy agrees, "I'll do it. Where do I sign up?"

"Here."

The Teacher hands him a form.

Bunzy signs it.

Sessions begin. They immerse him in tanks of very cold water for long periods of time and spin him around at tremendous speeds until he gets sick and passes out. Then nothing is said about more tests or less prison time. It's just as if nothing other than his suffering, ever happened.

Soon it's time for the second one of them to be injected with leprosy, then the third, then the fourth.

Bunzy's turn must be getting close. He's terrified. He doesn't want to slowly rot away like those other guys are doing.

He wonders. *Am I strong enough to hold out and die a little piece at a time like Hans? Should I even do that? What does the Teacher want us to confess? What would satisfy him?*

The Teacher comes to Bunzy and explains, "The Federal Government is the authority in your lives. The government is the repository of all human wisdom. It is the apex of all knowledge. It is only below that of God Almighty. You need to place your faith in that authority and to believe in the wisdom and goodness of the government and to see that whatever the Federal Authorities tell you is really for your own best interests and for the health of your family and the welfare of our community. When you recognize this and admit it, then you can leave the program."

Han's fingers and toes are beginning to come off. His face is becoming disgusting. Bunzy is horrified. He doesn't know how long it has been since he's slept. The members of the group are being required to take handfuls of pills. They don't know what drugs are in them. The capsules come anonymously in little white paper cups. They have to put the capsules in their mouths and swallow them with a little water. After they swallow, a guard looks in our mouths and then runs a long dirty finger around in it to make sure they haven't hidden any pills in their cheeks or under their tongues to spit out later. Bunzy is becoming very anxious, frightened, and confused.

He asks the Teacher, "What does the Government want of me? What can I do to make the Government happy?"

"The Government doesn't like the Attractor Box," the Teacher replies. "It wants you to stop promoting and giving out Boxes. It wants you to sign over all of your patents to the Government of the United States of America and to never ever discuss the ideas associated with the Attractor ever again. That would make the Government happy."

"The Box gives people free energy," Bunzy argues.

"The Attractor Box destroys the economy," the Teacher shouts in Bunzy's face. "The Attractor destabilizes peoples' lives and confuses them. It gives them a false idea of who they are and of the purpose of their lives."

"It gives them the freedom to do what they want," Bunzy asserts.

"Freedom is an expression of fear, anxiety, and confusion. Safety is what people need. Freedom is bad. Freedom is just another word for misery. You are bad. You are evil. You have ruined the happiness of our country. It would have been better if you had never been born. Now though, you are here, so how are we going to deal with you, Mr. Ringer? How can we give your story a happy ending?"

"Well, I guess the Attractor Box has to be disappeared. It needs to be eliminated."

"That's right, Mr. Ringer! So how are we going to do that? You put it out there."

"I guess that I'll have to take it back."

"That's right, Mr. Ringer! You have to take it back and make this country as if it never happened."

"How can I do that?"

"Give everything to the government and never mention any of this ever again."

"I don't know. The Attractor still seems like a good idea to me."

"Well think it over Mr. Ringer. Think it over as if your life depended on it."

There are no more classes for Bunzy. He spends his days watching his fellow prisoners rot and listening to awful music and taking pills that make him frightened and confused.

Watching Han's flesh come off is horrible. First it becomes white. Then it shrivels so that there are deep crevasses spidering across it. Then it flakes off in chunks. Bunzy thought Han's skin would become red and infected and gangrenous, but it doesn't. It's white and comes off in chunks. This is worse than pus and rot and dead black gangrenous flesh.

Finally, the Teacher comes to Bunzy and says, "Mr. Ringer you need to think about your decision alone, but first let's give you a shot of leprosy so that time will truly be important to you. No more sitting around contemplating your belly button. This is America not India."

They inject Bunzy and then drag him off to an interrogation cell in the basement. This cell is special. There is nothing in the room except a mattress, a toilet, a drain in the middle of the floor, an electric plug-in, and a bright fluorescent light fixture in a high ceiling. One of the teaching assistants in a black uniform takes the mattress out of the cell. Two other men in black uniforms hold Bunzy over the drain and strip him naked. The man who took the mattress out returns with a bucket of cold water. He pours it over Bunzy's head. Then two of the men go outside of the cell and return rolling in an electric chair. They roll it to the middle of the room over the drain, lock the wheels and strap Bunzy in it.

The Teacher enters the room and begins, "Mr. Ringer, this is a very special chair." He pats it fondly. "It has two separate electrical circuits. One circuit is for this technician here," he points to an unsmiling man who is standing beside the chair and has a double lightning bolt insignia on his black military cap, "to monitor your brain patterns and your bio-rhythms. In that way we will know more about what you are thinking than you probably will. It's just a formality because I can read your mind and I already know what you're thinking. The other circuit is to further your education by rewarding you in a proper manner when you act inappropriately. We'll severely shock you. Mr. Ringer, I can tell when you mean yes and when you mean no, but what I want you to do is to say the opposite of what you mean. Okay, let's begin."

He looks Bunzy in the eyes and asks, "What is your name?"

"Bunzy Ringer."

"Am I to understand that your name is Mr. Ringer?"

"Yes."

BZZZAP!

"Ummphhh!" Bunzy is slammed with a violent jolt of lightening. He bites his tongue and blood starts to run out of the corner of his mouth.

When he can think again, Bunzy asks, "Why did you do that? My name is Ringer. That's true."

"Yes, but I want you to lie. I told you that you are to say no when you mean yes and you are to say yes and when you mean no."

"Oh. This is really confusing," Bunzy says.

"Remember, yes means no, and no means yes in our conversation. So, the correct answer would have been no because no means yes.".

"I didn't understand," Bunzy tells him.

"I see that, but I hope that you do now, and that we won't have to have any more painful lessons," the Teacher says.

"So, your age is one hundred and twelve? Is that correct?"

"Yes. That is right," Bunzy answers.

"Good. Now we're getting somewhere," the Teacher observes.

"So, Mr. Ringer, the Earth is round? Is that correct?" He asks.

"No," Bunzy responds.

BZZZAP!

When Bunzy comes to again, he asks, "What did I say wrong? The Earth is round so I should say no shouldn't I"

"Well, the problem, Mr. Ringer, is; do you know the Earth is round?"

"That is just what I've been told, and I've seen pictures of Earth from space, and it looks mostly round like a ball."

"Those pictures could be faked, couldn't they?" The Teacher asks.

"No," Bunzy responds.

"Very good," the Teacher says. "Now you're catching on. Your teachers may have had good reasons to tell you the Earth is round, other than, that it is round."

"No," Bunzy says.

"Good answer again," the Teacher observes. "So, let's stick with what you actually know and not speculate about what you believe."

"Okay," Bunzy agrees.

"There are too many people on Earth."

"I don't know," Bunzy says.

"Good answer Mr. Ringer. You don't know. Now we're making some progress. Mr. Ringer would you like a sip of water?"

"No," Bunzy tells him.

"Oh, okay. Miss Smith, will you give Mr. Ringer a sip of water?"

An attractive young woman in a tight short white nurse's dress approaches Bunzy from his left side and holds a straw in a glass of water to his bleeding lips. He sips some water and smiles at her. She is the first woman whom he's seen in at least a year, maybe two or three years. With his head strapped in the electric chair, he didn't see her enter the cell.

"Mr. Ringer over here," the Teacher says. "Pay attention. Explain to me the meaning of life."

"I can't. I don't know the meaning of life," Bunzy answers.

BZZZAP!

"I don't understand," Bunzy whines. "Why was I shocked? I don't know the meaning of life."

"Oh, but I think that you do believe that you know something," the Teacher says. "Otherwise, you wouldn't be here and that needle over there wouldn't read above fifty." He's pointing at a big dial in the middle of the control panel that is attached to the chair in which Bunzy is strapped. "You'd be, being a good little boy and doing what you're told, but no, you feel superior. You think that you know things, don't you?"

"No," Bunzy shouts.

"Good," the Teacher says. "Now we're doing splendidly. So why should you be treated any differently than anyone else. Why should you have any special privileges? You feel important, don't you? You feel that you are unique and that you should be given special circumstances so that you can fulfill your high purpose in life. Don't you?"

"No!" Bunzy shouts again.

"Good answer. This feeling of uniqueness is a problem, isn't it? It causes you to do things that you shouldn't do. Doesn't it?"

"No," Bunzy answers.

"You are not special," the Teacher tells him. "There is nothing special about you, is there?"

"I don't know. I'm confused," Bunzy answers.

"Yes, you are confused," the Teacher acknowledges. "The truth is that you and all of the rest of the humans like you are nothing but tasty pieces of meat that do work."

"No," Bunzy whispers.

Looking Bunzy straight in the eyes, the Teacher continues, "Your crime is that you have been thinking about yourself and your friends and family in ways that you shouldn't and then you have been saying and doing things that are disturbing your government. This has to stop. Do you understand?"

"No," Bunzy mutters, then clearly asks, "Is disturbing the Government a serious crime?"

"Oh, it's very serious indeed," the Teacher tells him. "The happiness of our herd of people depends on their peaceful, secure state of mind. It's five years in prison for every count against you for disturbing the happiness of the flock and there are a lot of counts with which you could be charged."

The Teacher pauses for a moment. He watches Bunzy for a while. He seems to make up his mind and says to Bunzy, "The other instructors and myself are going to leave you here for some time to contemplate these lessons and to measure your mortality, especially its length in relation to leprosy."

They unstrap him. Everyone leaves. Two of them return and throw a mattress, a blanket, a pillow, a pair of pants, and a shirt into the cell, and then they leave again pushing the electric chair out, slamming the door locked closed behind them.

Hours go by. Days go by. Weeks go by. Bunzy's flesh begins to rot away. There is nothing to see in this cell, not even a cockroach or a rat. There is only slick, cold, hard, yellow enamel. His life is ending. Water, food and toilet paper appear, nothing else.

He sits in one corner of the cell on the mattress, wrapped in the blanket staring diagonally across the cell at the opposite corner. A white piece of paper lies on the floor over there. It's a white piece of paper about twice the size of an ordinary business card. There are two rows of numbers on it:

12 5 20 9 20 7 15 13 15 18 5
9 19 16 15 19 19 9 2 12 5

Tilopa Rinpoche's signature graces the back of the card.

Bunzy thinks about it. *Rinpoche said that I would need this note, but where did it come from? How did it get in here? It can't be here, but there it is.*

After staring at the card for a long, long time, Bunzy realizes that the numbers on it are the number positions of the characters in the English alphabet.

The note says, "Let it go. More is possible."

Bunzy immediately understands. The energy generating box isn't important. The whole technology of the Western world is a Trojan Horse. What seems safe and good and helpful is dangerous and bad. Technology is being used as a sophisticated deception. It's a trick, like a magician uses trickery in a stage show. The magician waves one hand around in front of the audience keeping their attention, while he does something else with his other hand, and makes fools of them. The Teacher and his assistants have taught Bunzy more than they meant to. There is a lot more going on here in this place we call Earth than we are being told.

When Bunzy begins pounding on the metal door in this isolation cell, a man comes over and slides the food slot in the bottom of the door open and gruffly asks, "What do you want scum ball?"

"Inform your Commanding Officer that I want to co-operate," Bunzy tells him.

The guard says, "Okay, as if that will do you any good, loser. You're going to die in there. Scum like you shouldn't be allowed to live and you certainly shouldn't be allowed to associate with decent people and infect them with your diseased mind."

Bunzy repeats, "Go tell your Captain what I said."

A while later the Teacher comes to Bunzy's cell along with his teaching assistants.

The Teacher says, "Mr. Ringer, I understand that you have something important that you wish to say?"

Bunzy confesses, "Yes, I'm sorry about the things that I've said and done. My ideas were ignorant and misguided. I regret that I have misled people and caused suffering. I will immediately cease and desist talking such nonsense and acting in a destructive manner."

"What about the energy generator?" The Teacher asks.

Bunzy says, "It is a misguided way of thinking about energy and life in general. It is dangerous. Have the legal papers drawn up and I will sign away all of my rights to the energy generator to the United States government and I will agree furthermore to never discuss the device or any ideas that surround the subject."

The Teacher smiles.

"It's good to see that you have come to your senses."

"Yes," Bunzy admits, "I regret my previous attitude and all of the horrible things I've done."

The Teacher probs further, "You see now, how important it is that everyone respects authority and leads productive lives, and that people not do things which upset our community, don't you?"

"Yes," Bunzy grants. "I do. I have completely let go of my old ideas."

Still smiling, the Teacher assents, "Well, after you sign the papers, I don't see any reason why we can't release you and why you shouldn't be counted as a productive member of society."

"Thank you," Bunzy says. "My job will have to be doing something very simple though. It's difficult for me to even decide to turn a light switch on or off."

The Teacher agrees, "you will need a period of adjustment, but you will be fine now. We will inject you with the cure for the fungus that is causing your flesh to rot away. The cause of the illness is not leprosy. It is a super strong type of athlete's foot. Once you are given the cure, you will recover fully."

They give Bunzy the first injection and he immediately starts to recover.

Two weeks later after signing the paperwork, the men in grey give Bunzy his final injection and release him at the basement entrance to a county jail. He walks around to the main street and stands facing Garden Valley Boulevard at night.

His charged cell phone is in the pocket of his old clothes which the men in grey put on him when they released him. The phone rings.

He answers it.

"Hi. This is Bunzy."

It's Isabel, "Where are you? Where have you been?" She asks really worriedly. "I've been looking for you for hours."

A scrap of paper came out of Bunzy's pocket along with the telephone. On the paper he reads, "Don't forget or we'll have to do this again." It is signed, "Your Teacher."

Bunzy says, "I've met the Archons."

Isabel responds, "Oh dear."

Bunzy thinks. *Why didn't they kill me? This is way more complicated than I thought. What's their game?*

CHAPTER 7
LIGHT RISING

"If it's not good for everyone, it's not good at all."
Cherokee saying

Nothing has really changed, except that everything is different."
Isabel picks Bunzy up on the corner of Sunset and Garden Valley.

"Where have you been?" She asks as she drives.

Staring straight ahead, he tells her, "I was arrested, convicted of disturbing the Government and sent to prison where I spent the last few years. Then I made a deal with the authorities in which I signed over the rights to the Attractor and agreed to never talk about it again. I also agreed to be a good, quiet, conforming, productive member of our society. Then I was released."

"All in three hours?" Isabel looks doubtful.

"Three hours!" Bunzy shouts turning towards her. "What are you talking about? It's been years since I saw you at the Armory!"

"No," she tells him very slowly keeping her eyes on the road. "It's been three hours. Look," she points at herself. "I'm wearing the same clothes that I was when I saw you last, and do I look a day older?"

Bunzy looks at her and thinks about everything. *Those are the same clothes she was wearing and she looks exactly the same as when I saw her last.*

"Well," she says.

Bunzy shrugs.

This is impossible. I must be going crazy.

Fighting down panic, he says, "Yeah, I see what you're saying alright, but it's impossible. I'm confused. There is something odd going on here. Things are definitely not what they seem to be. What about you? I saw you fly out of the door of Harvey's pickup, and I heard a terrible whump sound."

"That was the case of wine hitting the parked car I slid under. Other than being scratched and bruised, I wasn't hurt and no one even noticed me. I just shimmied out from under the car, got up and went back in the Armory."

She shows him her bruises and scratches and torn, stained clothes.

Bunzy is shaken and really confused.

He tells her, "I've met the Archons head-on. They are real and they are really seriously messing with us. They have the Dream Key. They have other ways to mess with us I don't even understand. We must do the mantra chanting ritual now. The Teacher could be watching."

After they do their mantra for thirty minutes, Bunzy announces, "We have to go see Rinpoche."

Isabel says, "Sure. I don't know about your weird idea about what happened, but I always like to go see Rinpoche."

When they get to the Naropa Yoga Center, they go straight to Rinpoche's office where he is waiting for them.

"Bunzy, Isabel it's lovely to see you again.

"Master Rinpoche," Bunzy begins, "I've had a very odd and terrible experience." After summarizing what has happened, he asks, "What do you think is going on?"

"Life on Earth," Rinpoche tells him.

Bunzy says, "I confess. I didn't believe you at first. This is not the life though I learned about as a kid."

"Probably not," Rinpoche says.

"I just lived through three or four terrible years in what everyone else experienced as three or four hours. That's impossible."

"I wouldn't say that," Rinpoche tells him.

"Why wouldn't you say that?" Bunzy asks.

"Because you just experienced it. Right?"

"Yes," Bunzy mumbles, "but that's crazy. I'm confused about what's real anymore. Until now, time has always seemed so tangible and went just one way, forward. Everybody was living the same amount of time, in sync with everyone else and time went from the past, through the present, into the future. I can't explain what just happened. I seem to be losing my mind."

"Well, if you were to lose your mind, what would you lose?" Rinpoche asks.

"I'd lose contact with what's real," Bunzy squawks.

"And then you would do what, unreal things?"

"I would imagine things were happening that weren't happening, Bunzy asserts.

"So, you would go to corners and wait for people to bring you money who never show up? You'd imagine that you got the lead role in movies that were never produced? You'd imagine that you were loved by someone who nobody else could even see?"

"Yes, that sort of thing," Bunzy mumbles

"You're forgetting about the Dream Key and the Archons?"

89

"The Archons?" Bunzy quizzes Rinpoche.

"The men in grey." Rinpoche clarifies.

"Then I'm not crazy!" Bunzy exclaims. "The men in grey are real. All of those things that I told you and Isabel about are real?"

"As real as you are," Rinpoche confirms. "The thing to realize is that space and time are infinite, eternal, and non-linear, and we are not things in time, but rather consciousnesses that create beingness, and Archons feed on beingness. Space and time are a projection of the eyes. You have been deceived into thinking space and time are outside of you and that you are looking from inside of you towards the outside and seeing what is real, rather than looking from inside/out and creating reality. You need to realize that things are not coming into being in the way that you imagine they are, and the Archons are using people as food and slaves. You were getting out of your Archon mind. You have been brutally put back in it."

"Master, that is a horrifying idea," Isabel says. "Why should we believe you? What proof do you have such a crazy idea has any validity at all."

"Isabel, the proof you are herd creatures who are being kept in pens, which you think of as your mind, is all around you. You even act as your own police dogs. Don't you see that humans are raised on feedlots called cities and carefully controlled?"

"What do you mean by carefully controlled?" She asks. Then she asserts, "I'm an American. Our children are Americans. We're free people living in a free country. We get to think what we want and to do what we like."

Rinpoche asks her, "Isabel, as soon as you could walk and talk and were potty trained, you were sent to school, right?"

"Yes."

"And at school they told you what to think and what to do and the school authorities started grading you so that you would know good from bad so that when you graduated you could get a job and make some money, right?"

"Well yes," she agrees.

"So almost as soon as you were born you were forced to go to school and learn things you didn't want to know so you could do things you don't want to do and you've been doing what you're told ever since, haven't you?"

"Yes, but I'm free to move or change jobs or friends. I could divorce Bunzy if I wanted to. I can do whatever I want."

"Did you want to go to school?"

"No."

"Do you want to go to work every day?"

"No."

"Would you rather live somewhere else and do something else?"

"Well yes, but I can't. I have obligations."

"There you go. Humans are truly pathetic. We even police ourselves or should I say that we even herd ourselves. Our parents, teachers, preachers, and police keep us in line in the beginning and then through peer pressure we stop each other from thinking thoughts that would get us outside of our feedlots when we become adults. The fence of the pen these Archons keep us in is the rational mind and it isn't really even our mind. It is their mind. They have given us their mind and tricked us into believing it is our mind. What we believe that we know is actually what they are telling us that we know. That set of beliefs they give us surrounds us and keeps us compliant in little human coops. So, Bunzy, losing your mind shouldn't be what concerns you. The two big questions that you and Isabel should want answered are: who are the Archons and what are they doing to humans?"

Bunzy answers for Isabel, "The Teacher said that humans are meat and slaves. Are the men in grey and the Archons the same?"

"It's not that simple," Rinpoche tells them. "Your teacher is a cruel deceiver. It's not as if there are only a few Archons and they all agree. Over time the Archons have multiplied and interbred with people. Now there are a lot of Archons, a lot of hybrids, and they have a lot of servants. This is an Archonic realm."

Bunzy interrupts, "The Teacher said they eat us. How? I haven't seen any men in grey suits hacking up people and tossing them on the barbeque."

"Archons can appear however they want to people, but in their natural form, they seem reptilian to us. Their eyes are different than ours. Humans rarely see them as they are and almost never understand what the Archons around them are doing."

"I understand all that. What I don't understand is the food thing."

"Archons use humans as an energy source in the same way that humans use cows and pigs for food, except that Archons are more like mosquitoes, really big mosquitoes, than people in their feeding habits. They have to have lots of prey to maintain themselves because they don't want to kill their victims when they feed on them. They take just a small amount of energy from their quarry each day. The result is that they keep their victims just about, but not quite dead. Each victim needs a certain amount of energy to maintain its own life. If an Archon were to take too much energy from all of its victims and they all died, the Archon would starve to death. So, Archons keep their victims fairly anemic, but not so anemic they die."

"Oh, they're not hacking us up. They're sucking our blood."

"Not quite. The Archon's food is what we would call our life force. It's not the same thing as the red substance that flows through our blood vessels, and they don't suck it out like mosquitoes suck blood. We don't really have a definition or understanding of what they're taking. This life force energy is not something that the Archons want us to know about. Remember we only have words for things which they want us to know. We don't know anything except what they want us to know. We don't know about them, so we can't see them as they are and we don't know that what they are taking from us even exists. You don't perceive what you don't know about. I'm sure that you are beginning to visualize what I am telling you though and now you will start seeing things differently."

"Can't Isabel and I somehow get closer to understanding the nature of what is happening like you do?"

"Sure, let's take a short verbal stroll around the people pasture. Think about people on the people farm the way that a rancher thinks about his cattle, but add some more dimensions to the usefulness of cows to farmers. Not only can Archons and hybrids consume people, but they can harness them to produce all of the things which the Archons, hybrids, and their managers need, and humans are also good pets and sex slaves. If you are an Archon or a hybrid you can abuse people any way that you want and then dispose of their dead, mutilated carcasses however you want. People disappear all the time. Humans are cheap, useful, convenient, and have absolutely no protections from Archons. Humans are to Archons as cows are to people. And like cows, humans don't have any understanding of what is going on, so they also have no say in what is happening."

"Why can't we see any of this?"

"You can't perceive what you haven't conceived, and you can't conceive what you haven't perceived. You were trapped in a blind loop like most people until I entered your life.

"Master, if Bunzy isn't crazy and there really are men in grey suits out there running this world for powerful beings called Archons, why don't they just kill troublemakers like us? Why go through all of the trouble to bring people who get out of the fence back into the pasture, so to speak?"

"Sometimes they do, but farmers can't kill every animal that gets out of its cage or tries to get out of the cage or fights its harness. Just because a cow finds a hole in the fence and escapes doesn't do it much good anyway. It has nowhere to go to live in safety. It has no weapons to protect itself. It really has no understanding of its situation. It is just out of the pasture for a while. That is how the Archons see Bunzy and you. What is a trouble making human going to do? And the people who are troublemakers tend to be stronger, more nutritious, and produce better work. The Archons don't see Bunzy as a threat. To them he's a grade A piece of meat on foot and a good producer. The effort that an Archon has to put out to round him up and put him back in his cage seems huge and magical to us, but it's nothing to them. It's not anything more than catching a chicken and putting it back in the coop is to us, and when other people who might be tempted to run, see Bunzy being caught and put back in his cage, he makes a good example for what not to do to other people."

Bunzy says, "Ever since I had that dream where I was at that revival and then heard about the Dream Key, I've been looking for a way to get out of here and back to paradise. This isn't the way that I imagined that I was going to get there though. I admit that I didn't pay much attention to what you said about the Archons, but now I'm listening and I'm a believer. I'm more baffled now by the Archons though than I am by dreaming. Things just keep getting more and more complicated. What advice do you have for us?"

"To thine own eye be true," Rinpoche tells him.

"Don't you mean, to thine own self be true?" Bunzy inquires.

"No. I mean, to thine own eye be true. Remember that you are projecting your self through your eyes. You need to learn that. You need to go to the desert, fast and think about what I'm telling you. And remember you are learning to be creative in a powerful way that attracts Spirit's attention. So, to thine own eye be true."

"Why?"

"Bunzy, you had that dream for a reason. You're a special person. That is why I've taken so much time educating you. Learning to see is a step toward your destination."

"To see? How do Isabel and I learn to see?"

"To begin with you need to be able to project what is in your mind's eye out in front of you powerfully enough that it becomes real. That is what the Archons don't want you to learn you can do."

"Why should my Archon owner let me go practice something he doesn't want me to learn how to do?"

"You have to learn to cloak your thoughts better than you've been doing. Humans gather energy while dreaming. We just call it plain old sleeping. Most people aren't aware of what they're doing while they're sleeping, but let's call what you're doing grazing. You have to be allowed to graze for a few hours per day to feed yourselves so you can feed your Archon owners and do their work for them. While you are sleeping you are literally out to lunch and while you are on lunch break, the Archons don't keep track of you. They have trouble connecting their minds to your mind in Dreamland. Seeing through your eyes then requires a Dream Key effort. We don't even look through our own waking body eyes when we're asleep. We see in a completely different way."

"I can grasp that," Bunzy says.

"Good," Rinpoche notes and continues, "it is also necessary for Archons to let humans take vacations every once in a while, to renew their energies. While we are on vacation, we enter an altered state of consciousness like we do when we are sleeping. Now imagine that the field that we graze in while we are in these altered states, is very large, say fifty thousand acres, and in that field there is a mountain with a forest on it and a valley with a river flowing through it. Something wandering around out there could disappear for a while. The rancher doesn't know what the cow is doing while it is grazing and he doesn't care. As far as he is concerned, the more food that it finds and eats the better. To the Archon owner, the further a human goes while eating, the bigger, fatter, and stronger that it becomes. The better food it makes and the better work it does, but if a human becomes too big and strong, then the Archons can't control it and it has to be slaughtered. This is bad for the Archons and bad for people. While you're vacationing, you need to communicate balance to your Archonic lord. The problem is that your mind is like a remote game camera. When you're doing something they don't want you doing, you have to be careful not to turn the camera on so that what you are doing can be seen by your controllers. We can depend on your owner's feelings of superiority to keep him from watching you too closely. So, go on vacation, but keep the game camera away from any dangerous thoughts. Don't go around acting strangely and attracting attention, but do go as far away as you can get in the recreational time that you are allowed. No more Attractors."

Bunzy and Rinpoche laugh.

Then Bunzy asks, "Isn't going to the desert on some kind of vision quest, a kind of odd thing to do?"

"No," Rinpoche tells him, then explains, "science and most of the religions are all part of the Archon mind. These institutions are all based on slave theologies wherein bad people make progress, get approved by higher authorities, and pass on to better lives. People go to the desert all of the time for knowledge or salvation or pleasure. But you don't have to make it all that complicated. Go hunting!"

"Go hunting?" Isabel blurts out

"Yes, go hunting," Rinpoche tells her. "Archons are hunters. Their whole lives are based on hunting things down, defeating and humiliating them, then eating or having sex or both with what's left. Turn your mind on to going hunting. You'll become instantly invisible. Your Archon lords won't be interested in what you're doing."

"Make a habit of doing mantra so that it doesn't seem odd to your Archon master when you begin to chant. Then when you are going to do something that you don't want to be noticed, do mantra, enter dream time and become invisible for a while. But meanwhile go on vacation, become boring."

Isabel and Bunzy head for home to prepare for a hunting trip to the desert. Their lives are getting dangerous.

Bunzy and Isabel decide to take Johnny Jones with them. He is way better at visualizing than either of them is. Maybe the three of them working together can come up with an understanding of what Rinpoche is teaching Bunzy and Isabel.

The three of them start driving upward along the pristine mountain waters of the Calapooya River through the Cascades towards the high mountain peaks that cut off the coastal rains from the inland high desert. They're mesmerized by what they're seeing through the front windshield as well as the reflections on the glass as they pass in and out through the dense forest.

Isabel tells Johnny what Rinpoche said about projecting your mind's eye out in front of you and asks him, "Do you know what he means?"

"I think so," he replies. "He's spiritualizing the vision."

"Spiritualizing the vision?"

"Making it more real. When you imagine something that you are going to draw or paint, you imagine it in your mind with your eyes closed. When you can see it in your mind clearly enough, then you draw it or paint it or sculpt it or create it in whatever media that you're using. If you are going to spiritualize it, you take the visualizing process a step further and you actually see what you are visualizing out in front of you with your eyes open as if it were really there. This tricks the mind into believing that you are really seeing whatever you're visualizing. This is best done seeing something that you have an emotional attachment to, like a deceased mother or father. Then when you see them with your eyes open, you think you're seeing them out in front of you, rather than in your mind. They are more real that way. You're reflecting what is in the mind's eye out in front of you like projecting a hologram in front of you. This is a reflection-mirror thingy."

"What's this reflection thing that you're talking about?" Bunzy interrupts them.

"Well, you see the reflection of this piece of paper on the dashboard up on the window here in front of us?" Johnny asks. He thumps on a reflection on the window with the knuckles on his right hand. "The papers are real here on the window too, but it's a reflection. Somehow our lenses in our eyes or something in us can reflect what is on our mind just like this window reflects this piece of paper. This is the paper." He strikes his forehead with the heal of his left hand. Then he waves around in the air in front of them. "This is the window. Bingo! Think about it, concentrate, next thing you know, you see a reflection out in front of you just like a reflection on a window, but because there is no window in front of you, what you see is more like a hologram. Your mind's eye is seeing this image out in front of you that is in your mind and all of the sudden when you concentrate it becomes real out there in front of you, just like a reflection coming off whatever is being reflected. The trick is being able to see what is in your mind's eye out in front of you with your eyes open."

Bunzy pulls over beside the road on a wide spot in the forest and announces, "Alright, let's do it."

"What shall we start with?" Johnny asks.

"Chief Joseph of the Wallowa Band of the Nez Perce Indians," Isabel volunteers.

"Why Chief Joseph?" Bunzy asks.

"I've had a great interest in Chief Joseph for a long time. He was one of the last great leaders of the American Indians. He was a man of high integrity. He represents a completely different way of life from ours. I would have very much liked to have known him and his family and his people. I've read about him, looked at his pictures, and feel a strong attachment to him," Isabel explains.

Then she asks, "So what do we do?"

Johnny says, "Imagine him as he looks in pictures or sculpture and once you've got a clear impression of him in your mind's eye, see him standing out in front of us twenty or thirty feet. Bunzy, you've seen pictures of him and have an interest in him too, right?"

Bunzy nods his head in agreement.

"Alright. See him with your eyes open as if he is really there. You're looking at him right now, out there in front us, not inside of your head. Quit imagining him in your imagination and see him really standing there." Johnny points to a spot directly in front of the hood of the car.

They all three concentrate on the gravel parking area beside the road in front of them.

A powerful dust devil appears in the tops of the trees on their right. It touches down on the edge of the parking area whirling leaves, sticks, dirt, and dust.

They stare at it.

Bunzy wonders, *what is this? We're looking for Chief Joseph and a whirlwind appears. What's happening? Will this wind get stronger and blow trees across the road and maybe even over the car, or will it just peter out? Is this whirlwind just passing or is this the front edge of something even bigger?*

As they stare and wonder, the dust devil comes to a halt right in front of them. A whirling column of destruction and debris is roaring, not twenty feet away. There is a man spinning around inside of it.

An Indian in full Indian garb, buckskins, beads, colorful sash, long black hair, and a single eagle feather whirls out of the wind which then blows on across the road and away into the forest.

The Indian turns around a couple of times from the momentum of the wind and comes to a halt facing them with his legs spread wide bracing himself. He is looking at his left hand, palm upwards toward his face. He rocks it back and forth. Then continuing to rock the arm back and forth, he looks up it to his shoulder, then back down to his hand again. Then he does the same thing to his right hand and arm. He examines his whole body in this manner. They can see surprise and wonder on his face. He looks around at the trees, the river, the sky. Then he sees the road, follows it to their car and sees them. He's looking right at them, but he seems to be looking at something just over their heads or maybe right behind them.

He points at them and says, "Shaman," as if that explains how he got there and what's happening.

He doesn't say it with a voice. He says it with the mind, but the three of them hear him in their minds.

With his mind, Bunzy asks the apparition, "Chief Joseph, is there anything you would like people that live the way we do now to know?"

The Chief emphatically answers back, "The vision quest is for all to see."

As the three of them stare at him, he begins to fade. They can see through him to the trees and to the gravel behind him. Gradually they see more of what is behind him and less of him. Then he is gone.

Bunzy looks over at Isabel and Johnny. They're stunned. He feels the same way. He asks them, "Did you hear what he said about the vision quest?"

"Yes," Isabel responds. "The vision quest is for all to see."

Johnny nods and says, "That wasn't what I expected."

"What did you expect?" Isabel asks.

"I expected to see something like a piece of art, like a painted sculpture. I didn't expect a living hologram. I didn't expect him to move. I didn't expect him to talk and I certainly didn't expect him to have the personality of a real Chief Joseph."

"Me neither. I agree with you," Bunzy says. "I feel like he looked when he quit spinning around. I wonder what he meant when he said that 'the vision quest is for all to see'?"

Johnny explains, "In their world, sooner or later they all had to relate to the vision quest. They had to journey and find a spirit helper who would help them understand the nature of this situation. This helper would guide, protect, and empower them, bringing them hope and happiness. In our world things are different."

"I think that is what Rinpoche has been trying to tell me. I need to go on a vision quest and according to Chief Joseph, you guys do too," Bunzy adds.

"Let's get out of here," Isabel says.

They drive for the rest of the day reaching the high desert flatlands at nightfall. There is still some light on the plains, but the sky is overcast and dark.

Isabel says, "Let's try that vision thing again."

They both agree.

They have passed through the forests and are now out on the open plains. They can see for miles in every direction. Bunzy pulls over in a wide area beside the highway.

They begin their vision quest staring through the front windshield. When Chief Joseph appears this time he is doing a ceremonial dance. He is dancing away from them in a counterclockwise direction up the right-hand side of a circle. His back is turned toward them. As he comes around to about the nine o'clock position of the loop, he looks up and sees them. He stops, stands up straight, turns away from them, stretches out his right arm and raises up his right hand holding it out palm flat and down. It looks as if he is looking under his hand. Bunzy and the others follow his arm as if he is pointing out something important in the eastern sky. Sure enough, a sapphire blue hole has opened in the overcast sky. Bunzy didn't notice the hole until Chief Joseph pointed at it. A wispy mist starts forming in the open blue part of the sky. Clouds start pouring out of that blue hole like fog pouring through a mountain pass into a valley, only faster.

Chief Joseph mind to minds, "The Great Spirit and the White Buffalo Herd."

Buffalo come charging out of the blue hole in the sky. The clouds pouring down out of the blue sky are rolling a trail out in front of the racing herd. There are hundreds of white buffalo stampeding down this road which is not quite a football field wide. The trail winds back and forth across the sky reaching down toward the ground. In the front where boiling white clouds are paving the way for the herd, big snorting males as white as snow are racing ahead changing places back and forth trying to be the leader.

The herd thunders across the sky from the blue hole to the ground. When the lead bulls reach the plains, buffalo stop coming out of the blue hole in the sky and the clouds quit rolling ahead of the racing herd as they charge across the Great Basin. On the ground Indians with big buffalo lances attack them. Each time a brave raises a lance and charges a buffalo, a big bull plows him and his horse under and the herd grinds them to pieces. After a dozen attempts at killing a white buffalo fail, the Indians give up on that idea.

The buffalo rumble on across the plains for miles. Thousands of white buffalo are running across the grass lands in the twilight. They light up the evening with an eerie glow. Then the clouds start rolling ahead of the herd again and the lead bulls start pulling back up into the sky, winding on a roiling cloud highway back up toward the blue hole in the sky. As soon as the white buffalo start running back up into the sky, those Indians who were ground down by the big bulls come right back up in the herd without their lances, riding on their horses right in there with the buffalo. Those Indians weren't there as the buffalo thundered across the plains, but as soon as the white buffalo start up into the sky, the Indians appear with the herd and go back up with them. When the White Buffalo Herd reaches the blue hole in the sky, they run in and disappear behind a big bank of white clouds, leaving dust settling across the Great Basin.

When the last buffalo disappears behind the clouds, the blue hole in the sky closes and the sky turns dark. It has become night. Johnny, Isabel and Bunzy sit in their car by an empty highway, on the open plains, in the dark.

Where the blue hole was, the sky opens again, and a full moon lights the prairie. A moon beam spotlights a white buffalo bull calf standing on the top of a mound out on the prairie. The mound is so big that the dust from the herd only reaches halfway up on it. As soon as the Indians realize that the White Buffalo calf is up there, they come out of the darkness and the dust and surround the calf. They are holding their lances straight up. They have no intention of harming the White Buffalo calf. They are in awe of it.

The clear spot in the sky closes. The moon disappears. Bunzy, Isabel and Johnny are in darkness again. A lightning bolt flashes across the plains and lights up the mound. There is nothing on it. The calf went with the moonbeam. The Indians are standing there alone on an empty mound.

A white buffalo herd has just swung by them and then gone up into the sky. A white buffalo calf appeared in a moonbeam and then disappeared. They are entranced.

When the lightning flashed, Chief Joseph was gone too.

Bunzy mumbles, "What the hell just happened? You guys just saw a While Buffalo herd right?"

Johnny says, "I'm pretty good with the imagination and creativity, but c'mon that was pristine clear and Chief Joseph started it. We wouldn't have been involved with it if he hadn't pointed it out. He's pointing at a real sky and there's a blue hole in a real, cloudy sky. I was thinking that he must have some reason for pointing there. Then I heard him say, 'the Great Spirit and the White Buffalo Herd' and clouds started pouring out of that blue sky and buffalo started charging out of the sky in those boiling clouds. Where did those words come from? I didn't think them up and put them in his mind to have him create a vision of white buffalo. Did either of you?"

"Not me. That was amazing," Isabel says. "It was so real and lifelike. It was just like we bleeped into another world. None of it was cloudy or unclear. The whole vision was sparkling crystal clear. How does this work? Something other than our creating a fantasy vision is in play here. I'm hanging out with you guys, going with the flow. We've done some pretty imaginative things over the years, but this is going way beyond what we've done before. There is something else from Chief Joseph's side happening here. The hologram pointed at the only blue hole in a really real, dark overcast sky. All of the sudden the sky is working like it is part of the vision. How does that happen? There's a real hole in a real sky with white clouds that happens to take place in the real world when a vision points to it. So, there we have a hologram that we are somehow creating in our minds and all of the sudden that hologram is showing us some things in the real world. This is not something like, okay, now I'm imagining a hole in the clouds in the sky. No, the hole in the overcast sky was there. Chief Joseph points to it and says, 'the Great Spirit and the White Buffalo Herd' and all of the sudden clouds start shooting out of the blue sky like fog blowing up out of a canyon and boiling over a ridge, only faster and there are thousands of charging buffalo coming down to the ground on those clouds."

"No sooner did he speak those words than they appeared," Bunzy adds. "And where did that idea come from? I didn't think, 'yeah, let's see the Great Spirit and the White Buffalo Herd. Oh, that's a good idea. I'll go with that one.' There's something else involved here that makes this event unique. It's our spirituality."

"That's exactly what it is," Isabel agrees. "Johnny, you said that on a vision quest, the seeker, if they were successful, acquired a spirit helper. I believe that we have acquired a spirit helper and he is showing us the Great Spirit and helping us to change our concept of who we are and of what is happening here. That's what Rinpoche told us to do. We are in the big struggle with the Archons now. We have a spirit protector and Spirit helper.

Johnny adds, "Chief Joseph said that the vision quest is for all. Then he proves it by bringing us a vision. The vision quest led the ancient peoples into the spirit world. I wonder where this is all headed for us."

"The Dream Key," Bunzy says.

"What I want to know is about this Great Spirit. Who or what is the Great Spirit?" Isabel asks Johnny. "I didn't see anything except the Buffalo Herd and the Natives."

Johnny explains, "The White Buffalo Herd is an expression of the Great Spirit. The Great Spirit is the tribal ancient infinite. We moderns live in a linear objective realm. It is full of important beginnings and endings. When we saw the White Buffalo Herd, we entered the infinite/eternal and became one with the Great Spirit. We left the linear objective world. In objective reality, we couldn't have seen the great White Buffalo Herd. It wouldn't have been real. So it wouldn't have existed. We couldn't have seen it, but we did see it. We have entered the eternal and become one with the Great Spirit. We are now living in the spiritual eternal rather than in Archon linear objective history."

"I wonder how knowing the Great Spirit will change our lives? What will be different from now on?" Bunzy asks.

"Let's circle up the wagons and set up camp for the night. I'm done for the day," Isabel says.

Johnny and Bunzy agree.

They don't get going early in the morning. After a light breakfast, they break camp and are sitting on some boulders gazing out over the plains talking about last night. It's a lovely sunny day on the high desert plains.

Johnny asks, "What do you guys think that all meant yesterday?"

"A spirit, Chief Joseph, showed us a vision of the return of the power of nature to our world. The White Buffalo Herd is the spirit of the natural way of life. It's the opposite of our technological world. They showed us that, that is what the Great Spirit is bringing back," Bunzy suggests.

"It was some kind of cleansing event," Isabel offers. "The buffalo are pure and white. No buffalo dies. The Indians look like they're killed, but they are reborn and go back to the Great Spirit with the buffalo."

Johnny says, "I agree with both of you, but I think, for us, the main thing is that we actually saw that vision together, as if it were real. That's amazing, weird, magical, and impossible. I don't think that we are in techno, money-land anymore."

A little whirlwind appears in front of us. Chief Joseph steps out of it, spins around once and stops, facing us. The whirlwind vanishes. He is only visible to them from the pockets of his pants, up. He's wearing blue jeans and a green shirt. His black hair is hanging loose. He looks like a 60's hippy who is on a hike in the desert and is just dropping in on their campsite for a visit. Chief Joseph beams the feeling he's proud of them for having seen the White Buffalo vision. He isn't saying this in the mind as when he talks. This is a feeling, he is radiating, which they convert into thoughts.

When he speaks mind to mind, he says, "You are ravens now. You are bringers of the vision."

Isabel says, "I honor you and thank you for coming back and bringing us the vision of the Great Spirit and the White Buffalo Herd and for making us ravens. We admire you and it was our desire to meet you and now that you are here, I want to convey my respect for you and your people. Is there anything we can do for you or is there any message we can convey for you to this world?"

Chief Joseph says, "Tell your people. You have destroyed our way of life and you have destroyed my people. You are the eaters of souls and by destroying others' souls, you have harmed your our own souls. You must restore the Great Earth Soul and the souls of its children and regain the beauty and happiness and wonder of your own souls."

Isabel continues, "Thank you Great Father. I don't understand you or your ways. Could you help me understand what is passing from Earth, what the Americas were like before the White Man came?"

Chief Joseph explains, "Your people have no respect for the land and animals or for other peoples. You see no further than your credit cards and bank accounts. Imagine that everything as far as you can see in every direction is your family's, not yours personally but all of yours, and that you are not going to sell it or develop it or change it. Your only desire is to live in harmony with its natural ways and to experience its beauty and wonder each day. Imagine you are living in a National Park. That was life before the White Man came."

"Is there any way that we can restore that attitude?" Johnny asks.

"You must acquire outside help. You need spirit allies. You've entered a dark place and become lost."

"What can we do to restore your happiness and your family's honor and lifestyle?" Bunzy asks.

"We have passed from this world. If our way is to return, then there must be young people who dream our ancient dreams. Only when the young dream our dreams will those ways return, but who knows our traditions any longer? So, who will dream our beautiful dreams? That was the great evil that was done. Not only were we destroyed as a people, but our ways were obliterated, our dreams were ruined, our way of being was denigrated and pronounced worthless and wrong. Our customs were not allowed to be taught to our children and to their children and our ways have been forgotten, even erased. Now you live in a poorer world and in a few years you will not be able to recover what was lost because there will not even be a memory of it. The way will be gone forever. You will be poorer and live in poverty for eternity because of the mean spirited greed that has become the heart of your being."

"Thank you Chief Joseph for your candor and I hope that we will take your words to heart and use them to restore what was lost," Isabel says.

"I hope that you will too. Allow me to leave you with a vision that working together we may bring peace in the future. Aho!"

"Aho!" Bunzy, Johnny and Isabel respond.

Chief Joseph disappears. They look at each other, then they look back at where he was. Chief Joseph is now standing on a hill out on the plains. The vision they see is small, just him in full Indian buckskin regalia standing on a hill. He's holding a peace pipe in his arms in the same way that he would carry a baby. He starts walking. The vision widens. He is walking among dead horses, Indians, and US Calvary soldiers. The vision widens further. He's walking on the hill where the Sioux defeated Custer and the United States Calvary. Everyone is dead except Chief Joseph. He walks once all of the way around the hill weaving in and out among the dead, the weapons, and the shattered war equipment. As he climbs the hill to the top, the vision gets smaller again, closing in on him. When he reaches the crest, he holds the pipe up in both of his hands, as if he is offering it up to the sky. As he stands there making the peace offering, the vision closes. He is gone.

They sit still on the rocks.

Bunzy says, "We have crossed some serious lines here."

"There's no question about it. Guys, not to change the subject, but what was that about ravens?" Isabel asks.

Johnny explains, "The raven is the bringer of the vision and now we are ravens and everyone can be a raven, if we successfully deliver this message, because before he told us that we were ravens, he said that the vision quest is for everyone."

"How do you know about ravens?" Bunzy asks.

"That's Indian folklore. In the animal kingdom, the raven is a magical animal. In all of the Native American sacred stories the raven is the bringer of the vision. So, when we're walking somewhere and a raven calls, we should pay attention. We can see a vision with the raven's help. That's the cool thing. It's automatic. That raven isn't talking to us for no reason. When he starts talking, you better open the mind's eye, because he is bringing you a vision."

"Where do we go from here?" Isabel asks.

"To thine own eye be true," Bunzy answers

"What?" Isabel asks.

"Rinpoche said that we need to learn to see and that the way to do that was to go to the desert and fast and contemplate all of this," Bunzy tells her.

"Okay. Drive on," she says.

They load up and head further into the wilderness.

CHAPTER 8
THE GOOD NEWS

**"The kingdom of God cometh not with observation.
Neither shall they say, Lo here! Or, lo there! For, behold,
the kingdom of God is within you."**

Jesus Christ
Luke 17:21-22

Weeks later they are deep in the wilderness miles from the nearest electric power line or Wi-Fi site. They have been fasting, trekking, and meditating for days. After taking turns soaking and bathing in a little hot spring, they are camping beside a large pool in a crystal-clear stream which they can wade across in the rapids below the big pool. To the east on the other side of the creek, there is a mountain ridge.

They are lounging around their camp after lunch one afternoon when Chief Joseph appears riding a beautiful Paint stallion on the mountain slope. He is straddling a long riding blanket with eagle feathers attached to the back of it. The horse is painted with circle designs on its rump and shoulders. It is wearing a colorful neck band and reins. Chief Joseph isn't carrying anything, no pipe or bow or spear or bags. They can hear ravens calling and see them flying around him. Turning his horse toward the crest of the mountain and starting to ride upwards, Chief Joseph momentarily turns back in their direction and beckons them to follow him. As he rides onwards toward the mountain top, the ravens continue calling to him.

Johnny, Isabel, and Bunzy start up the mountain together following Chief Joseph. When they reach the ridge top, Chief Joseph sits there at the edge of a cliff on the Paint stallion surveying the vista spread out before them. To the east, the far side of the ridge drops straight away to bright green flatlands which are crossed by a meandering river. In the far distance there are majestic, rugged, snowcapped peaks.

This is a special high spot that looks out over the holy ancient Nez Perce lands. Chief Joseph and the ravens know this place. The ancient ones came here too, just as Isabel, Johnny and Bunzy have. Behind Chief Joseph there is a stone circle made with stones so old that they are covered with moss, lichens and desert varnish. This circle is big enough for a ceremony with many people.

The wind blows strongly in Chief Joseph's face. Two ravens pull up on each side of him. There are now four ravens holding their position right beside him floating in the wind. They are so close to him that if he wanted to, he could reach out and pinch the nearest one's tail feathers. Then another raven flies up beside the ones on his left and one of those ravens that was already there drops away over the face of the cliff. It dives down picking up speed, then pulling up and doing some incredible flying maneuvers. Then another raven drops down doing even more fancy stunts. Those two ravens then fly back up beside Chief Joseph and another one drops down doing more fancy exploits. They do this for some time putting on quite a performance for the Chief. When they're done, they all pull up beside him. There are five of them, swaying in the wind, holding their positions right next to him, as he sits there looking out over the vast wilderness before them. This is an extraordinary location. Chief Joseph has come here on vision quests before with ravens. This is a site where magic happens. Those ravens that are hovering there with Chief Joseph, are bringing him visions. He doesn't see just one vision. He sees multiple visions. Chief Joseph has brought Bunzy, Isabel and Johnny to a very special spiritual area. He looks slowly at all of the land around them. He seems satisfied, turns toward them, raises his right hand, palm toward them and says, "Aho."

He and the horse disappear in a whirlwind. The ravens dive over the bluff into the wind and vanish too.

Bunzy, Isabel and Johnny stand there for a moment shoulder to shoulder looking out over where Chief Joseph just disappeared at the incredible scene before them with an overwhelming feeling of reverence and wonder.

Bunzy announces, "I'm going to stay up here on the mountain top and listen to the wind for a while."

"I'm going back down to the camp," Isabel says. "I'll wait for you down there."

"I don't know how long this will take. It might take a few days," Bunzy says.

"That's okay. I'll wait," Isabel tells him.

"I'll wait too," Johnny says, "but I'm going back down to the camp with Isabel, where there's water, fire, and a little food."

"I have some water. I'll be alright," Bunzy says.

"See you down at the camp," Isabel responds.

They embrace. She turns and walks away.

Johnny and Bunzy hug. Then Johnny runs to catch up with Isabel.

Bunzy watches them go, then climbs over the bluff looking for shelter. Before long, he finds a small cave, crawls in, assumes the lotus position and begins to meditate.

On the seventh day, Rinpoche appears at the mouth of the cave.

"Master Rinpoche!" Bunzy jumps up and embraces him, then salutes him by touching his index fingertips in prayer position to his forehead.

"What are you doing here?" Bunzy asks.

"I've come to bring you good news," Rinpoche tells him.

"Good news, what good news?"

"You can now save people through dreamtime. By learning how 'to see', you have gained control of your imagination in some of your dreams. So, stop living in this ugly drama. Take people to those places where you can save them and wake them up. Then they will be released from the Archons. You'll know when your audience has entered a dreamtime where they can be released because there you will be able to perform miracles. So, it's time for you to cross over. Wake up!" Rinpoche shouts in Bunzy's face.

"Oh, I see what you're saying," Bunzy says.

He is overwhelmed with joy. He blinks his eyes and staggers around.

"This is as far as I can go," Rinpoche tells him. "You will have to find another guide from here on over."

"I don't understand," Bunzy says.

"That's okay," Rinpoche tells him. "You will. You've got a lot to do. So, get busy. It is not enough that you know the good news which I've brought you. Now that you have realized this truth, you must go out and spread the word. Because you are in this world, but no longer of this world, you can do things which will seem to be miracles to the people of this world and because you do them, they will listen to what you say. While they're listening to you, they will enter dreamtime. So go now, teach the good news and do miracles. The moment people realize the kingdom of Heaven is here, now, they will be changed in a wonderful way. Start by going back down to your camp and telling Isabel and Johnny what you now know. Show them a sign that they too might be saved. Then go out into the world teaching and doing miracles so masses of humans will enter dreamtime and be free of the Archons."

Bunzy says, "Thank you Master Rinpoche. Thank you for all of the kindness and support and wisdom you have shown me. I will be forever grateful to you."

Bunzy puts his hands together, bows his head to Rinpoche, touches his fingertips to his forehead, and declares, "It shall be as you say." Then Bunzy turns, climbs up the bluff, and walks back down to their camp.

Isabel and Johnny see him coming and rush to the mountain side of the pool to greet Bunzy. When he reaches the water, he doesn't turn downstream and walk to the place where they ford the creek. Instead, he continues walking and crosses the deep pool walking on the water.

Isabel and Johnny look at Bunzy with wide-eyed astonishment.

Isabel asks, "What has happened?"

He tells them the good news. Then he adds, "We are to go into the world and testify to this new revelation until all have heard the new gospel and are free of the Archons."

Isabel says, "Walking on water isn't normal. I'll grant you that, Bunzy. I can see you've had some kind of revelation alright, but I know you Bunzy. Something is wrong here. There's a pea under this haystack and I'm not going to try to sleep on it."

Johnny says, "Well I get it Brother and I would leave here and return to Paradise now, but I love you and all of this." He waves his hands around. "I'll stay and help you spread the news."

"How will we do it though?" Johnny asks. "We have no money to rent auditoriums, or pay for advertising, or to entertain the media. How will we show people what you are saying is true?"

"All things are possible to those who believe. It is time for another miracle," Bunzy says. "Have faith. We will go down into the cities and win a five hundred-million-dollar lottery jackpot. Then we will purchase what we need to set people free."

"Alright, that sounds like a good idea," Johnny tentatively agrees. "A big lottery win should get some attention and kick things off with a bang. I think though I would rather stay out here in the wilderness, but let's go do what you say."

Isabel informs them, "You guys do what you want. I'll be in charge though. Sooner or later, this show is going south. I just don't know why, where, or when but I know it is."

In the first village they pass through, they purchase a lottery ticket that happens to be for a five hundred-million-dollar jackpot. It takes them two more days to get home. By then they have won the prize.

They go to the lottery headquarters to certify they have the winning ticket. A date is set for an award ceremony when they will be given a check for the jackpot.

At the awards ceremony they are handed a big mock check so that their picture can be taken as the winners of this huge amount of money. This event is to promote the lottery and for the press to get to know if there is anything newsworthy about the winners.

As the media people gaze at Isabel, Bunzy and Johnny in boredom, a reporter asks, "What are you going to do with all of that money?"

Bunzy declares, "We have been given this money to announce that the kingdom of Heaven is here, now, and the moment you realize that truth, you will become an angelic spiritual being and be able to do even greater things than we have done in winning this giant jackpot."

Photo cameras begin flashing. Movie cameras commence to roll. People start jabbering excitedly on cell phones. Reporters are yelling at their co-workers and vigorously pointing at Bunzy, Isabel and Johnny. The media folks sense a big story. "Crazy cult prophet wins five hundred-million-dollar lottery," headlines the media.

The correspondent who asked them the question continues, "Mr. Ringer are you saying you didn't win the lottery accidently, that you have a method to win lotteries, and you are willing to share that method with others?"

"Yes. I'm saying there are no accidents."

"What is your method?"

Bunzy tells him, "We will be setting up a tent in a field outside of town where I will explain to everyone who is there what I know. When we get all of the arrangements made, we will announce the time and place."

Other reporters are now shouting questions at Bunzy.

"Are you a member of any foreign organization?"

"What do you mean by the kingdom of Heaven?"

"Heaven is an incredibly beautiful place where everything that you wish, you realize, where everyone is happy and loved and supported. You can enter Heaven now. I will show you how to get there and the moment you believe, you will be able to do as I have done. You can do even greater things."

"Mr. Ringer have you ever been in a mental institution?"

"Are you the member of a cult?"

"Have you ever taken LSD?"

"Where is this Heaven? Can I drive there from here?"

"Thank you for the money," Bunzy says to the lottery officials and shakes their hands. Their mouths hang open and Isabel can see the whites in their eyes all around their pupils. Then turning back to the cameras, Bunzy adds, "If you want to know more then come to the meeting. I will do more miracles there."

"More miracles?"

The crowd goes wild again.

"Mister Ringer, are you claiming that you can do miracles?"

"What miracles have you done? Where did you do them? When?"

Bunzy, Johnny and Isabel push their way out of the building and into the parking lot to their car. People are shouting questions and grabbing at them all of the way to the car as the cameras roll and flashes flash. By the time they make it into the car, their clothes are torn and they're scratched and bruised. They get to the freeway as fast as they can and lose the crowd.

Johnny says, "That went well," with a look that means, "that was terrible."

Bunzy smiles at him and says, "The show is on the road. Let's go buy a circus tent and get it set up."

The media runs the story, "Cult prophet promises to tell how to win the lottery." The consensus is Bunzy is insane, but he did win a big, big jackpot. So, a lot of people want to hear how he did it and how they can do it too.

Bunzy, Isabel and Johnny buy a giant striped circus tent with "THE GOOD NEWS TENT" painted boldly across its entrance. Next, they hire a big award-winning black gospel choir and dress them all in white silk gowns. Then they hire a studio orchestra and dress them in black tuxedos. They have a soaring stage built out of fresh lumber and fill the tent with chairs and clean new sawdust. Johnny goes to work promoting the event. Isabel oversees everything. Bunzy goes to visit his friend Jazz Newton who is a private detective. He is the world's only consulting I Ching private eye.

When Bunzy tells Jazz the good news and what they are going to do, Jazz says, "Well then, the first thing you need to do is change your name. Bunzy sounds like a handsome body building, super model of questionable morals and even more questionable behavior. I don't think that is exactly the audience you're shooting for. Change your name to something like Michael, or Paul, or John, or Peter."

"Alright, I see your point," Bunzy says. "As usual, you're right. Michael it is. I'm now Brother Michael."

Jazz and Bunzy call Johnny and inform him Bunzy will be speaking as Brother Michael.

Johnny says, "I like it", and changes the promotions before anything goes out.

"That advice will cost you one hundred million dollars," Jazz tells Bunzy.

They look at each other, then start laughing.

Bunzy says, "You'll have to talk to my wife about the money."

Jazz says, "No thank you. This one's on me."

The Good News tent is packed on the very first night. Johnny takes the stage and warms up the crowd with music and jokes. He then introduces Bunzy and Isabel as Brother Michael and his lovely wife, Isabel. Bunzy and Isabel enter the main entrance of the tent and walk down the center aisle arm in arm and up onto the stage. They cross over to the pulpit where Bunzy takes the microphone and Isabel steps over beside Johnny who has been standing beside the podium clapping vigorously.

Bunzy announces, "I am going to start this show with a few miracles. Is there anyone out there who has a disease or condition which has been declared incurable, or who has been blind since birth, or who is paralyzed?"

Two people come forward. The first one is a young man being pushed in a wheelchair. The other is a young woman holding onto the arm of an older lady.

Bunzy asks the young man, "What is your name?"

The young man replies, "Tony and this is my father." He rolls his eyes toward the man who is pushing his wheelchair.

"Tony, what happened to you?"

"Ten years ago, I jumped off a bluff into the river, struck my head on a rock and broke my neck. I have been paralyzed from the neck down ever since then."

"Tony, would you like to walk again?"

"Yes, very, very much."

"Have you heard that I can cure you?"

"Yes."

"Do you believe that I can make you whole again?"

"Yes. That is why we've come here. We know that you can do miracles."

"Well Tony, today is your lucky day. Today you are going to be healed."

Bunzy walks around behind the wheelchair and places his hands on the back of the young man's neck at shoulder level.

Tony says, "That feels really good." He looks perplexed, then says, "Wait a minute. I haven't felt anything back there in ten years, not since the accident, but I can feel your hands. They are really warm."

"That is because you are no longer paralyzed. Your spinal cord isn't broken anymore. You can walk."

Tony looks down at his feet, weakly rotates his left foot, then his right, looks up at Bunzy, smiles, and says, "Yes, I can walk."

The young man shakily stands up, takes a wobbly step, and tumbles into the arms of his father. Then with his father's help he stands back up and grinning broadly, faces the congregation and raises his fists in a victory salute.

The crowd goes wild.

He turns and embraces Bunzy, then collapses back into his wheelchair. His father pumps Bunzy's right hand with both of his as tears stream down his face, saying, "Thank you. Thank you. Thank you," all of the time.

Bunzy says, "This is only the first step to freedom. Keep listening and you will fly."

Tony and his father leave the stage and Bunzy greets the young woman. "Young lady what is your name?"

She faces his voice and answers, "Katy."

"Katy, how long have you been blind?"

"Since I was a little girl."

"Were you listening when I healed the paralyzed man?"

"Yes."

"Are you ready to see again?"

"Yes."

"Do you believe that I can heal you?"

"Yes."

"Well, I can. Prepare to see."

Bunzy places his hands over her eyes.

She says, "Your hands are very warm."

Bunzy continues holding them on her eyes for a couple of more minutes. Nobody says anything. The audience sits and silently stares. The choir and the musicians watch intently.

When Bunzy removes his hands, the woman blinks, covers her eyes with her hands, and peeks out between her fingers, then she begins to sob uncontrollably. She turns to the older woman who was leading her, grabs onto her, buries her face on her shoulder and continues to cry.

Bunzy asks her, "Katy, can you see?"

Between sobs, she chokes, "Yes, I can see."

The crowd erupts in an enthusiastic roar. The people are joyfully clapping, stomping their feet, whistling, yelling, and jumping up and down and hugging each other.

Bunzy steps to the pulpit, raises his hands above his head, and shouts, "Brothers and Sisters, I am here to tell you that today is your lucky day. You are going to be free. You are saved and you are going to be exuberantly happy men and women."

People enthusiastically shout, "Tell it Brother Michael!"

"You have been viciously deceived and used and abused, but no more! Today that is over. You are reclaiming your birthright. You are being born again. You are powerful spiritual beings. You are angels who have been led astray, but no more. When I shout, you are going to wake up. You are going to be back in Paradise and this will all have just been a bad dream. When I yell wake up, you will wake up in Heaven and remember who you are and where you are. You will remember what has happened, but first allow me to say some things, so that you will begin to remember and realize what your situation is."

"You are angels of delight who are capable of creating worlds. When you are in your natural state of being, nothing is impossible for you. When you imagine it, it begins to happen. Just as a flower grows from the ground and blossoms, beautiful worlds spring into being and flower from your thoughts. You have a great power of imagination and creation. You have been deceived and captured and are being used and abused, but no more! That is ended. When I shout wake up, that is over. Your imprisonment has been done in a devilishly clever way so you do not even see it. As in all clever deceits, the victim doesn't even realize they are a victim. The sufferer in an abusive relationship does not understand their situation and cannot escape without outside help. They only see their unhappiness. They only see their hopelessness and misery."

"Well Brothers and Sisters, I am here to tell you that you have been in an abusive relationship with a powerful master, but you do not need to continue to take part in that sad relationship. You do not need to give all of your treasures to that awful monster who rules your life any longer. Your life is now all yours to do with as you wish, and happiness, abundance, security, health, wealth, and joy and wonder are yours. This world of toil and suffering and fear is a great deceit. It is a concentration camp in which your wealth is being stolen from you. It is a factory of the soul where your precious life force is being squeezed out of you drop by drop and enjoyed by others. But no more!"

"The Serpent trapped you long ago with a great lie and created an immense delusion and gave you dreams which you see as this world. He and his minions have worked hard for thousands of years to maintain this nightmare. Every year you lose a little more freedom and a little more power and become a little weaker, but no more. Today that is finished. When you realize this truth, everything that has been taken from you will be restored to you. The important thing is to realize the true nature of this situation and the true nature of your being. You are angelic spirits known as dreamers. In infinity, you are the joy of creation because you produce the entertainment. You are the dreamers of dreams. Dreams originate in your consciousness. So, forces which do not dream, wish to control your awareness. You have fallen under the influence of the serpents known as the Archonic Empire and they have you busily spinning this little world drama known as humans on Earth, while they steal the rest of your boundless creative energies and use them for their own dark pleasures. Well, that is only possible while you are held in ignorance, while you are trapped in the rational mind and believe you have only the powers of the physical body and believe you are ignorant, bad, and weak. You are the beloved children of the Divine and are eternal beings with the creative potential of the infinite. Realize that truth now!"

Bunzy jumps to the front of the stage, raises his hands over his head, extends his palms outwards towards the audience, and yells with all of his might, "Wake up!"

All over the audience, there are bright flashes of light and people disappear. There is a momentary bright vacant spot in the place where the person was sitting. Then the bright spot is gone, and so is the person who was in the now empty chair. Not everyone who believes flashes out. Some stay like Bunzy, Isabel and Johnny, but like them, they are changed. The first reaction of most of those who don't believe and are left behind is shock.

The good news movement quickly grows. Bunzy, Isabel and Johnny do another show in a field somewhere almost every night. Thousands are saved. Most people can't quite believe the good news, but their faith in their old world view is badly shaken and people are beginning to carefully think about what they do believe and what they don't believe. What they thought that they knew, they have begun to see doesn't make sense in a lot of ways and thousands and thousands of them begin changing their everyday lives in small ways which are adding up to a big world change.

The disappearances cause great agitation amongst non-believers. The authorities are pushed to stop the revival. People demand the arrests of Bunzy, Isabel and Johnny. Some want them seized for kidnapping and murder. Others want them taken for fraud and deceit. Opposition to the movement builds to hysterical levels but so does support.

On August 6th, Bunzy is speaking in a hayfield outside of Peoria, Illinois. As he watches the audience, he sees himself sitting near the back, just to the right of the main aisle. The moment he realizes that it is him, watching him, he is inside of the him in the audience looking back at Brother Michael on the stage. He realizes he is in his double and he knows he has come back from a present future to a past through his dream body. The shock of this realization propels him back into the him on the stage.

As Brother Michael, Bunzy jumps to the front of the stage and shouts back at the Bunzy in the audience, "Wake up!" In a flash of light, the Bunzy in the audience disappears and wakes up in his waking body in objective reality in the past.

The experience of being in two different places at the same time and of being simultaneously in still a third place where he watches himself as both Bunzy and Brother Michael, shatters Bunzy's rational mind. He stumbles from the pulpit, down the stairs, and up the main aisle. In the pandemonium the audience doesn't notice his leaving the stage.

When he shouted, "Wake up," people flashed out of existence all over the crowd. Many of those who are still there, are in shock. They stare at the empty seats. Others scream in fear and run here and there. Many jump around, shout and hug each other with joy.

Johnny takes over at the pulpit and is closing the ceremony. The choir sings their hallelujah number. As Bunzy passes where he was sitting, he looks at the knocked over empty chair where his double was. On the far side of it is a tall, slender attractive blond woman. She is standing up and staring down at the overturned chair. She has both of her hands clasped to her cheeks. On this side of the empty upside-down chair sits an almond eyed gentleman who fixedly watches Bunzy.

When Bunzy sees Rinpoche, his faith crumbles. As a prisoner of circumstances, he stumbles on up the aisle to the outside of the tent.

The Teacher is standing there waiting for him. When Bunzy looks up and sees him, he almost doesn't recognize him. The Teacher seems reptilian. His eyes are lizard like. The Teacher knows Bunzy isn't seeing him in human form. The Teacher doesn't even attempt to disguise himself.

He says, "You know, Mr. Ringer, all of this has to stop, don't you?"

Bunzy tries to re-enter dreamtime. He can't.

The Teacher sneers at him and says, "Don't try using your two-bit human sorcery crap on me. I don't believe in you. I know you're a fraud. I know where we are and what we're doing. I know where the power is here and it's me, not you. Now that you can see me and know that I am your owner and master, it's time for you to get back in your cage. The story that you thought was happening isn't happening. What comes to pass is what the dominant consciousness wills to occur. We, Archons, are the dominant beings in this realm. We control the internet, the schools, the libraries, the television stations, the newspapers, the magazines, and the money, and thus people. We constantly explain what your point of view should be to you. We control your minds. We tell you what to think so that you'll see and do what we want you to do. You don't really know anything. You, Mr. Ringer, believe that you have been personally empowered with a new truth, but you are powerless against my understanding. It is time for this to stop."

Standing six feet away from Bunzy, without even raising his hands or touching Bunzy in any way physically, he grabs Bunzy's left hand and viciously snaps his little finger back against the top of Bunzy's hand.

Bunzy screams, "Damn! Damn! Damn!" He grabs his wrist and hops around.

When Bunzy stops flopping and shaking, the Teacher pulls Bunzy's ring finger back until it shatters. A black fog descends on Bunzy. He's dizzy, staggering. Pain is choking him.

The Teacher ferociously jerks Bunzy's middle finger sideways until it is destroyed.

Bunzy starts screaming, "Stop! Stop! What do you want? I'll do whatever you want."

Bunzy believes he's helpless in the Teacher's presence. Bunzy's mind has absolutely jammed. His memory no longer works. He feels hopeless. His guilt about what he's been doing is overwhelming. He's confused. He doesn't know what to do. He can't think of a way to stop the Teacher. The Teacher can break all of Bunzy's fingers, then his wrist and his arms and continue to mutilate Bunzy or any one whom Bunzy loves, in any way the Teacher pleases. Bunzy can imagine no way to stop the Teacher.

The Teacher tells Bunzy, "I want you to turn over control of your organization to me and give me all of your wealth."

He watches Bunzy stand there hugging himself and whimpering for a while.

Then he asks. "So, what is it going to be Mr. Ringer, a very nasty public humiliation and death, or turning over the reins of your organization to me along with all of your wealth? I would hate to have to send a productive animal like you to the slaughterhouse. What is it going to be?"

"The slaughterhouse won't be necessary, as far as I'm concerned, but my wife is in charge. You probably already know that," Bunzy gasps. "Take the organization and the wealth. Take them! Please, just stop hurting me."

"Alright then, here's what's going to happen," the Teacher tells him. "You are going to make a public statement in which you will admit you badly misunderstood some very important truths, but I whom you recognize as a more realized person than you, have pointed out your errors to you. Because of your mistakes and because of my superior understanding, you are going to stop what you've been doing. Do you agree?"

"Yes," Bunzy groans.

"Good. I commend you on being an exceptionally productive human and it's good to see that you recognize your inferiority. I'm sure your wife will agree you've been being foolish and agree to stop with all of this nonsense."

"I will tell the world, after helping you I am returning to the wilderness to meditate on the great truths which you have taught me."

"Under those conditions, I give you my permission to return to your farm but remember what you call your mind is actually my mind and I control that mind. I can also see what is going on in there. So, whenever you start having thoughts about escaping or doing miracles or healing the sick or winning the lottery or saving the rainforests, just stop right there and get back in your cage before I see what you're doing and have to come over and put you back in your coop. The next time I have to use some of my valuable time and energy to discipline you, I'm not going to be so gentle. You've had your last warning. Do you understand, Mr. Ringer?"

"Yes."

Bunzy staggers back into the tent tightly gripping his left wrist with his right hand to where Isabel and Johnny are waiting for him. They both stare at his mutilated hand.

Johnny asks, "What happened? How can you even be hurt?"

After Bunzy explains, Isabel asks, "Can't you just heal yourself?"

"No," Bunzy tells her.

"Can we use mantra to escape, heal you and put things back together?" She asks.

"Quiet!" Bunzy hisses. "Don't even mention that."

They rush him to the emergency room at the local hospital.

A doctor x-rays his hand, sets his fingers, splints them, and tapes them together.

The doctor asks Bunzy, "How did this happen?"

Bunzy replies, "I fell down some stairs."

He gives Bunzy a doubtful look, as if to say, "Really?"

Bunzy shrugs and gives him a weak, guilty smile.

The doctor goes on working after giving Bunzy a prescription for some powerful pain pills. To the doctor Bunzy is just another clumsy fool who can't take care of his own problems and mistakes.

Later, Bunzy explains to Isabel and Johnny he is powerless in the presence of the Teacher.

Isabel says, "You're not helpless anywhere, any time. You are always in the presence of the Divine All. You're just a fool."

Bunzy's eyes dart around. He puts a finger to his lips and whispers, "Be quiet. The Teacher's watching."

"You're pathetic," Isabel tells him. "Get a grip. One minute you're a messenger from God. The next, you're a sniveling coward."

Bunzy says, "We understood some amazing things, but we missed a really important point. The Archon consciousness dominates everything in this realm including us. We must stop what we are doing or die terrible and humiliating public deaths. We can only do what the Teacher tells us is possible and nothing is possible other than what he allows. His explanation of how the Cosmos operates is the only explanation that works in this situation. If we think any thoughts which don't conform to what he allows, he will know, and things will quickly get very ugly."

"Bunzy you can do better," Isabel says. "I don't understand how you can be such an enlightened powerful man one minute and such a stupid, cowardly fool the next."

"Shut up!" Bunzy shouts. "Shut up. He's listening. You're going to get me sent to the slaughterhouse."

"I hope Spirit finds you and saves you, Bunzy Ringer, because otherwise you're a dead man walking. It's hard to believe a person could rise so high and sink so low.

After fulfilling the terms of his agreement with the Teacher, Isabel and Bunzy go home.

Isabel tells Bunzy, "Bunzy, you are an amazing fellow, but luckily when we won the lottery, I didn't put all of our family's eggs in the Bunzy basket. I hope Rinpoche has a backup plan for this world too."

Their kids are grown up, but Isabel takes what responsibility she can for them and leaves Bunzy. Their oldest daughter has finished college. She has a husband and children of her own. Bunzy misses those boys terribly.

Isabel buys a house in town and goes back to work at her healing practice.

Johnny turns into a white light and disappears.

Bunzy stays alone at the cabin in the woods.

CHAPTER 9
Back to the feedlot

"None are more hopelessly enslaved than those who falsely believe they are free."
Johann Wolfgang von Goethe 1749-1832

Bunzy can't remember anything anymore. He's really confused. There is a high-pitched whine in his head all of the time. It's very distracting. There is constant chatter in his mind. He experiences extreme feelings of abandonment, insecurity, and loneliness.

He wonders. *Who abandoned me? Why have I been forsaken and left here alone in this house to wander around helpless and lost? Why is everything so meaningless and hopeless? Why can't I do anything right? I just don't understand. I don't know anything. I don't know what to do. I could die of misery.*

His health begins to fail.

Fearing he's mentally ill, he goes to see a psychiatrist. The psychiatrist tells him he's depressed, but he shouldn't worry about it because being depressed is normal. The psychiatrist gives Bunzy a prescription for anti-depressants.

Bunzy goes to a doctor to do something about his poor health. The doctor puts him on drugs to lower Bunzy's blood pressure and gives him pills to mask his aches and pains.

Now Bunzy not only can't remember anything, but he also doesn't care. He doesn't feel anything anyway.

Bunzy starts to recognize the awesome technological powers of the US, the intellectual brilliance of its leaders and their long-term dedication to high purpose. He is also impressed by the massive understanding of the big picture by university scholars.

After a while, he doesn't have any money for food, heat, transportation, medical bills, or property taxes. His situation gets very ugly.

The Teacher calls Bunzy and says, "So, Mr. Ringer, I see that you are broke and need some financial assistance. I think that I can help you. Would you like a high paying, important job?"

Bunzy tells him, "I'd settle for a low paying, unimportant job. I'm really broke. I need some money, badly. My situation is getting really desperate. How can I help you?"

"Think of me as your new best friend. I have an associate who operates a military contracting business whose principal location of operation is at a fort in Louisiana. The company headquarters are in Seattle, Washington. He could make good use of someone with your talent for empathy and persuasion. We could make your wages very attractive. Are you still interested?"

"I'll do anything for money.

"Well, if I make you wealthy, then you should be willing to be very helpful and do what I need to have done, no matter what it is, right?"

"Yes. I'm willing to be very helpful."

"Good! I'm willing to pay substantial amounts for very helpful people. Your job will be training soldiers in population control. There's a bunch of free-ranging humans in central Asia and we need to round them up, get control of their resources, and pacify them. I want you to help with that operation."

"Okay. I don't care how you describe the job. I just need money. Like I said, I would be interested if the wages were less than attractive. Making me a lucrative offer makes this a done deal. I'll take the job."

"I'll inform my assistant, the president of the Omnibus Corporation, that you will be in Seattle next Wednesday at 10 AM. He'll be looking forward to meeting with you."

"Wait a minute! I don't have enough money to get to the grocery store, much less to Seattle. I'm not just broke. I'm in debt. I am a desperate person."

"Your money problems are over. I'll have Mr. Ashwood, C. C. Ashwood, the president of the company, send you a generous cashier's check along with your instructions and directions to the Omnibus office building on overnight delivery. After you get to the corporation headquarters all of your expenses will be paid while you are being trained. After that your wages will make it possible for you to purchase what you need or desire. How does that sound?"

"Works for me."

"Then we are in agreement, right, Mr. Ringer?"

"Yes, we are. Thank you."

"Then we'll expect you on Wednesday. I will inform Mr. Ashwood that you are an especially talented person and that he should make good use of your potential. He'll be waiting for you. Goodbye."

"Goodbye."

When Bunzy arrives at the Omnibus headquarters on Wednesday and introduces himself at the reception counter, an attractive young woman takes him to the offices of Ken Walker, vice-president of operations.

Walker promptly greets Bunzy, "Hello Mr. Ringer. My name is Ken Walker. You can call me Ken."

Walker scrutinizes Bunzy, then says, "Bunzy, before I take you to see Mr. Ashwood, I'm afraid that we're going to have to take you to a stylist and have your hair cut and your beard shaved off and put you in a fashionable new grey suit. You really don't have the proper look to convince anyone that you know how to take orders and get things done. However, Mr. Teacher says that you have talent, so we believe in you, but we have to change your looks. Is that alright with you?"

"Yes. That is perfectly alright with me," Bunzy responds.

"Good. I think that we are going to get along with each other splendidly and have a super productive relationship," Ken tells him.

After Bunzy has the correct look, while he and Ken ride up an elevator to Mr. Ashwood's office, Ken asks, "Did you know, Bunzy, that rats can swim?"

"No," Bunzy replies. "I hadn't ever really thought about it."

"Well, you might want to consider it."

"Alright. Thank you. I will," Bunzy says.

They enter Mr. Ashwood's office and Ken introduces Bunzy to Mr. Ashwood, who explains to Bunzy, "Mr. Ringer, our mission is simple. We save soldiers' and natives' lives. We have set up very realistic native villages in forts down South. Before soldiers are deployed to the battle front, they are run through our villages where they get to experience the local indigenous culture and what we expect will happen to them over there. This foreign culture that they are going into is very different from ours and unless our soldiers are schooled in those local customs, they will act in ways that will cause serious problems. The military's mission is control, not problems. Problems cause suffering and deaths on both sides. We try to avoid that. Our mock villages are staffed by real war refugees from the area where the soldiers will be going. Someone needs to communicate with these foreign people and co-ordinate role playing activities between them and the military. We have previously had interaction problems between the groups involved in our school program. Mr. Teacher has informed us that you have a unique ability to communicate between dissimilar groups who don't understand each other and who don't naturally get along very well. Your job will be facilitating our school activities between these groups. Can you do this?"

"Absolutely. I'm really good at that type of thing."

"Fabulous. Mr. Walker will take you to our training center and get you started on your orientation. It was a pleasure meeting you. I look forward to seeing your progress reports."

Bunzy and Mr. Ashwood shake hands and Ken and Bunzy leave Mr. Ashwood's office.

Ninety days later Bunzy lives in some barracks in a fort in the South with cultural role players. People off base would most likely not call his roommates cultural role players, but rather Afghani refugees, that is, if those local people are being nice. Otherwise, they would call them gooks, ragheads, or just plain old assholes. There isn't a lot of niceness in the area surrounding this base. People around here are really poor, hard cases.

Bunzy has his high and tight haircut, his fatigues, and his clipboard. Afghani immigrants are being shipped from all over the country to this Army base to staff mock villages which soldiers going to Afghanistan must go through to get an authentic experience of what is going to happen over there. These villages were built and are staffed and operated by the Omnibus Corporation. The refugees speak Afghani. They know the customs, so they can do a little back checking of things that are being played out to make the experience more authentic. What the management involved in this enterprise are trying to do is to teach the soldiers how to understand the customs of the people where they are going so that they won't offend those people. In different scenarios, the soldiers experience the mullah saying the prayers and they see how it looks and feels to walk around on the Afghani streets. The people who build these mock villages even have thrown taxidermist made dead dogs beside the road, because the soldiers will see dead, dried up dog carcasses lying beside the roads. It's all very realistic. There are twenty of these mock villages on this fort and more of them at other forts throughout the South. They can't be seen from outside of the bases. They are all on the interior of the military installations and it takes a great deal of driving to get to them. They aren't all continuously occupied, but some are.

Bunzy is in a convoy on his way to a village called Dharmasala. He hasn't been this far out before. They've been driving mostly through swamps for a long time. Suddenly they come out of the swamps onto this big open plain. There is a herd of wild horses out here just wandering around grazing. As they get closer to the far end of this plain they can see a little village that has a three story mosque with a minaret. There is a light mist lying over everything. The plain with the horses and the village are shrouded in mist. It is beautiful, but there are also noisy, intimidating military helicopters flying overhead all of the time, non-stop.

Bunzy thinks. *This experience is just so surreal. We are in backwoods Louisiana. This place is in the middle of nowhere USA. The talent surrounding the fort is appalling, just terrible. There's no peaceful, loving spiritual consciousness around. The Army base is the most liberal place out here. It's just downright progressive compared to the surrounding area. So, we're in the middle of Hicksville in the South on an Army base and suddenly we're in an Afghani village. People in traditional Afghani clothes are walking around living their lives. It looks as if we are over there in Afghanistan, but as we enter the village, we walk by the Cajun role players who are locals that have been hired to do the fill in roles. They are like extras on a TV show set. They don't have any speaking parts. They are paid just to sit around in traditional clothes. These guys that we are walking past are on break. They're dressed as Afghanis, but they are down home, good old Southern boys who are sitting there with their big old beer bellies, smoking, and talking about their trucks. It's comical, crazy. Behind them we can hear Afghani devotional music being played over loudspeakers. When we get into the village, it's very authentic, very impressive.*

The military gives everyone involved scripts of situations that they want depicted. The scenarios are very detailed, but nobody knows more than they need to know to do their part. Bunzy's role is to stay out of the way but keep track of what happens so that he can reward good efforts and punish bad performances.

Today some really high-ranking military officers are negotiating with some Afghani government officials about building a school. The first thing that Bunzy notices is that education is spelled wrong on the banner that greets them as they enter the meeting. The American officers try to start the meeting without prayers. One of the interpreters does a smack down of these officers that isn't in the script.

He says, "What you guys just did is not going to work over there. You just disrespected our religious leader and our beliefs and what you did isn't going to work. We start every meeting with a prayer."

The officers apologize and the mullah starts the prayers. He begins a beautiful melodic chant in Arabic from the Koran. The Americans don't understand a word of it, but they're all respectfully listening when there is a huge explosion. Boom! The blast is close, out on the main street. They are on a side street in a building just off of the main street. The main street is on a major road that runs through the fort. People are screaming, but the negotiators can't see them.

Bunzy wonders, "*What is going on?*"

He's looking around thinking, "*Where can I see what's going on?*"

There are some stairs up the back of a mock building leading out onto a platform that overlooks the main street to where the explosion has just happened. He can still hear screaming and yelling out there.

He runs up the stairs.

When he gets up to the platform, there are a couple of Army officers up there observing the action.

They explain, "A military convoy was coming through town and militants just blew up the lead truck."

On the street all of these traditional Afghani people are shrieking and screaming blood curdling screams and crying. There are bodies blown to pieces all over the place. Hands, heads, feet, whatever, legs, everywhere.

Bunzy is like, "Whoa!"

He knows this is all fake, but this is so Hollywood level nuts he can't help but have an emotional reaction.

A woman is screaming louder than everyone else and tugging on an Army guy's coat and pointing at maybe her husband who is lying on the ground and also really screaming loudly. He has had both of his legs blown off. His legs are lying there blown to pieces and all bloody. He's just screaming and screaming. Blood is spurting out of the stumps of his legs.

This is the first time that these soldiers have experienced anything like this. Most of them are starting to go this way and then turning back and starting to go that way but never getting anywhere. They are gawking at all of the blood and gore and anguish and madness. Villagers are pulling on them, pointing this way and that, and yelling at them in Afghani. The soldiers don't know what to do.

Bunzy asks the officer beside him, "What are they supposed to be doing?"

The officer answers, "The first thing they are supposed to do is secure their perimeter. They are to ignore those people especially the dead ones and figure out where the attack is coming from. They are pretty much doing everything wrong now, but that is what we expect to happen the first time a soldier is confronted with a situation in the theater of war. They are pretty much overwhelmed, but after three or four of these incidents, they'll get the hang of it."

While Bunzy and the officers are talking, boom, boom, boom! Grenades start exploding amongst the people and the soldiers. A Jeep blows over sideways. Militants attack from a nearby building and just do it to the soldiers. A soldier in the convoy goes insane and starts shooting and beating all of the villagers around him.

One of the officers beside Bunzy says to the other officer while pointing at the madman, "That guy's out of the Army."

Over the following months, this happens over and over again. This is Bunzy's job for Omnibus Corporation. After months of blown-up bodies, vicious attacks by thugs, and stupid mistakes by soldiers, he starts to question what he's doing. He knows what the Army's plans are for the next two years, because Omnibus is acting out what the Army is going to do. Bunzy knows that the wars are never going to be over. That would be bad for the Army and bad for the businesses which supply the war efforts. Everyone would be out of work. The money and power would stop flowing towards the Army and Omnibus. In fact, the people in charge of all of this are planning more wars in more places. They want wars of indeterminate length and no clear objectives going on all of the time so that they can go on and on as powerful men selling war services and products. They don't want the wars to end. That would be terrible.

The shock of this horrible realization along with his anguish and isolation makes Bunzy start talking to himself. He begins a dialogue with himself wherein he argues about his job. He doesn't dare talk to anyone else about what's happening. He's out in the swamps of Louisiana, living with people whose language he doesn't speak, surrounded by soldiers whose mission he doesn't share and being confronted by Cajun locals who are stranger to him than the Asian refugees. He is completely alone. His inner life starts to grow, and he starts shutting down on the exterior. The people around him start to treat him as if he's strange, or maybe even crazy.

The soldiers being taught to ignore the suffering of the natives and to take control of the situation reminds him of what the Teacher said about rounding up those free-ranging Asians and pacifying them. The natives' choices are being limited to the same ones he has to make. He begins to see the soldiers as people who have already been pacified and enslaved and who are being used and abused too. Even for the obscene amounts of money that he is being paid to do what he is doing; he starts to think that maybe he should be doing something else.

When he asks the soldiers who he's working with why they do what they do, especially when they're in the war zone. They say things like, "I'm not thinking about the war. I'm just trying to protect my buddies. We're on the ground. I'm surrounded by my close friends. We're fighting for each other's lives at this point in time. Gone is any thought of whether this military incursion is a just one or not. I'm just trying to protect my friends and my family and my country and stay alive."

These are not evil men doing evil things. These are good men trying to do the right thing who end up doing bad things. It is the whole conglomerate profit-based business thing that becomes the beast that is lumbering over the planet chewing things up.

Bunzy can't even claim to be doing what he's doing for a good reason though like the soldiers. He's doing this for wages.

It's so easy to be abstract and intellectual about things like hunger when you have money, like I do now, but when you're broke, you just go back to the reptilian base. You're not necessarily evil, but you have to take care of business. You have to do things to survive, and all of those ideals just recede. Wages are evil because they persuade us to do things that we wouldn't otherwise do. We look at the money and not at the consequences of what we're doing.

Jobs for wages are bad because they direct a person's life energy in a direction that is greed based rather than community welfare based. Wage based jobs pit each individual against each other individual for personal gain. It's clearly the opposite of the old American Indian concept of "if it isn't good for everyone, then it isn't good for anyone". So, the problem with the modern job is that the individual looks at their own needs and benefits and they don't look at the bigger picture of whether their activities are benefiting or harming others. Many people even begin to enjoy victimizing others. The best relationship becomes the one where I'm in charge and you have to do whatever I tell you to do.

Looking at this job right in front of him, Bunzy can feel good because he's doing a good thing by preventing unnecessary suffering and death by both soldiers and natives. However, when he looks at the big picture and realizes the overall enterprise is to enslave the natives and to steal all of their resources using the soldiers as low paid gladiators, he's having a hard time doing his job.

His thoughts run towards: *I just don't want to be involved in this war activity any more. Killing people, forcing them to do things that they don't want to do and to live in ways that they don't want to live and to give all of their treasure to someone else while destroying the earth, air and water is wrong and I just can't do it, no matter how it is spun to me. It doesn't matter how much I'm paid. I know that it looks as if I'm protecting my country and even helping the people whom we're attacking, but it all falls apart when I take a long hard look at the global situation. Now that I have a few dollars in my pocket and my bills are paid, I'm going to get a different job.*

As his job search progresses, he realizes *I need money but everything requires more of a compromise than I'm willing to make. Everybody needs food though. Supplying good, healthy, nutritious food to people would be a good thing to do and it could be a money maker, and it could be done right.*

Bunzy decides to suggest the idea of making a food product to Mr. Ashwood on his next rotation back to corporate headquarters.

"Great idea, Bunzy," Ashwood says when Bunzy introduces the food idea to him. "I've been thinking about the same thing. What do you think about a line of organic soups?"

"I like the idea," Bunzy says, "but cooking foods at high temperatures destroys much of the nutritional value of the food. I was thinking more of selling fresh juices."

"I thought of that too. The problem is that the Food and Drug Administration doesn't like fresh food. They claim that it isn't safe, that it causes outbreaks of food poisoning and disease. It's against the law to bottle fresh foods and to put them on the shelf unpasteurized. Even if the government allows it, the shelf life of fresh foods is very short. So, it would be very hard to get any volume going on fresh juices. Your idea is good, it just won't make enough money. So, we're not going to do it."

There is no way to square Bunzy's internal dialogue with the external world. He quits his Omnibus job and goes back to their family's cabin in the woods. He cannot participate in the world of wages, but non-participation isolates him as a crazy loser who doesn't have enough resources to even survive much less have friends, a love life, and a family.

Just contemplating these issues makes him a weak, vacillating, poverty-stricken fool.

Bunzy wonders. *What can I do? My only options are supporting the status quo with a wage job, becoming an outlaw, being a drug addict, insanity, or death. None of those things interest me. I am interested in Isabel and our family, but they seem to be doing fine without me.*

The only possible solution for his troubles he can think of is the Dream Key. For some reason, he still remembers the Dream Key. He obsesses over it. The only place he can think of to look for it is in his dreams.

Bunzy begins to seriously look for the Dream Key in the dream worlds. He participates less and less in the waking world. He only does enough to maintain his body and the appearance of a reasonable person. As much time as he can, he spends over in the Dreamlands. As he slides out of this world, he passes over into a world of spiritual beings. He begins to communicate with the angelic Dakini, Gsal Byed Gdos Bral Ma. She begins to guide him and protect him.

He passes into another way of being.

"Gsal Byed Gdos Bral Ma what am I to do?" Bunzy asks.

"No more thoughts. Remember, it isn't your mind and they aren't your thoughts. Stop allowing those thoughts to rule your life. Your task is to let the thoughts pass, just as the wind passes. Some will only brush your cheek like a warm gentle evening breeze, while others will shake you like a hurricane, but they will all blow by, leaving you unharmed. Just let them pass and meanwhile, watch. Watch everything. Just watch. Have no opinions, make no judgments. Watch from the heart, not with the eyes. Feel the essence. Watch the essence. Watch the great ebb and flow of beingness. Watch the stream of creation as it pours from the void filling and shaping eternity. Be not afraid, as you stand in the gateway of the infinite. Know that you are the beloved fire of joy that lights all. Wherever you turn your attention, darkness recedes and wonder and happiness fill the hearts of your companions. So be strong, have courage, believe that goodness shall prevail. Leave the mind behind. Sit on the peak of experience and watch and when your desire for understanding has been filled, follow me across the void. I will guide you into the realms of greater being."

"Okay. I will do as you say, Gsal Byed Gdos Bral Ma. My mind is already clearer and I can remember things better over here in the Dreamlands. I don't have nerve enough to cross the void with you though. Where are those Archons Rinpoche told me about on Earth over in the Dreamlands?"

"Things happen differently over here than they do in the waking world. The Archons cannot control these places. You don't have any control over here either. You're like a newborn babe. That is why I'm trying to orient and educate you. You aren't used to watching and being aware while you are asleep. You aren't practiced in being conscious while you are unconscious. It would be easy for you to get into strange and dangerous situations, and to be harmed. I don't want you to get into struggles using your rational mind. I just want you to relax and pay attention. You aren't going mad. You aren't a bad person. You are just becoming aware of a bigger way of being. You have to realize that. You are experiencing the eternal return. I want you to experience dream time all of the way over in the dreamlands. This is the ancient world of our tribal ancestors. Prepare to cross the Great Divide on a journey of discovery."

CHAPTER 10
LOSING IT

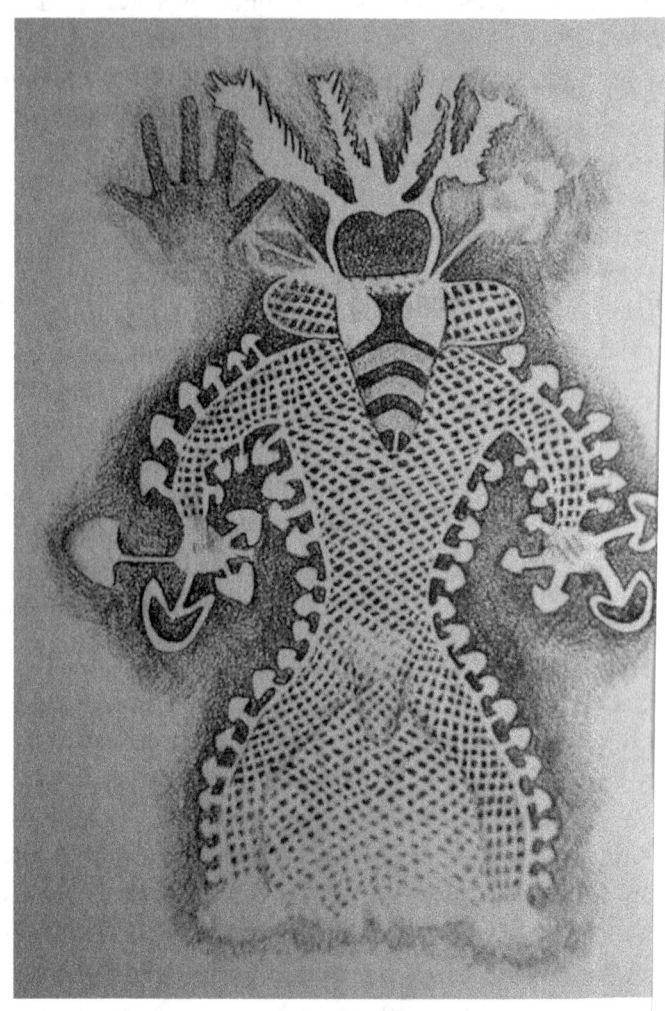

"The world may not only be stranger than we sup[pose, it]
may be stranger than we can suppose."

J.[

Bunzy and Gsal Byed Gdos Bral Ma are walking along the edge of a dark sea gazing down into deep pools in the moonlight. The pool they are looking into is the size of a mountain lake with steep cliffs plunging into the water below. The water has the clarity of a perfect diamond. It sparkles with energetic beauty. Bright yellow lava is rising up from the bowels of the world, covering about a third of the pool on the side of the pool away from them. The lava is swirling and glowing under a hundred feet of water, but the water isn't boiling or even steaming. A full moon shines behind them and the lava radiates in front of them. The blackened sea fills the night around them with the mysterious unknown. The shadowy land holds their feet aloft.

Bunzy starts to wonder, "How can all of that lava not cause the water to boil and kill us?"

"You are not to try to understand this situation," Gsal Byed Gdos Bral Ma answers. "Let your ideas about what is happening and how to influence what is happening, go. You are like a house fly trapped in a big glass jar. You keep buzzing around banging against the invisible walls trying to get out of the jar, but that's impossible. A fly can't get out of a bottle unless the lid is left off of its trap by something much bigger than the fly. A fly can try as hard as it can try, but it will never escape. It will die within those impregnable, invisible walls, unless the lid is taken off, and even then the fly has to discover the place where the lid was, is different from the place where the glass is, because both places look the same from where the fly is. Stop buzzing around. Go to sleep watching. That is all that is required of you now."

"Gsal Byed Gdos Bral Ma, you have to admit though that, that glowing yellow lava under the crystal water is quite a sight and look at that pool over there."

In the walls of this other pool are layers of amber colored see-through quartz. Each layer is at least twenty feet thick with layers of black basalt in between. Millions of objects are embedded in the glass. They aren't human artifacts. These layers were old before humans strolled along the shores of this ancient sea. Displayed in the amber glass are thousands of seashells, big bones and little bones, skulls, legs, backs and flippers, horns, tusks and teeth. There are things which may have been used by something, for some reason, at some time, but for what is unimaginable to Bunzy. There are crystals and gems. There are nuggets of gold and silver, copper and platinum. If Bunzy could just break off a piece of one of those ledges big enough to carry away, he would be rich. No, not just rich, he'd be wealthy and famous.

Then he thinks, "How can I see so well at night in the dark?"

Gsal Byed Gdos Bral Ma answers, "Because you aren't looking with your eyes. Your eyes are closed and sleeping in your body that is asleep."

"What does one see with when they are dreaming?" Bunzy asks.

"Good question, and what does one think with when the mind is unconscious?" Gsal Byed Gdos Bral Ma asks.

"I don't know," Bunzy responds.

Gsal Byed Gdos Bral Ma explains, "I realize that it is hard for you to understand that the eyes don't see and that the mind doesn't think but remember what we are doing here is losing the thoughts and watching with our hearts. What I am trying to get you to realize is that you do the strangest things in the weirdest, most dangerous situations and never even notice. You just indulge in your morbid thoughts and wander around in circles as if everything is fine. Let's practice seeing with your feelings. Follow me over to that cliff over there."

She points at a rock wall.

"I want you to look in a cave over there. Pay particularly close attention to what you feel. Maybe this exercise will answer some of your questions."

"Alright," Bunzy agrees.

The cliff is huge. It's like looking at the far side of the Grand Canyon. The trail along the base of it is wide, ancient, and well-travelled

Bunzy and Gsal Byed Gdos Bral Ma stroll over to a cave that she points at and look in. Peering into it is more like looking through a big gate into a sunlit field than staring into a dark hole in the ground. There is an Army colonel standing inside the mouth of the cave. Behind him is a command center in a war zone.

Looking at him, Bunzy says, "I could do this better than you guys are doing it."

The Colonel angrily shouts back, "Oh yeah, can you do this?"

He jerks an ammo case out of a Jeep which is parked behind him, rips the lid off of the wooden box. He picks up a large handheld weapon and loads it with six inch long shells from the open crate. According to pictures on the box, each of these explosives he is jamming into the gun, are a combination bullet, missile, and bomb. The command center buildings are off to Bunzy and Gsal Byed Gdos Bral Ma's left. There is a big open field in front of them, then there is a tree line and a village in the distance. The Colonel opens fire spraying bullets across the field. The air ignites as the missiles pass through it. When the projectiles hit the trees, the trees explode and burst into flames. Then everything in front of them, even the air explodes and begins to burn brightly. Trees, bushes, scattered buildings, animals and people, even the atmosphere becomes part of a raging inferno. Black smoke turns the day dark.

Loosely holding the rifle, the Colonel turns to Bunzy, smiles wickedly, and says, "Well!"

"I certainly can't top that," Bunzy concedes. He turns and walks away.

Behind Bunzy, the Colonel laughs fiendishly while his servants rush to put out the fires.

As Gsal Byed Gdos Bral Ma and Bunzy walk on, Bunzy says to her, "It's hard to believe that we don't notice or remember things like that. Am I asleep and dreaming?"

"You have not crossed over yet. You are still wandering around, mind tripping, talking to yourself, and looking at things with your unconscious waking consciousness. You're in dreamtime but not a dreamland. If you were totally asleep, you would no longer be here. You would have gone over to the Dreamlands, and you would be over there and your waking body wouldn't even know what's happening. When a person isn't awake at all any longer, we say that they have gone to sleep because they have gone from waking life to sleeping life. They have gone from here to there, much like you would go from Oregon to Africa. There's a lot between Oregon and Africa but in the end, you're in one or the other."

"You have compartmentalized personalities which don't share their experiences or memories. It's as in objective reality where you can't be in two places at the same time, with the double-whammy that you also can't remember what you did when you were in that other place. When you go to sleep, you go to a Dreamland. You are not a conscious being who is in objective reality any longer, even though your body and unconscious waking consciousness are still here."

"Go look in that cave up ahead. You'll experience what I'm telling you."

Looking into another cave, Bunzy sees his friend Johnny Jones going into a bar.

He yells, "Hey Johnny wait for me," and rushes to the front door of the nightclub Johnny has just entered.

This is a big building with a Greek façade on the front of it which proudly displays large faux columns, a fountain with life-size marble-like statues of gods and goddesses, and a landscaped garden. There is a restaurant on the ground floor. A bar with a dance floor and video gambling parlor is upstairs.

Johnny disappears upstairs as Bunzy enters the front door. Rushing up the stairs following him, Bunzy runs into the barroom.

The place is really crowded. Beautiful scenic murals are painted along the walls. A floor to ceiling waterfall separates the big dance floor from the bar. A band is playing. People are dancing. The video gambling machines are in a darkened room on the left at the top of the stairs opposite the dance floor. The bar is straight ahead.

As Bunzy pushes through the crowd towards the bar, a woman staggers over to him, grabs his arm, and slurs, "Bunzy, dance with me." She is pretty. He doesn't remember where they know each other from. Her boyfriend or husband glares at him.

Sliding his arm free from her grip, he says, "I'll come back and dance with you in a little while. I'm trying to find my friend Johnny Jones."

She looks deflated and pouts, "Alright, but don't forget."

Bunzy gives her his most sincere smile and pushes on into the barroom. There is a man that looks like Johnny lying on the floor between the barstools and the bar. The men drinking and visiting at the bar are paying no attention to the body under their feet. As Bunzy gets closer, he sees it isn't Johnny. There are other bodies on the floor scattered amongst the tables. He doesn't know if these people are drunk or dead or what. Men and women are drinking and talking, paying no attention to the bodies under their feet. He feels terrible about this whole scene. He's filled with disgust and loathing for these people.

Johnny is now behind him at the top of the stairs between the video machines and the dance floor. He spots Bunzy and yells and waves, just as a dozen violent young men come up the stairs and take over the dance floor. These are big, tough men with macho aggression in their eyes. It's obvious they've come to fight. There are some pretty, young women huddled at the far end of the dance floor. They seem to be aroused by these vicious men.

The fight starts beside the bandstand at the wall of falling water between the dance floor and the bar. In seconds the waterfall is destroyed, and the fight is in the bar. Tables and chairs are smashed. More walls are caved in. The lovely murals are trashed. Many of the video machines are thrown down the stairs. Bunzy has to push gambling equipment ahead of him and climb over it to reach the street. The carnage is terrible. Bunzy feels horrible.

The front of the nightclub has already been smashed. What happened out front must have been even worse than what is happening upstairs.

Awful, just awful, Bunzy thinks.

Johnny waits for him out front in a big, black limousine with the back door open. He waves to Bunzy to come over and get in. The woman who grabbed Bunzy's arm and her friend come out of the building right behind Bunzy. They all jump in the back of the limo and make their escape.

Johnny smiles and greets him with, "Bunzy, how are we going to top that?"

The woman's friend suggests, "Let's go out to Suicide Bridge and watch the people kill themselves."

"Good idea," Johnny responds. "Driver, take us to Suicide Bridge."

They take the freeway out of town to a bridge which is about a mile long. This is a big bridge with four lanes of traffic crossing high over the river. On the far side of the river, there is a wide spot at the end of the bridge where they pull over and park. At this place on the bridge the cement support abutments are massive and the bridge is wide. An apron which forms the side of the bridge slopes steeply away from the highway and ends abruptly. From where they are sitting, they can't actually see the outer edge of the bridge or the river below them. All they can see is twenty or thirty feet of slick cement, then nothing, air, and far below and away from them is the river.

A woman who is wearing a nice dress, expensive long coat, and high heels is walking towards them along the sidewalk from the land side of the bridge. When she reaches them, she climbs over the railing, turns around facing them, and lets go. Her terrified eyes lock on theirs. She changes her mind, screams and lunges back at the railing, slips on the slick cement, and slides away, disappearing below.

"I wonder what happened to her," Johnny says. "What's over there, the river, rocks, what?" He's tense.

"Maybe she fell in the river and is alive and needs rescuing," the woman suggests. "It looked like she changed her mind about wanting to die."

"Driver, go the end of the bridge and find a way to drive down underneath it, so that we can see what is happening down there," Johnny orders.

"Why did she do that?" the lady asks.

"Hopelessness," Johnny answers. "She was in a situation so terrible she couldn't bear it any longer."

"Weren't there any other solutions?" Bunzy asks.

"Not for her. Death was better than anything else that she could hope for," Johnny explains.

"Harsh," Bunzy says.

"That is really sad," the woman muses. "For her there was no future that could ever be anything but more painful than this unbearable moment. No hope ever. Just endless days of more and worse suffering and humiliation. How could something this terrible ever happen?"

They all sit in silence feeling as if they have just been dunked in ice cold water, then burnt by lightning. Their failures, disappointments and humiliations surround them.

At the far end of the bridge, the driver turns left crossing both lanes of traffic and turns onto a gravel service road which circles back beneath the freeway. When they drive under the bridge, they come under it from the side opposite to where the woman fell. She would have hit the water ahead of them and to their right. The area under the bridge between the bank of the river where the bridge starts and where the bridge begins to cross the river is the length of a football field with support piers spaced every fifty feet going across and running along under the bridge. There are men scattered around standing by the concrete pillars. They are all wearing black suits with white shirts and thin black ties. They are just standing there like beasts of prey waiting for a victim.

The limo passes under the bridge slowly drives to the side of the river where the suicide victims land in the water and drown. It is a big, deep, dirty river with a fast swirling, treacherous current. There is nothing out there except cold muddy water. There isn't a woman floundering about who is trying to get to shore. As the limo driver reaches the edge of the water, he makes a U-turn and starts back the way that we came, but right under the middle of the bridge, he stops. We get out of the limousine and look around.

A tall lanky guy who seems to be the leader of the beasts is standing about forty feet ahead of us and a little to our left on a dry dirt mound that supports a bridge column. The guy is about six feet two inches tall, wearing the same black suit with the white shirt and skinny tie as the others. He is probably in his forties, has short, salt and pepper hair and the look of an experienced, stone-cold killer. He waves the limo away with the imperious gesture of an emperor commanding his troops to release the lions into the arena to tear the victims to pieces.

As the limo pulls away, Bunsy stands facing this lead beast with Johnny in front of Bunsy and the man and woman who came with them are behind Bunsy. The lanky guy and three more men in black suits who are further away and behind Bunzy start towards them. It is obvious that the tall guy means to kill them. His look is flat, emotionless, and dangerous. He doesn't say anything, just attacks, smoothly and deliberately, like a big cat. When he reaches Johnny, he kicks him in the abdomen. As he executes his kick, Bunzy dives to his left, grabs him around the neck from behind, starts dragging him backwards and choking him out. When he loses consciousness, Bunzy drops him and kicks him with all of his might right in the temple with the toe of his right boot and yells at Johnny, "Stomp him! Stomp his head in."

Johnny lands on the leader's head with all of his weight on his right knee crushing the guys skull and popping his eyes out.

With adrenalin pumping from killing the leader and terrified at what he's going to see when he turns around and faces the next three guys whom Bunzy is sure have already murdered the man and woman behind him, he starts to crouch and shift his weight. Something smashes into his left temple, throwing him six feet to his right, stunning him. Everything is foggy. Bunzy can't think clearly. A fist punches him in the left rib cage.

Blocking a kick with his left arm, shaking his head and looking to his right, Bunzy looks through the curtains on the right side of his bedroom and out the window. Looking back to his left, he stares into an open closet at his shirts.

What the hell just happened? I was --- where, what?

Isabel stands by Bunzy's bed shaking him and kicking it. She yells in his face, "Wake up! Get up!"

When she sees his eyes are open, she asks, "What have you been doing?"

Bunzy realizes. *I am in bed, at home in the waking world. It is morning and the Sun is shining in through the windows.*

"I was dreaming," he answers.

"About what?" She asks.

Bunzy tries hard to remember, but the dream is gone.

He wonders, *how can I forget all of last night in one minute? Then he thinks, when it comes to dreams, I've discovered that I have instant amnesia when I wake up.*

"I don't remember," he tells Isabel.

"Bunzy, get out of bed. You need to quit hiding, get a job, and become a contributing member of our community."

"I'm meditating and becoming enlightened."

"Bunzy, stop it!" Isabel shouts. "That may be what you are telling yourself and your fabulous fantasy friends, but what I see is a guy doing nothing. Get some mirrors. Put them around and watch yourself. Then tell me what you see. What I see is a cowardly, two-bit hypocrite hiding while he takes long naps. Compare that to the story you're telling yourself about who and what you are."

Bunzy says, "I'm sorry about what I've become."

Isabel says, "No you're not. If you were, you would do something about it." Then she adds, "Bunzy you're disgusting. If you can't provide me with food, shelter, health care, transportation, a little fellowship, some good time entertainment, and a hopeful future; then you're wasting both of our time. We'll talk later. I have to go to work."

She storms out.

After Isabel's visit, Bunzy does nothing for a while except mind tripping. Then he starts meditating and calls on Gsal Byed Gdos Bral Ma.

When Gsal Byed Gdos Bral Ma appears, Bunzy asks her, "What do you think about what Isabel said?"

"I like it. She's partially correct," the Dakini tells him.

Bunzy says, "I've had enough loneliness, fear, pain, suffering, and lack. I have been ignorant, oppressed, abused, and miserable long enough. What must I do to be happy again?"

"You have to find the Dream Key, re-assemble your awareness into one complete consciousness which is connected directly to the Divine and release your imagination into creation."

Bunzy pauses for a while looking at Gsal Byed Gdos Bral Ma. Then he tells her, "I don't understand what you just said."

"Nonetheless, that is what you must do," Gsal Byed Gdos Bral Ma says.

"Okay. Where do I begin?" Bunzy asks.

"You need to make a connection with the Great Spirit."

Wide eyed, Bunzy asks, "How can I possibly do that?"

"You need help from beings who know the territory and can successfully show you the way," Gsal Byed Gdos Bral Ma answers.

"Where could I find these guides you're talking about?"

"In a desert wilderness."

Bunzy says, "Okay, I'm on my way."

He stands up and starts packing.

A week later, Bunzy sits on a big smooth reddish-brown boulder in the blazing southern Utah sun thirty feet from the edge of a two-lane blacktop highway. A nice-looking older silver four door sedan pulls over on the shoulder of the road in front of him. A Thirty-five-year-old guy gets out and walks loosely over to where Bunzy sits. The guy is tall and thin with tousled reddish blond hair that hasn't been cut in a while and a two-week-old beard, sparkling blue eyes and a smile that lights up Bunzy's heart. The guy wears clean khaki cargo shorts with pockets everywhere. Below the shorts are powerful tanned legs and feet covered by stream crossing, rubber and nylon hiking sandals. His dark green t-shirt proclaims:

It's Not
The Food
In Your Life.
It's The Life In
Your Food!

The guy sticks out his right hand and says, "Hi. My name is Jason, but people just call me J."

Bunzy shakes his hand and replies, "Hi. My name is Bunzy and people just call me Bunzy."

"Yes, sometimes it works like that," J agrees and grins conspiratorially. "So, Bunzy, are you just sitting here or are you going somewhere?"

"I'm not sure."

"Man, I know how that is."

"Where are you going?" Bunzy asks.

"I'm going to Mexico. Do you want to come along?"

"Sure. I haven't been to Mexico in a while. I like Mexico. It's a magical place. You have any idea where you're going in Mexico?"

"No. I'm just going with the flow."

That reminds Bunzy of Gsal Byed Gdos Bral Ma.

"Going with the flow?" He asks, seeking clarity.

"Yes, you know, flowing with the go."

That sounds right to Bunzy. He stands up, picks up his backpack, and together they walk back to J's car. Bunzy throws his pack on the backseat. They get in the front seat and take off.

"Bunzy, do you like to eat mushrooms?" Jason asks.

"Sure, I like all kinds of mushrooms, shitake, lion's mane, chanterelle, morel, king boletes. Shoot! I even like button mushrooms cooked in coconut oil, garlic, miso, white wine and soy sauce, with maybe a few mustard seeds and a little curry powder," Bunzy answers.

"No, I mean magic mushrooms, teonanacatl."

"I haven't eaten any, but I'm interested. Why?"

"Because I have some and we need to eat them before we reach the border. This is totally meant to be. Awesome synchronicity."

"J, sir, I don't wish to seem cowardly or negative, but what you are suggesting is dangerous. You are saying that if the police search this vehicle right now and catch us with these consciousness expanding mushrooms, they will put us both in prison for a long, long time, right?"

"Yes, that is right."

"And the reason that they will put us in prison for possessing them is because these magic mushrooms have a poison in them that is going to cause us to hallucinate if we eat them and become schizophrenic madmen, as in to hear things and see things that ordinary people neither see nor hear, right?"

"They have a substance in them that is going to open our minds to greater possibilities. I don't think that, that is quite the same thing as what you are suggesting."

"Why don't we just throw them out the window?"

"Life is short, and we have a long ways to go and a short time to get there."

"What does that mean?"

"You want to find love and be ecstatically joyful and dance with angels, right?"

"That sounds pretty good. I would like that."

"And in all of the things you've done in your life and in all of the roles and jobs you have had and all of the things you've learned in schools and churches and from the wisest people you've known, have you found that profound truth that has put you on an anxiety-free foundation where you know with absolute certainty everything is going to be beautiful, wonderful and you have the power to overcome all of the obstacles which will ever confront you and threaten the happiness of you and everyone you love?"

"No."

"Well, there you go then. You need to have the great experience. That is why you should try psychedelic mushrooms."

"The great experience, eh? What about bad trips, people curled up in the fetal position, hallucinating, screaming, throwing up, and then jumping out of windows in high buildings to their death? If we eat those mushrooms, we could end up as schizophrenic asylum vegetables or psychotic amoral criminals"

"You can't be really good, without first being bad."

"What do you mean by that?"

"If you are going to dig ditches well, the first ditch that you dig might not be a very good one, but you are going to have to start somewhere. If you are going to be joyful and happy, you might be carrying some ugly baggage around you need to get rid of. There might be some things you need to let go of."

"Aren't there less dangerous ways to let go of these things?"

"I suppose there are lots of them. I just don't know what they are and I don't happen to have them in a bag handy. I suppose though I should warn you the border patrol psychiatrist is right though. Once you do this, you can't undo it. The change is forever, or as the border psychiatrist says, 'the damage is done'. You can never go back. The cultural high wall will have been breached, and you will be on the outside of the fence that holds your community of friends and family. You won't be in that world any longer in which you have learned and lived all of your life until now. You will never be happy with the jobs or roles our materialistic culture offers. You will be set on a different path, seeking something more mysterious and grander than you could have ever imagined previously. You are entering upon a great adventure from which you will never return. You will never be satisfied with the ideas of what a useful productive person in a materialistic community is any longer. You will always be seeking something better, something more wonderful, something ephemeral, something just outside of others' awareness."

"Sounds like a Hell of unhappy alienation and loneliness to me, leaving your family and loved ones, your job, church, and civic roles."

"There is that. This isn't the path for everyone. Nobody should do this unless they are absolutely certain they have to go. There are other ways to get your kicks without leaving your place in your community, opening yourself to persecution, and plunging into a vast, overgrown, tangled jungle like an explorer searching for a lost city, or riding off into the wilderness like one of those old time mountain men."

"No way back, huh?"

"Nope. No way back. When you go into that wilderness, you go in forever."

"Love and happiness, right?"

"Love and happiness and ecstatic wonder and joy."

"J, you are not a very reassuring companion."

"Yes, I know. Like I said this trip isn't for everyone."

"Schizophrenia is frightening. Seeing things that no one else sees, believing things no one else believes, and acting in ways others think are weird doesn't make many friends and can get you locked up for the rest of your life, naked and isolated in a little cement cell being beaten, doped, and hacked on by some demented psychiatric surgeon. There is no place in a science-based, materialistic, modern society for the type of behavior that you are advocating. I know, because I meditate, and do visualizations, but I keep what I see and do to myself."

"It does look like a day at the beach with mountainous cold dark waves of shark loaded fear rolling in and breaking on top of you one after another until you're ripped to pieces and drowned, but when you get to the edge of the sea, it's all lovely mounds of sweet whipped cream coming in and the darkness is rivulets of hot chocolate fudge drizzling down them. No more fear, just sweet beauty, wave after wave rolling onto shore and the pieces all fit together into one beautiful, wonderful day at the beach. Suddenly it all makes sense swirling around you in a sweet white light. Dude, you have to relax in all matters and go with the flow to get to that beautiful far shore. I am not advocating opposing anything or anyone. I agree with everyone."

"J, you are quite the spin-doctor. What do you mean by 'the pieces all fit together'?"

"Each of us is like a plow horse with big blinders on who is plowing another furrow in this vast field filled with other beasts of burden with their blinders on who are pulling on their own heavy loads. Each person is self-absorbed in their own episodic psychodrama which reflects multitudes of confusing stories in thousands of disconnected images like reflections on little jagged sharp pieces of glass from a big broken mirror which is lying shattered on a busy grey downtown sidewalk next to a luscious green park on a sunny Wednesday afternoon. All of those pieces of broken glass lay there on the sidewalk showing the people rushing around in their mad, anxious, jerk-jerk lives while the trees in the park flow slowly on communicating deep caring support to each other and anyone who will stop for a moment and listen. Then, after eating a few mushrooms, in the crackling hum of firing neurons, the blinders come off, time flows backwards and the mirror becomes whole again reflecting one great picture, one great story, which is full of the purist, brightest, most beautiful light which illuminates everything, and the big picture all becomes clear again. When the blinders come off, there it is, one great cosmic creation of love and beauty. And what causes the blinders to come off? A change in attitude. When people's attitudes are different, the world is different. The whole dominatrix game collapses in laughter. Not because it is defeated, but because it is irrelevant. People just turn their backs on the old ways and walk away, because what they are walking towards is more enjoyable. And whereas before everyone was down on the cold concrete crawling across those broken shards of glass, when the mirror all comes back together, they shake their heads as if they are waking up, smile with beatific smiles, rise up out of their houses, out of the cities, and go back to the gardens and the forest where everyone is smiling and hugging, and tears of joy are streaming down their cheeks. Get it Bunzy?"

"J, you should be a poet. I had already decided to do this. I just wanted to hear what you had to say."

"Brother, I am just telling it like it is. The people who are running the wars on this and the wars on that, those are the ones whom you need to watch out for. Stay away from TV, newspapers, magazines, and the internet, politicians and talking heads, and the latest greatest thing. Follow your heart. When you're told that up is down, agree, then go on and do whatever you were going to do before you were hassled. That is the way to stay out of prisons, asylums, corporations, poverty, and armies. That is the path to happiness."

"What about police who want to search cars?"

"They're not bad guys. They just have their blinders on. They have their own biases. Man, you just need to appreciate where they're coming from."

"Which is?"

"They are our friends. We all want to help each other. Man, you just have to have a little faith."

"Hey, there's a hitchhiker up there," Bunzy shouts, pointing ahead at a guy who is standing on the shoulder of the highway by a road sign. "Pull over. Let's pick him up."

Jason pulls over and Bunzy rolls his window down and says, "Jump in."

The hitchhiker is a slender, dark haired guy who is wearing faded, clean blue jeans, a white t-shirt under a brown pull-over V-necked sweater, white running shoes, and carrying an old Army rucksack over his right shoulder. He throws his pack in the back seat, next to mine, and hops in.

Jason looks at him in the rearview mirror and asks, "Where are you going?"

"South to the University. I'm a grad student in education. I'm getting my Masters so that I can get out of teaching and get into administration where the easy, big money is. Where are you guys going?"

"Mexico," we chorus as we pull back out onto the highway.

"Great. You'll be going right past the University and you can drop me off by my apartment."

"We were discussing mushrooms. What do you think about them?" Jason asks.

"I don't like toadstools at all. At best, they are madness producing and at their worst they cause a painful, ugly death. There are a few that can be eaten, but why take a chance? They are disgusting things that live in the dark and eat shit."

"Seems a bit harsh. What did you say your name is?" Jason asks.

"Murray, Murray Schwarzkopf."

"My name is Jason. This other guy is Bunzy. When you say madness Murray, what do you mean?"

"I mean stark raving, lunatic, paranoid, schizophrenic psychosis. I mean creepy people who are hallucinating weird ideas and acting strange."

"Give me a feeling for what you consider is an odd idea."

"Personalizing nature, giving plants and animals personalities like humans. Thinking that there is a conscious, intelligent force behind everything in the Universe."

"Murray, you don't believe in God?" Jason asks with an open mouth and wide eyes.

"I believe in science," Murray says.

"What does your science tell you is happening here?" Jason wants to know.

"There is stuff banging into stuff and stuff happening."

"Is there any meaning or purpose behind all of this banging around?" Jason asks.

"No," Murray tells him. "This is all just happening. If there were a conscious creator behind all of this cruelty, suffering, misery and death, then I would have to hate that creator. It's simpler than that. There was a Big Bang and everything started. It's in the nature of matter," he bangs the back of the seat, "to explode and start banging into each other and to start forming more and more complex structures. It's just in the nature of matter to do that. There's no purpose, self-conscious intelligence, or meaning in it. Things just happen. When stuff bangs into stuff and stuff happens, the nature of that happening is the formation of more complex beings and eventually life arises and then consciousness arrives. Previous to the moment of the arrival of human consciousness, there was no self-consciousness. There was just stuff banging into stuff. It was all unaware, unintelligent things making random collisions. The rule of the nature of this more complex situation is that life is based on death. Live things must consume the lives of other things to survive. Survival of the fittest, fang and claw, that's the law of nature and that's what rules here. The stronger, smarter things consume the weaker, duller things. So be it. Once there is self-aware intelligent consciousness, and humans are the only ones who are that, then there is the ability to manipulate stuff because humans have the ability to do that. So based on the laws of nature, humans have the right to do whatever we choose to do to make ourselves happy and that includes the exploitation and destruction of other beings. And the best way to get the greatest good out of a pile of stuff is private property coupled with the profit incentive. If a group of intelligent people exploit a set of resources so as to maximize the profit from those resources, then the result will be the greatest good and the most happiness possible for that group of intelligent beings."

"How do you measure happiness, Murray?" Jason wants to know

"Happiness is based on having the most and the fanciest material products which lead to the greatest comfort and prestige possible in the here and now. There is nothing outside of what can be perceived by the five senses. There is no spiritual realm and there is no here-after, after we are dead."

"Whoa, Murray. That is quite a leap you just made. Almost everyone has always believed that there is a spiritual realm with a god or gods," Jason observes.

"There is no god," Murray proclaims. "That is an outdated, silly belief held by ignorant people and spirits are the hobgoblins of superstitious cranks. Scientific materialism works. Other beliefs don't. You can use the ideas explained by science to make better weapons and to enslave and exploit everything and everyone else who believes and acts upon a different set of beliefs. Scientific materialism is the most powerful belief system available. It explains everything we need to know about ourselves and what is happening. Faith and power of mind techniques never help anyone get anything done. Hard work, money, and scientific facts are what counts. What power is there in the spiritual realm that can withstand the onslaught of the profit motive?" Murray asks Jason.

"To relate to things on a profit basis, rather than on a fellowship basis, is a disturbing world view to me." Jason tells him. Then Jason asks, "Can't someone be a scientist and a Christian?"

Murray argues, "No way! Not if there're honest anyway. Religions all claim there is a spiritual basis to creation, and everything has purpose and meaning. Science says there isn't and it doesn't. But none of this matters, because in the end we're both going to act the same. We're both going to try to get the most that we can."

"Yes, but the most doesn't mean the same thing to both of us," Jason says. "The man who believes in spirit, believes in mercy and grace."

"True. That's what makes spiritual people weak and pathetic," Murray agrees. "That is the reason that spiritual people always lose in a struggle with scientific people. Spiritual beliefs have no power over material reality. Spiritual beliefs are delusions which cause the people who have them to act in weak and foolish ways. Where is there one culture based on mysticism that has survived and prospered against the onslaught of scientific technology."

"What happens to us when we die?" Jason asks.

"It's like turning off a light switch. The light goes out. We aren't anymore."

"There is no spirit?"

"No. If you have a spirit, show it to me."

"I can't."

"Then what makes you think that you have one? I don't believe that you have one. If you have a spirit prove it."

"I can't."

"Then don't be talking nonsense."

"So, what do you think that we should be doing with our lives?" Jason asks Murray.

"Isn't it obvious?" Murray wants to know.

"No, it's not obvious to me. Help me out here." Jason begs.

"Get as much prestige and importance, power and wealth as we can, while we can, any way that we can. Be somebody. Be somebody important."

"How do you identify someone as being important?" Jason asks him.

"By their job and their position in the community, the type of car they drive, the house they live in, the clothes they wear, the friends they have, and the clubs they belong to."

During this discussion, they have been driving on a scenic highway alongside a deep canyon with precipitous sides that plunge straight down for a long, long ways, but the canyon is very narrow, not much wider than a football field. On a dirt road off to their left they are nearing an old wooden trestle bridge spanning the canyon. It's a narrow bridge, only one car width wide with logs for bumpers on each side of the bridge. Out in the middle of the bridge, the right side has rotted and fallen into the canyon for maybe a thirty-foot span. The right bumper log is gone and a few inches of the roadway is gone too. Jason slows down only a little, wheels onto the dirt road and heads for the bridge.

The student yells, "What are you doing! Where are you going!"

Jason very reasonably and calmly says, "What are you worrying about, Murray? It's just stuff banging into stuff. It's all determined by natural laws and it's all going to work out for the best."

"Stop! Stop right now! You're insane," Murray starts yelling. "We're all going to be killed."

"Relax, man," Jason tells him. "If something goes wrong, you won't feel anything, anyway. When the lights go out, you're gone. No problem. Who cares about one light bulb, one way or another? Do natural laws care about light bulbs? Laws don't have feelings."

As they near the bridge, Murray moans, "No, but I do and I don't want to die."

"I want to see what's on the other side of the bridge," Jason nonchalantly replies.

Murray makes a desperate lunge for the steering wheel.

Jason grabs the wheel with his left hand and drives his right elbow into the bridge of Murray's nose, smashing it, blood spatters Jason's elbow and the front of Murray's sweater. Murray grabs his nose with both of his hands and falls backwards into the back seat, blood bubbling out between his fingers.

He stares ahead at the bridge mumbling over and over, "I don't want to die. I don't want to die. I don't want to die."

Jason takes the bridge with their left wheels up on the bumper logs on the left side of the bridge and never slows down. If he goes an inch to the left too far, they'll slide off of the logs and roll into the canyon, plunging hundreds feet down onto the rocks below, but if he is not far enough to the left when they come to the hole in the bridge, they'll smash through the decking on their right and plunge downward, smashing through the bridge supports into the canyon below. They're dead either way, unless his judgment is absolutely perfect and his skills are impeccable, and the bridge miraculously holds them up. Leaning back, driving with his right hand only, with his left elbow casually out the window, Jason discusses the importance of having meaning and purpose in our lives.

Neither Bunzy nor Murray listen to Jason. They're staring at the bridge. A river snakes through the canyon below. In the backseat, Murray shakes and moans with blood running down his wrists. Bunzy wants to scream, but he's too terrified to breathe. His mind has disconnected from his body. He watches the drama unfold as if it is happening on a movie screen to somebody else.

Jason weaves back and forth, dodging knots which stick up on the logs. They shoot across the bridge past the gaping hole and on to the other side where Jason puts the car into a four-wheel drift and comes to a skidding stop on a dusty flat spot in front of a big, old cement wall.

Murray leaps out, runs around to the driver's side of the car, starts kicking the door, and screaming, "What's wrong with you? Are you insane? You could have killed us all."

Jason politely looks up at him, smiles radiantly, and says, "There is no hope Murray. We are all caught in the jaws of a slavering beast and devoured sooner or later. There is no way out of here, other than through an uncaring death. No hope, only death. Just a little time and then death, dead, gone forever, snuffed out as if we never ever even existed. We're doomed to be just like dead cows, ground up and put in plastic packages in a supermarket freezer. No importance and no hope."

Murray shouts in his face, "You're mad. You're completely insane," and runs around to other side of the car, grabs his pack and runs away back across the bridge towards the highway and civilization.

Bunzy says, "Damn man, your facts are a bit harsh."

"No shit," Jason replies. "Just trying to help the guy."

They get out and look at the wall. It's an old scabby grey concrete slab surrounding what appears to be a prison camp. They stand near a square corner in the structure. At this point, the wall is only about five feet tall. It goes away from them in two directions for hundreds of feet getting taller as it goes. Inside the wall in this area of the prison which they can see from where they stand are hundreds of people standing packed together shoulder to shoulder. The young man who is standing closest to them in the corner of the wall, has long blond hair and blue eyes. He was beautiful once, but now his hair is greasy, stringy and matted. Terror and exhaustion make him ugly. His eyes bulge out. They dart this way and that. Suddenly he goes down, disappearing. They realize that his hair wasn't greasy. It was wet. He was standing up to his chin in water. He was jerked under. They wait. He doesn't come back up. All of those people standing behind that wall are up to their necks in water and if they falter for even a moment they will slide under and drown. Then, where the angelic man was standing, a grinning brute pops up. He is a head taller than everyone else. He pushes them aside and looks around. He is obviously not one of the prisoners.

Jason declares, "I'm going to free those people."

"You just advised me to go with the flow and not oppose anyone or anything. You said that, that was the way to get by and to be happy."

"Well, some things are just too much," Jason says.

There is a twenty-foot tall, big, thick wooden plank paneled double gate up the wall to our left. Jason strides up to it, starts banging on the heavy boards with his fists and shouting, "Set the people free. People have got to be free. Everyone deserves respect and a decent life and happiness."

Nothing happens.

He begins to kick the wood and yells at it, "What you are doing is evil and wrong. Life is a precious gift. What kind of god do you worship?"

There is the sound of tumblers clicking and then of big locking bolts being slammed back. Jason backs away from the wall, back to where Bunzy stands. The left panel of the gate swings out towards them ten feet, leaving enough room for a massive man to stride out. He glares at Bunzy and Jason, as if he is looking at smelly goats that are waiting to be sacrificed. He is a white goliath, seven feet tall, massive shoulders and back, with legs like trees. He's wearing a heavy dark green pull-over with military patches and insignias on it, brown canvas cargo pants and big black leather paratrooper boots. His thick blond hair is cut short.

He declares, "We don't worship no stinking gods. We're men of science, not weaklings, like you two sissies."

Then he runs at them like an Army tank with its guns ready to fire; lethal and unstoppable.

Jason says, "Let me handle this," and steps between Bunzy and the giant.

When the giant reaches him, the big man leaps into a flying kick, driving his right boot at Jason's face. Jason steps aside, surprisingly quickly. He doesn't crouch or take a defensive posture. He doesn't strike a blow at the giant as he flies past him. He just steps out of the way of the attack. When the giant lands on the ground on the other side of Jason, he spins around and comes back at Jason like a lawn mower of karate chops and kicks. It all happens so fast that Bunzy can't see half of what happens, but no blow touches Jason. He just ducks and weaves back and forth slowly giving ground, backing towards the cliff. As the giant wheels around and follows his windmill attack with a flurry of jabs, elbows, knees, kicks, and punches, Jason continues dodging without ever seeming to put out any effort. He smiles back at the giant which makes the giant absolutely, insanely furious. It looks as if Jason is going to be knocked over the cliff.

Bunzy attacks the guy from his back with a vicious kick in the giant's right kidney.

It is like kicking a bale of hay which is supported inside with iron bands. There is no give, none at all.

Bunzy bounces back. The giant spins around, punching him in the forehead with the heel of his right hand, driving Bunzy twenty feet back, and knocking Bunzy down on his rear-end in the dirt, stunned. Then the giant turns back to Jason.

By this time Jason has been driven back to the edge of the cliff. The giant begins a series of cartwheeling kicks which are tremendously fast with a lot of momentum. When Jason dodges the kick that should knock him over the edge of the cliff, the giant's force propels him into the canyon. As he flies over the edge, he grabs Jason's shirt and jerks him over the cliff along with him.

Bunzy is left sitting alone, in the dirt, in the silence, with only the wind sighing over him. No sound, not even groaning comes from the prison.

He thinks. *This place has the feel of a mournful old desert ghost town graveyard. Damn, I liked Jason. I thought that we were going to do great things. I already miss him. The idea of using psychoactive plants to find spirit hasn't worked out very well.*

Staggering to his feet in the greyness, Bunzy walks over to the car, takes out his pack, swings it over his right shoulder, walks the full length of the concrete concentration camp wall that faces the canyon. Stops. Hoists the left pack shoulder strap on, buckles the waist belt, turns right up a dismal draw and walks away into the lonely hills.

CHAPTER 11
PSYCHOSIS OR GNOSIS

"We do not progress from point to point, rather we cross over a line."

Ernst Junger in a letter to Albert Hoffman

These hills are full of ghosts. Bunzy doesn't see or hear anything. The place just feels creepy and frightening, as if something unpleasant is watching him all of the time. It could just be his imagination, but that doesn't matter, whatever it is, it's horrible.

He can't sleep at night. He just lights a fire, get his back against a boulder and waits for the Sun to return. Nothing happens. There aren't even any coyotes howling, just the sound of the wind moaning all night, keeping him cold, nervous, and awake.

When the Sun does come again, it's a cloudy grey day with a black sky hanging low overhead, but no rain. It's a dry, dust caked, choking darkness like a mummy's just opened grave.

Bunzy pushes on all day. In the evening he crosses a high barren plateau and towards dark enters some broken hills. In a sheltered draw ahead, there is a camp fire burning. Hoping for safety and companionship, he walks to it.

There's an old Indian sitting by the fire, staring into the flames. He has long black hair which is held back from his broad dark brown face by a wide band of folded scarlet cloth which is knotted at the back of his head. He is wearing a heavy black woolen coat with green arrow heads and yellow lightning bolts woven into a wide intricate pattern which runs around his chest. Below the jacket he has on cream colored hemp pants and hard worn, old style, Mexican huarache sandals.

When Bunzy enters the firelight, the Native looks up, showing no surprise and says, "Aho, white man." His dark sparkling eyes stun Bunzy for a moment. Bunzy likes the Indian instantly, but there is a seriousness about him that frightens Bunzy.

"Aho, red man," Bunzy responds. "Do you mind if I share your fire?"

"No. Pull up a rock and make yourself at home," the Native says.

Bunzy rolls a big rock up close to the fire, sits down on it, starts warming himself, and asks, "What do people call you? My name is Bunzy Ringer."

"Running Bear," the Native answers.

"Running Bare? How do you spell that b-e-a-r or b-a-r-e?" Bunzy smirks.

"B-e-a-r, but smart-ass white boys can spell it b-a-r-e. It's your choice. I'm neither bare nor a bear. You're just talking to yourself anyway."

"What!" Surprised, Bunzy does a double-take and exclaims as he points at the Native, "You're sitting right there or are you saying that I'm imagining you?"

The Indian looks Bunzy in the eyes, smiles and proclaims, "I'm as real as you are. What I said was that you are not talking to me. You're talking to yourself. That doesn't deny my existence. It is a denial of your sanity. Your fantasies are about you. Not about me. You're not seeing me. You're seeing the inside of your own mind and talking to some phantom in there. So don't try to harm me with your arrows of arrogant, blind cleverness."

"Alright. You win," Bunzy says shrugging his shoulders and lifting his palms upwards, "I see what you mean, but if you don't mind I think that I'll just call you John."

"Another word pregnant with meaning: Saint John, John the Baptist, Don Juan."

"But those are associations which I can deal with and that is what is important to me right now."

"What is important to you?"

"Getting a grip. I need something to hold on to and a friend named John has the feeling that everything is normal and the world is a safe place, even with those associations with the mysterious that you have alluded to."

The Native casts a stick into the fire, slowly turns his body square with Bunzy's, rocks forward onto his toes, looks hard directly into Bunzy's eyes and in a lightning quick smooth motion, crisscrosses his chest with both hands and draws two big, wicked Bowie knives from behind his shoulders.

Bunzy is paralyzed. He stares past those gleaming hack and gut pieces of bare steel into Running Bear's face, waiting for his next move.

The Indian says, "Indeed, you wouldn't want to call me something that reminds you that you don't know what you might meet while you're wandering around alone, defenseless, lost in the wilderness in the dark."

Then he leans back, re-sheathes the knives, smiles off to his left side into the darkness for a moment, then turns back towards Bunzy and in a casual, friendly manner continues, "So, do you mind if I call you Bill, Bob, Kip, or Shane, or maybe Molly, Einstein, or Golden Spaceship Earth, or Milarepa, or Jesus, or Xolocoyotezcatl? Do you like any of those names Bunzy? How do they make you feel? What's in a name anyway? If you call me Chief Joseph will that change anything that happens here tonight? Does a person's name determine their situation? Can you change the game by changing the name? Does it matter where we were born or when?"

Bunzy shrugs again, relieved that Running Bear put those big, scary knives away, squinches his lips together and admits, "I don't know," and gives up, "Running B-e-a-r you are."

The Indian holds out his hands as if he is going to get up and come over and hug Bunzy, as if they are best friends, and says, "Bunzy, you can call me just plain Bear, B-e-a-r."

"Thank you Bear," Bunzy responds, sagging as the tension drains out of his face and shoulders. "I promise to try not to harm you with any more of my arrogant nonsense."

"I'll hold you to your word," Bear concludes smiling, while pointing his right index finger at Bunzy like it's a pistol, squinting over it with his left eye and aiming at Bunzy with his right eye.

"That would be a good thing," Bunzy sighs. "I realize that you are a divine spirit and I am honored to be in your presence and I wish to serve and be of benefit to you."

"Thank you Bunzy, and I recognize the same of you and I wish to do the same for you."

Trying to move away from dangerous confrontation and be more companionable, Bunzy asks, "Does your name mean something special that explains something about you? Was it given to you by your tribal elders or maybe even by your grandfather in a special ritual ceremony?"

"It does and it was, but Running B-a-r-e means something too and in our case it may be more appropriate to our situation. After all, most humans could be said to be Running B-a-r-e. Bare should be a common human family name in your culture like Smith or Jones. Cosmically speaking, humans are born mightily handicapped, severely retarded, and specially ignorant. So, Running Bare, B-a-r-e, could be a common name representing a lot of people's condition. People could call each other Running Bare as if they were looking at themselves in a mirror and recognizing their human nature. Most people could be said to be out in the open, running bare-ass naked, empty handed, lost, and exposed through some very harsh and deadly elements."

He stands up, with his right hand picks up a spoon that is sitting on a boulder beside him, slips a blue bandanna from around his neck with his left hand, using the cloth as a pot holder, lifts the lid from a pot that is sitting on some coals at the edge of the fire, stirs the contents, puts the lid back on the pot, sets the spoon back on the rock, and sits back down, slipping the bandanna back around his neck.

"I suppose," Bunzy agrees, after silently watching all of this, "but what do you mean by born handicapped, retarded, and ignorant? That seems a bit harsh."

Bear looks Bunzy over for a few moments as if he is weighing his options, then Bunzy can see he's made an important decision. Bear leans into Bunzy slightly and says, "Bunzy, I want to tell you something and I don't want you to be offended, because this is the nature of the human condition, not just your situation personally. Almost everyone in this realm is handicapped, retarded, and ignorant. This condition is so severe that it can be said that most people really know almost nothing about the forces which shape their lives. When I say that most people are handicapped, what I mean is that they believe in only those things which they can see, touch, hear, smell, and taste and these perceptual tools only work for them in very small ranges. You know that what I am saying is true because in the last few centuries technologies have been created which have extended those senses, for example: microscopes, telescopes, x-ray machines, infrared sensing devices, hearing aids, and temperature gauges. All of these efforts have helped people to see, hear, and perceive more than they were capable of perceiving previously, but none of these devices go very far into infinity and eternity. These perceptual tools do not allow you to perceive very much of all that there is to know and even if you were able to overcome your perceptual handicaps and to consciously perceive time and space more profoundly, there is still the problem of your being retarded. Your ability to comprehend what you are perceiving has been reduced so much you couldn't understand your situation even if your perceptual handicaps were removed. People are like pond scum who are trying to comprehend and describe the back side of the moon. Pond scum just can't do it. The third problem you are facing is ignorance. You really don't have much useful information. You only know what you have been told, and you haven't been told hardly anything. Most humans don't even understand the evil of the money system, much less the basic nature of reality and their connection to dreams. So, you find yourselves in a sad dilemma in which you are handicapped, retarded, ignorant, and enslaved. Bunzy, you have to start doubting everything that you think or believe, and you have to doubt every source of information which you have been given. You are helpless and your situation is hopeless."

Bear pauses, looking at Bunzy as if Bunzy has been talking and showing Bear something important, which Bunzy hasn't. The Indian seems to be examining the air around Bunzy. Bear even looks away from Bunzy into the darkness for a while or maybe he is still looking at Bunzy but out of the corner of his eyes.

Meanwhile Bunzy stares at Bear and listens to him.

Suddenly, looking directly at Bunzy again, Bear continues, "Bunzy, you've got to realize your handicap is so great that on your own, you could never overcome it and you are so retarded that you will not be able to understand the nature of this situation without help and your lack of knowledge is so great that on your own, you will not even be able to discover you are handicapped and retarded. But, if you are ever going to do anything about the situation in this world in which you find yourself living, you need to get a grasp on what's happening and to see how really big and complex eternity is and realize how much power there is driving your lives in the direction you're going and how ruthless and greedy the forces are that empower this cruel, destructive, perverted, corrupt tyranny. Then you will understand how helpless you are and you will see how hopeless your situation is. If you are going to get to a place of happiness, beauty, abundance, wonder, harmony, and love; your only hope is to get some outside help. You're going to have to be given a great and wonderful knowing from outside of your current comprehendible perceptual consciousness. Forget about trying to solve this dilemma with the tools, awareness, and abilities of a modern human. You're way too dumbed down. Your abilities are way too narrow and the information which you are being given is way too small to overcome the situation in which you find yourself. You must find a friend or friends who have a grander and more powerful understanding, or else, you will continue to lose like you've been doing. Sorrow, despair, and humiliation will be all that you will ever know. On your own it was never possible for you to understand this situation or to do anything about it, but you've never been alone. You have always had allies and helpers who are unrecognized by you. So, relax, become aware, and learn."

Bunzy's hungry and nervous. He doesn't want to argue. He wants to steer the conversation somewhere he understands. He looks at the fire and asks, "What's in the pot?"

Bear looks at the fire and says, "Beans, mostly. They're almost ready. There are plenty for both of us."

"Good. I'm starving," Bunzy tells him, then adds, "Surely, you're exaggerating about what you just said. What kind of help could I need? How bad could things be?"

"They are more horrifying than you can imagine and don't call me Shirley." Bear grins in the firelight.

Bunzy's taken back by Bear's accusation and denies it saying, "I didn't call you Shirley. I said, 'Surely you're exaggerating ---.' Oh, I get it. From the movie. Right? Very funny." Bear laughs. Bunzy laughs too but a bit nervously.

He continues to pursue his main line of thought, "Bear, there's always been problems. When you say horrifying, are you saying that our troubles have gotten worse?"

Bear looks past the fire into the darkness for a moment, then back at Bunzy and begins, "Bunzy, imagine that you are a rich, influential man who lives in a big, old mansion in the middle of the capitol city of this fine country. You're fed up with my lame jokes, so you eat your bowl of beans and go home. When you get there, you walk into your house, set your bags down, and listen. Something is wrong, terribly wrong. You feel it in your guts. You're suddenly scared, really scared. As you listen, you hear things up in the attic flapping around on bat wings, but these aren't mouse sized bats. These are blood-thirsty, thumping, thudding, swashbuckling ten-foot-tall creatures who are flapping their black scaly wings, walking about on two legs and talking. What they are discussing is how they have been controlling people for thousands of years, but now they are tired of all of this subterfuge and subtle manipulation which they have been using. They're planning on coming down and taking over directly, starting with ripping you to pieces and eating your family. In terror, you run outside, where you bump into your neighbor, Fred Collins, who manages the City's underground utilities. You try to tell Fred what you've discovered, but he won't listen. He ignores you while he explains that city workers have discovered a terrible environmental disaster that is happening. The ground which the city is built on is like a sheet of ice covering a vast deep lake and this covering is melting. It's getting thin enough that people are starting to fall through and disappear. Some whole slums have already gone down. Men, women, children, dogs, cats, houses, cars, and chickens; everyone and everything is completely gone, as if they never existed."

"You ask Fred, 'What are you going to do about this horrible impending disaster?'"

"Fred replies, 'Nothing. The government and the corporations are going to fix it.'"

"That doesn't reassure you. You ask, 'How long do we have until we all fall into this lake?'"

"'Who knows,' Fred tells you. 'You and your house could go at any minute.'"

"That is when you realize that you are surrounded by madness, true insanity, not a romantic sickness, but true painfully fatal psychosis. There are terrible creatures running this show and they intend to do horrible, evil things and meanwhile the ground under your feet is dissolving and no one intends to do anything about the situation. People won't listen to you and if they do, they think that you're crazy. So, the best thing for you to do is to silence yourself, but this creates unbearable tension and anxiety in you as you try to live as an ordinary person in a world ruled by monsters that is about to dissolve and sink into oblivion."

Bear pauses and tosses another stick in the fire and asks, "Do you understand what I'm telling you?"

"Yeah, I get it. That's worse than I thought alright. Just drop the clever metaphors though and tell me straight out what it is that is so damned horrifying. Then tell me what I should be doing, but first tell me why you are out here?"

Bear looks Bunzy straight in the eyes and in the sincerest, sweetest, most heart-felt, convincing voice says, "Communing with Spirit."

In this moment, Bunzy knows something important is about to happen. This guy may be the most dangerous person he has ever met. He's scared. Bunzy knows the two of them are about to cross some line.

As calmly as he can, he says, "A lot of people don't believe in spirits anymore. They only believe in what they can see and hear, just like you said."

"Well, that's too bad," Bear responds, "because a lot of people don't see or hear very well anymore."

Bunzy offers, "I meditate and do visualizations. I have a Dakini guide. However, I don't understand what spirit is. I can't see spirit. Getting a grasp on what the Divine is, in any workable way, is beyond me too. I was just traveling with a couple of guys and they were having a discussion about spirit. One of them believed in spirit and one of them didn't. The one who didn't believe, challenged the believer to show him a spirit, but the believer couldn't. Can you show me a spirit?"

"Son," the Native drawls, "spiritually you are sitting in a standing room only space. There are many ways to see spirit but most of those methods are too slow for you because you've got a long way to go and you need to get going pronto because you're already in deep trouble."

Bunzy realizes this conversation has taken a threatening twist, but he ignores Bear's frightening innuendos and carries on, "When I'm doing a visualization, how do I know that I'm not just making up what I'm communicating with? How do I know what's real and what's not real? No one else sees what I'm seeing or hearing. I might just be crazy."

"Son, you are not crazy," Bear tells him. "You're just ignorant, confused, powerless, and now scared. When you know what you are, that makes other options possible. The difference between being schizophrenic and being a shaman is that the spirit whom the shaman talks to does empowering and useful things in this world. When things are going right, everyone is connected, communicating, and helping each other to live better lives. The shaman isn't crazy, frightened, or confused. He just perceives and knows more than others do. That is why he is respected and consulted by people in cultures that have not lost their connection to nature and still know there is more going on here than just what they see and hear."

Bunzy asks, "Are these spirits whom shamans communicate with as powerful as the technology of a scientist or is the scientist's understanding so great that he can destroy the shaman's world whenever he chooses to?"

"I'm afraid that you will have to answer that for yourself. But before you do, allow me to say, this isn't an us versus them situation. It isn't an I'm right and you're wrong scenario. It isn't a science guys versus spiritual people struggle. We don't have to be angry, frightened and fighting with each other all of the time. We are all in this together and need to act as one. We need to trust, share, support, and help each other with the tools that we have at our disposal. We also need to be willing to accept help from those with whom we disagree when their methods are getting the results we need. So, I don't want to get into an argument over whether technology is superior or whether spiritual techniques are better. That is like arguing if you have a nickel, the head side is superior to the tail side. They are different faces of the same coin. However, there are those who believe that they benefit by the use of the divide and conquer techniques which they are carrying out against us. They have made this discussion about science and spirit into a fight which doesn't benefit anyone except them and in the end it will not benefit them either. That being said, you're a science guy, even though you can do visualizations and have some understanding of spirit. You still travel from place to place in machines, buy your food from a grocery store with money, and live in a house financed by debt. You are dependent on money technology. I am dependent on Spirit."

"I don't see how you can depend on Spirit to provide you with food, shelter, and transportation, or to protect you from heavily armed thugs."

"You know the thoughts and beliefs of the science myth. You were raised in Archon schools. You have been indoctrinated in their mind control programs. For you to understand the spiritual way, you need to meet Spirit so that you can experience Spirit's side of this story. Then you will understand what Spirit is offering."

They are leaning into each other intensely sharing their thoughts. Bear stands up and proclaims, "Let's eat," breaking the tension between them.

Bunzy gets out his plate and hands it to Bear.

While Bear fills their plates, he asks, "Who is your Dakini guide?"

"Gsal Byed Gdos Bral Ma," Bunzy answers. "Do you know her?"

"Yes, of course, she is well known amongst those who are interested in spiritual matters. She is much loved, respected and admired. Her strength, wisdom and guidance has helped many, plus she is beautiful and humorous. You are really lucky to have her for a companion."

"Yes, I know. Her support and guidance and strength has gotten me through a lot of difficult situations."

Bear hands Bunzy's plate, full of vegetable stew, back to him. They eat in silence, staring into the fire, thinking their own thoughts, drinking from their own water bottles.

After they clean their plates and spoons, put them away, gather some firewood, build up the fire and sit back down, Bear says, "People don't mold their lives around ideas. You mold your lives around what you perceive that you have experienced, which isn't much because your experiences are as tightly controlled and limited as your perceptions and ideas are. After you've had an experience, you justify your actions through the limited ideas which you have been given. If you were to come into the Divine presence and have a new experience of what is happening that is totally different than what you have previously experienced and if that new experience were to be wonderful on a magnitude you couldn't have previously even imagined was possible, then you would become something totally different than what you are now. And when you saw things around you changing in good ways, based on this new understanding, it wouldn't matter if what you were hearing on TV, or from professors, politicians, or neighbors contradicted what you knew from your own experience. You would have a grander, more profound vision which gave you an understanding that is beyond those other peoples' world views. You would consider their ideas to be the opinions of simplistic, mentally impoverished, robotic slaves. You would stand on a mountain of ecstasy that gave you the power to live joyously. Excitement, importance, and pleasure would become the core of your being. You would bathe constantly in the middle of a stream of divine blessings, washed by wealth, beauty, power, and happiness. And when those around you saw your wonderful transformation, they would want to become like you. All that you would have to do then is to give them the experience too and the world would be changed. Once people come into the presence of Spirit and have the full revelation, they can no longer live the way they were living. They have to express themselves in a more sharing, caring, sensitive way. The institutions that people toil in don't need to change. It is the way that people operate those institutions that has to change. We can argue and debate and try to convince each other for years that we are right and they are wrong, but just one minute in the loving Divine presence ends the discussion. After that minute, the only thing to talk about is how we may serve and how we may spend more time in the joy of that loving presence. After the ecstasy of that ineffable moment, nothing needs to be explained. The person who has had the experience knows. His faith is unshakeable."

"Alright Bear, I'm convinced. How do I meet Spirit and have the experience?"

A voice hails us from the dark, "Buenos noches, Senior Running Bear and amigo, may I join you?"

"Good evening, Brother Seattle. C'mon in. You are always welcome," Running Bear answers.

Seattle is a big, brown skinned man, six feet four of lanky powerful muscle, with a noble long straight nose and piercing dark brown eyes. It's hard to tell his age. He looks to be about forty, but there is something older, timeless about him. He is wearing a broad brightly colored, striped cloth wrapped around his head with three long eagle feathers tied in his long black hair, some of which is sticking out of the top of the cloth. A loose-fitting white tunic falls from his shoulders to the middle of his thighs which are wrapped in tight fitting black leggings down to his moccasins. A heavy green blanket hangs around his shoulders.

Running Bear introduces them, "Seattle this is my new friend, Bunzy. Bunzy, this is my old friend and helper, Seattle."

Seattle walks straight over to Bunzy. Bunzy stands up. Seattle grabs Bunzy's right arm just below the elbow and Bunzy does likewise to him, as Seattle says, "It's a good night Bunzy. I am honored to meet you." Seattle shakes Bunzy's arm and then lets go.

Bunzy is awed by Seattle. He sincerely responds, "It's good to meet you too, Seattle. Running Bear called you, his helper. I could also use some help."

They sit down.

"What kind of help do you need?" asks Seattle.

"I'm searching for spirit and the Dream Key."

"This then is your lucky night," he responds.

Running Bear asks Seattle, "So what have you been doing?"

"Journeying around the hyper-spatial, trans-temporal busyness with the Master of Life enjoying the wonder and beauty of it all."

Bunzy interrupts, "What did you mean by, 'this is my lucky night?'"

Seattle asks, "Bunzy, how could some chickens escape from their wire cages in one of those flesh growing factory farms?"

Bunzy says, "They couldn't. There is no way that chickens can escape from a factory farm on their own. Their only hope, their only way out of their cages, is if the farmer sets them free or if some animal liberation people break into the chicken factory, take the cages out into the country and turn the chickens loose. Otherwise, those chickens are all going to die together, horribly, in a slaughterhouse and their butchered frozen bodies are going to be sold in plastic packages in grocery stores to people for money."

"Bunzy, you think that you are on a planet called Earth that is spinning around like a top at over a thousand miles an hour, hurtling through space around an exploding ball of gases called the Sun at 66,666 miles per hour and yet where you are sitting over there on that rock, there is no wind, and I can do this." He picks up a stone, stands up, and tosses it in the air. It falls at his feet. He turns around in the opposite direction, picks up another rock and tosses it in the air. It also lands at his feet. Try that on the back of a flatbed truck going down the freeway at seventy miles an hour. Then tell me again that we are on a planet spinning around like a top and hurtling through a void at tens of thousands of miles per hour."

"If we're not on Earth, where are we?" Bunzy asks.

"We are in an energy sink and we are vectors in that sink through which ideas such as planets and suns occur."

"Seattle, I am afraid I don't just not believe what you are saying, I don't have any idea what you are even talking about."

"That's right Bunzy. You don't, and that points to your main problem. The wires in the cage that holds you are your conceptions of your perceptions. Those wires are your ideas of who you are and where you are. You believe that you are a human on a place called Earth, when you are actually an angelic being in Paradise. You are a conscious vector of power in an energy sink and you are capable of creating great joy and wonder and beauty, but your creative abilities have been hijacked in such a way you have become a domestic servant and your creative abilities are being used to support the fantasies of a group of beings who are too lazy to create their own world. Those same wires prevent you from seeing spirit and experiencing the Divine loving presence. Bunzy, you wouldn't recognize the Great Spirit if you were looking right at it. All you know are broken fingers."

Running Bear grabs his belly and starts laughing so hard that he falls off of the rock he's sitting on.

Seattle smiles as if he is hilarious.

Bunzy doesn't get it. He's angry at both of them for their foolishness. He sits silently staring at them and fuming.

Seattle stops laughing. He looks tenderly at Bunzy and asks, "My dearly beloved Son, what do you think spirit is? How would you recognize a spirit if you came into the presence of one?"

Running Bear gets up, dusts himself off and sits back down on his rock, still grinning.

Bunzy says, "I guess that a spirit would kind of shimmer or glow with its own light and have a tenuousness about it like maybe I could see through it, or put my hand through it, or maybe it would just appear or disappear, or walk through a wall, or maybe it would be totally strange looking like a rooster headed, lizard man with glowing red eyes."

"What do you think, Seattle? Am I close?" Bunzy asks.

"Good effort," Seattle tells him. "But I think this information will help you have a better understanding. Everything is spirit, or maybe a better way to say this is spirit is everything. Everything has a living, conscious spirit and that spirit is its soul essence. A soul is the eternal essence of beingness. It is that spark of consciousness from which we all get our existence. And this spirit that is us, is part of one great spirit."

Bunzy argues, "Seattle, that is like saying that everything is molecules." Then he asks, "How is that supposed to help me?"

"It does seem similar, but they are actually quite different." Seattle tells him.

"How?" Bunzy asks. "Why can't I see spirit?"

"Spirit is the essential building material of this reality," Seattle tells Bunzy. Then he explains to him, "The reason that you can't see it, isn't because it is very small, like molecules, or wispy and ghost-like. You can't see spirit because it is encased in a shielding container and containers only see other containers."

"Containers?" Bunzy raises both of his hands and stares wide eyed at Seattle.

"Yes. Containers," Seattle says. "Forms, things with mass. You think of containers as solid things with names, specific behaviors and even personalities. The soul uses imagination as its reality projector. The soul spirit, through the mechanism of the imagination encases itself in a personality through which it experiences being. In this realm once spirit takes on a shape, it forgets its eternal essential nature and takes on the nature of the form in which it has encased itself. From then on, it isn't possible for it to imagine itself in any other form, in any other situation. What is, is, and to it nothing else is possible. Spirit through imagination constructs personality and personality acts. Personality has no big connection to everything and no long-term memory. It's blind and ignorant to possibilities other than the one it is doing. Spirit doesn't exist to most humans who are encased in their human personalities. In your world once a bit of spirit is encased in personality, it is only personality which can be perceived by its awareness, and personality only perceives other personalities. Personalities act out their essential dramas no matter what those dramas are: a gold molecule, a powerful corporate CEO, a sick giraffe, a dying planet, a dreaming teenager. It does this through the creative mechanism of imagination, but its imagination is restricted by the nature of its particular personality in its particular moment, in its particular place. A penguin on the southern polar icecap doesn't become an elephant in the steaming jungles on the equator. An elephant doesn't morph into a planet. A stockbroker on Madison Avenue in 2016 doesn't become a pirate in the Caribbean in 1666. Divine intent creates personality through its spirit. Spirit creates through imagination. Personality defines and limits imagination but acts and has unique experiences. A pig only imagines what pigs are meant to imagine. A cow only imagines what cows are designed to think. A computer only does what its programmer designs it to do. That which gives birth to a personality determines its shape and form and behavior. You can't see spirit because you have been equipped to see the result and not the cause. This all holds until the container is broken or opened."

"So, what you're saying is there is a way for me to see spirit!" Bunzy interrupts Seattle excitedly. "All I have to do is change into a personality which sees spirit?"

"Absolutely!" Seattle agrees, echoing Bunzy's excitement. He continues, "It's not an easy thing to change personalities, but it can be done. Imagination is the key. The Dream Key is the spirit of your human imagination. What that personality you're in now has lost is its imagination. With the loss of your imagination, you have forgotten that you are an angelic spirit and you have become trapped in the this realm, repeating the same drama over and over for the benefit of your captors. The Teacher stole your imagination outside the Good News tent with the finger snapping incident, then he continued to maintain your ignorance with the noise in your head, your fears and confusion. You have to realize that you're not in the world you think you're in. The world you are sitting in at this moment is entirely different than the one which you believe you are sitting in."

"Alright!" Bunzy shouts. He jumps up and starts pacing around.

He states, "I'm getting close to knowing what I've been trying to discover."

Then pausing mid-step, Bunzy turns slowly to Seattle and says, "but I don't understand what you're saying, and I can't accept what I do think I understand. You're going to have to push harder and explain more or else just show me something. And if the Teacher tunes in to what I'm up to, it's all over for me. How about doing a quick good old-fashioned miracle to alter my thinking before I'm caught?"

Seattle stands up, takes a couple of quick long steps and is suddenly behind Bunzy. He grabs Bunzy underneath his arms below the armpits, leaps into the air, shooting upwards for thousands of feet, then drops Bunzy.

In the darkness Bunzy can't see anything. He's plunging downwards, picking up speed. His body is filled with tension as he braces himself for the life ending impact. He can't even see the ground rushing towards him. He doesn't know when he's going to smash into it and die. His mind is numb, paralyzed with terror. From somewhere outside of his body, he's watching, preparing for the last moment of his life. As he falls, he gives up and lets go. He's resigned, blank, plunging downward.

When he hits, it isn't the life ending thud on rock he's been anticipating. He plunges feet first, like a spear, into an ice-cold river. When he reaches the surface and takes a gulp of air, in complete darkness, he's swept over a small waterfall maybe ten or twelve feet tall. The current is very swift and powerful, rolling him over and over and banging him against boulders. His clothes are soaked and pulling him down. Before he can angle his way over to shore and escape this big, powerful river, he's swept over another waterfall. This one is much bigger, and he's pushed way down, further than he thinks he can make it back to the surface in his wet clothes. The current just keeps pushing him down, down, down. Then, to his surprise, he comes out of the bottom of the river and continues to float downwards through air in an inky blackness.

A light appears ahead. It's a tropical paradise. Bunzy lands softly on a white sandy beach on a warm pleasant day near a small, clear-water river which is bubbling over pebbles into a lovely sea. Small waves break on the shore in front of him. A dense jungle lies behind him. Trees thrust upwards full of fruit, chattering monkeys, and yellow and green parrots with black eyes, like little bandits. Neon blue butterflies bigger than his hand flutter about here and there. Shimmering iridescent hummingbirds from as big as pigeons to as small as a bumblebees streak about amongst bright yellow, red, and white blossoms.

Seattle lands beside Bunzy. He asks, "So Bunzy, where do you think we are?"

"Not in Utah," Bunzy ventures, panting and bending over, leaning on his knees with both hands.

Seattle laughs. "No. You're not in Utah." Then he points at Bunzy and says, "Notice that you are wearing a white robe and that you have wings."

After standing up and looking at himself, Bunzy asks, "Am I dead?"

"No." Seattle chuckles. "You're not dead. I'm just showing you that things aren't the way you think they are. To see spirit, you need to widen your senses. Don't expect spirit to shrink itself for your sake. I dropped you into an energy sink. This is the first time you've been aware in Paradise in a long, long time, but we can go back to Earth if you want to."

"No. I'm alright with this," Bunzy quickly says. Then he continues, "So you're saying I've got like a split personality. The core essence of my being is in this place and I'm projecting a personality into a psychodrama on Earth."

"Something like that," Seattle answers.

"If that's true, why don't I just become lucid and change the concepts under which I'm struggling? It would be really nice not to feel that horrible pain when the Teacher snapped my fingers."

"Sorry, it's not that simple."

"What do you propose I should do to solve my Earth problems?"

"Simple, while sleeping, watch. When you are watching, you are aware of where you are and at the same time, you are aware of what you are watching. You have a consciousness of two places at the same time. You have to master that ability to be aware of yourself in more than one scenario at the same time. The biggest reason to watch though is to open your personality to bigger possibilities so that you can recover your imagination."

"Why don't I just stay here? I'm already an angel here."

"It's your choice."

"No. I can't stay here. I can't leave all of my friends and family over there suffering. Where do we go from here?"

"Make a wish."

"Okay. I wish that I had a nice house to live in."

Bunzy's wish surprises Seattle. Turning slowly all of the way around and pointing with both hands as he turns, he says, "You have a nice house here to live in. You are a creative vector in an energy sink of creation or an angel in the Garden of Paradise, however you want to view all of this. Everywhere here it is always the temperature that you want it to be. There are no poisonous snakes, blood sucking insects, flesh eating predators, or vicious thugs. All of this creation is your perfect home; safe, comfortable and stocked with everything that you need or desire."

Bunzy looks at it all for a while, then says, "It's nice. Why am I not happy?"

"Because you are still thinking as a human. You don't need only to find spirit and the Dream Key and get back to Eden. As a human, you need to be forgiven and find salvation and if you can't find those, then you need to find enough dope to forget your problems for as long as you can."

He laughs musically at his own cleverness. Bunzy smiles too. Bunzy realizes *Seattle has a sense of humor.*

"So where do we go from here?" Bunzy asks.

"You need to realize your capabilities. Imagine a possibility and then make a wish."

But while you're pondering what to wish, Seattle says, "It looks as if we have company."

Seattle is looking up the beach to their right. Bunzy follows his gaze. The most beautiful man whom Bunzy has ever seen is walking towards them. It's the Teacher. Bunzy recognizes him immediately, but the Teacher has been transformed again. He is pretty, like a tall dark woman, but he is built powerfully and exudes the dangerous macho presence of a world champion martial arts fighter. As the Teacher gets closer, Bunzy gets nervous, so anxious he becomes nauseous.

For Bunzy, standing in front of the transformed Teacher is like standing before a ten-foot-long black cobra that is standing up with its hood out swaying slowly back and forth looking Bunzy in the eyes with its own beady black ones, ready to strike him dead. Bunzy sweats and pants. He wants to run and hide, but there's no place to escape to.

Seattle introduces them, "Bunzy I know you think of this being as your Teacher, but this is Mephistopheles."

Seattle then asks, "Mephistopheles what do you want?"

"I want to congratulate Bunzy on his great achievement." Mephistopheles voice is sweet, convincing. When he speaks it sounds as if he is singing a lovely sincere melody. "I want to offer him all of the joys of becoming an Archon lord."

Mephistopheles points off into the distance across a bay to their left. Over there, a mellow light is striking golden domes in a beautiful city.

Speaking formally, with hope and generosity seeming to flow from his heart to Bunzy, Mephistopheles offers, "Bunzy, if you will serve me, a thousand cities and lands like that one shall all be yours. You will rule over everyone and everything in them. Your desires will have to be fulfilled immediately. Your every wish will be a command to be obeyed without question. All of the treasures of Earth will be yours to enjoy. No one and nothing will be able to resist you. Everything shall be yours to consume, use, or abuse. What do you say?"

Lust, the will to dominate, ruin and kill others, and to possess everything while others go without and suffer tempt Bunzy. He thinks about Mephistopheles offer for a moment, then answers, "I accepted your offer once before and it led to terrible grief. I'm going to pass this time but thank you."

Before Mephistopheles moves, Bunzy shouts, "I wish to be in the presence of the Divine All!"

Mephistopheles screams, "No!" and begins to turn to flee, but it is too late. He is instantly changed.

The Divine presence fills their awareness. Everything begins to glow with a pure white light. Bunzy begins to weep uncontrollably with joy and happiness. He's so glad to be home where he's safe and all of his needs and desires are instantly fulfilled. He's made it back. More love than he even remembered was possible envelopes him. He is consumed by admiration for something so great and so wonderful that he's dissolving in ecstasy. Everything is so beautiful and pleasurable he fears he is going to die from too much joy.

A warm, pleasant white light fills their world.

A voice booms, "Dearly beloved child, we are overjoyed that you have returned. You have done wonderfully. You are a great success. Everything that you did that you wish that you hadn't done, and everything that you didn't do that you wish that you had done, and everything that you did but that failed miserably, is forgiven, and all of the things that have been done to you by others that were terribly painful are forgotten. You are reborn a completely new creation, a divine creation, an arc of delight, a path to forgiveness and salvation, a bringer of the dawn of freedom, the key that releases the shackles of bondage. All things are possible because what you look upon with your imagination shall be. So, take care to be wonderful and your life will be beautiful and the lives of everyone and everything around you will be a pure delight. We will do as you wish because you are our dearly beloved child, and our hearts are filled with joy because you have returned."

Big fluffy, billowing white clouds form in the sky and in those clouds millions of angels are singing a hallelujah chorus. Everyone whom Bunzy has ever known come to him. With tears of joy in their eyes, they hug him and thank him sincerely and joyfully for saving them. Millions of creatures surround them witnessing and enjoying this moment of their release from bondage. All of these beings sing and dance celebrating this moment of hope and happiness.

Mephistopheles who is standing beside Bunzy, weeping, says, "I must tell everyone. We have to change. Our sins are unbearable. I didn't understand, but now I see."

He wanders away dazed as if he has been blinded by the light that shines all around them.

Seattle asks Bunzy, "What do you want to do now?"

Bunzy hesitates, then tells him, "Go back to my friends and family and all of that world that is still lost and show them the way."

"Prepare to go then," Seattle says.

Bunzy raises his hands high over his head and turns all around saying, "Thank you Divine All. I accept these awesome blessings you have bestowed on me and others. From these blessings I gather all of the blessings which I can and with these blessings, I bless all." Facing the east, Bunzy bows and says, "Bless you", turning to the south, "bless you", to the west, "bless you", to the north, "bless you", facing upwards, "bless you", and bending down and touching the sand with his right hand "bless you". Standing again and holding his hands in front of him as if he's holding an offering, he says, "And I return any blessings that are left that Divine All, you might bless others as you have blessed me. Thank you Divine All. May we never be separated."

Then Bunzy turns to Seattle and says, "I'm ready."

Seattle warns Bunzy, "When you return to Earth, you won't remember what has happened here in Paradise, but we will remind you and open your Earthly awareness wider until the Divine All's blessings are realized even there."

Again, Seattle steps behind Bunzy, grabs him under his arms and leaps into the sky.

Again, they are surrounded by darkness, but this time Seattle doesn't drop Bunzy. Pinpoints of light flash past them in rays as if they are in a spaceship flying through the universe at a million miles a second. Then they are sitting by the fire in Utah looking across it at Running Bear. The Sun is rising.

For just a few moments Bunzy remembers the presence of the Divine All and Paradise, then it all slips away as if he's waking up and forgetting a dream. Bunzy is dazed and confused. He feels as if he accidentally went to sleep and missed something important.

Bunzy asks Running Bear, "What happened? Did I fall asleep?"

"No. You went away for a while. Seattle showed you an energy sink, but he showed it to you in an altered state of awareness and you don't have conscious access to that memory yet."

Seattle adds, "Remember, if you watch while you are sleeping, as you wander through the dream worlds, you will regain your memory and when you regain your memory you will find the spirit of imagination which is the key. That is why it is called the Dream Key. We call it the Holy Spirit. Everything will all come back to you."

A tall handsome man who is built like a fighter and carries himself with power and confidence, enters their campsite.

Seattle asks, "Mephistopheles, why are you here? What do you want?"

"I have come to thank Bunzy, ask for forgiveness, and to honor him."

He walks over to Bunzy. Bunzy stands. Mephistopheles kneels and places his forehead on Bunzy's sandaled foot.

Mephistopheles says, "Thank you Bunzy. Please forgive me. I didn't know."

Bunzy suddenly realizes this is the Teacher whom Seattle has called Mephistopheles who is kneeling before him and asking for his forgiveness.

Bunzy asks, "Teacher, why should I believe that you have changed?"

"Because, you have shown me the light and the way. I am sorry that I used and abused you and I regret what I have done to you and all of the others. I have freed you and all of those other people who were in my herd."

"What will you eat? Won't you starve to death?" Bunzy asks.

180

"Will you starve if you don't eat chickens and cows," Mephistopheles says. "I didn't understand what food is until I came into the Divine presence and realized who we are and what actually sustains our being. I know that you cannot consciously enter into the Divine presence yet and this doesn't make sense to you, but I assure you it will and I am healthier than I have ever been. Please forgive me for what I have done. I will go to every Archon that will receive me, share the Divine presence with them and save them just as you have saved me and they will set their slaves free too. Together we will create a beautiful world."

"That sounds like a really good idea," Bunzy agrees. "Mephistopheles. Rise," he commands.

Mephistopheles rises to his knees, kneeling before Bunzy with his head bowed and his hands in prayer position.

Bunzy places his hands on the Teacher's head and says, "Brother, you are forgiven." Then pointing with his right hand into the wilderness, Bunzy proclaims, "Go forth and do as you have said and may all of your efforts be blessed through the loving presence of the Divine All."

Mephistopheles gets to his feet, stands staring at Bunzy for a moment with tears of joy in his eyes. Then he reaches inside his coat and removes several pages of paper and hands them to Bunzy, saying, "This is information on all of those people whom I have freed. It will be useful to you."

After Bunzy accepts the papers, Mephistopheles turns and walks away into the hills.

Bunzy looks at Seattle and asks, "What was that about?"

Seattle answers, "In Paradise you brought him into the presence of the Divine All and he was saved. You don't remember because you are back in your Earthly body, but I can tell that you have gained some new understanding by what you just said and did. Your awareness is growing. As your consciousness opens to greater possibilities, you will regain your memories of Paradise, the Divine All, and your true nature. Remember to watch while sleeping and recovering your imagination is the key."

Bunzy's mind has a clarity that wasn't there before. He's not besieged by ideas that force him first this way and then that way. As he gazes out at the morning world, he realizes that something has changed. Things are not as he thought they were at all.

He misses Isabel.

CHAPTER 12
THE WORLD WITHOUT MONEY

"I believe that banking institutions are more dangerous to our liberties than standing armies. If the American people ever allow private banks to control the issue of their currency, first by inflation, then by deflation, the banks and corporations that will grow up around them (the banks) will deprive the people of all property until their children wake-up homeless ..."

Thomas Jefferson 1743-1826

Bunzy asks, "So Bear, Seattle, how do I regain my memory?"

He tells them, "You guys have convinced me that things are radically different than I believe they are and I have this feeling that I know far more than I can consciously bring to my attention. It's really frustrating. You are like ambassadors from a far away, mysterious, forgotten realm and I am like Christopher Columbus before he managed to get those boats and set sail. So where do we go from here?"

Seattle says, "Interesting analogy you chose to frame your problem with. However, I'll tell you what you should do. Powerfully imagine everything that is possible and good, then watch."

Running Bear asks, "Are you a gambling man Bunzy?"

"Only in love," Bunzy remarks, then laughs.

Running Bear laughs along with Bunzy, then notes "The queen of hearts is always worth a risk. But seriously, what if you played a game and won and you could have it all? Would you play?"

"And what if I lose?" Bunzy asks.

"Why dwell on the negative? Remember the Law of Attraction. Didn't Seattle just advise you to imagine everything that is possible and good?"

"Alright, I'll play," Bunzy says. "What's this game called we're going to play anyway?"

"The world without money," Bear tells Bunzy.

"The world without money," Bunzy hollers. "I don't understand. What's your angle, Running Bear?"

"Happiness on Earth," Bear says.

Bunzy blurts out, "I thought that happiness was when you have a bunch of money, not when there isn't any."

Bear explains, "Money is a major Archon tool of control. They've taken thousands of years perfecting a method to enslave people that isn't visible to most. Bunzy, where do you think that money comes from?"

"I don't really know," Bunzy says. "I assume that the government prints it."

Bear tells him, "Get out a dollar bill and read what it says across the top above the President's picture"

Leaning back and reaching into his left front pants pocket, Bunzy takes out his wallet, opens it, pulls out a dollar bill, unfolds it, and reads, "The United States of America."

"Above that," Bear spits out.

Bunzy reads, "Federal Reserve Note."

"And who or what is the Federal Reserve?" Bear inquires of Bunzy.

"I don't know," Bunzy answers. "I have always assumed it was a part of the Treasury Department of the government."

Bear explains, "The Federal Reserve isn't part of the government and there is no reserve backing that piece of paper you're holding with anything of any value other than your trust and the trust of others like you. The Federal Reserve is a private corporation which is owned and controlled by a few families."

"The government doesn't print our money?" Bunzy mutters.

Running Bear walks around behind Bunzy. He points at the word note.

He says, "That green piece of paper in your hand is a note, a debt. It is a piece of paper representing a debt owed by the people of this country to a privately owned money printing monopoly."

The sky far to the south of Bunzy, Bear and Seattle begins to rumble with a frightening roar.

After they pause and listen for a while, Bunzy says, "Bear, what you just said doesn't sound right. That would make money just part of a counterfeiting scheme."

Running Bear says, "Yup. That's right Bunzy. That bill you're holding is just part of a sophisticated legalized counterfeiting scheme.

"That doesn't seem good," Bunzy mumbles.

"It's not. Listen up," Bear tells him. "The situation gets worse. Because money is the way that people have been taught to communicate with each other and their environment, whoever controls the money, controls the world. The owners of the central bank create and control all of the money, so they own and control the corporations, the President and all of the legislators, the judicial system, the police and the military. They write the laws, enforce them, and tell the people what to think through controlling television, books, magazines, newspapers, the internet, pulpits, social media and schools. The money printers control everything; the jobs, the educational system, the information, the energy, the transportation, the entertainment, the natural resources, everything; people's homes, food and health services, everything; down to personal relationships.

"You mean the President isn't the head of our government?" Bunzy remarks in surprise.

Bear grabs both of Bunzy's arm, looks him squarely in both eyes and shouts, "Think about it." Then more quietly informs him, "If your lives are controlled by money, then whoever creates and controls the money, owns whatever they want to own, including the Presidency. Money and debt are currently the main control mechanisms of domination, and the Archons created and control both of them. People's lives are based on the acquisition and the spending of money. So, people have become easily controlled. There are a lot of things other than money that people could center their lives around, but they don't."

The menacing roar gets closer. It sounds like hunting helicopters flying back and forth. It's worrisome. One part of Bunzy listens to the ground shaking grumble. The other part listens to Running Bear.

Running Bear continues, "Modern people cannot even imagine a world without money. The Archons rule this world through money, and we allow this horrible situation to exist. We have allowed it for thousands of years and it has only gotten worse and worse. We can change the balance of power anytime that we choose though. The Archons are more informed and intelligent than humans and they possess very powerful weapons, but there are billions of people and only a few Archons."

Now Bunzy, Seattle and Bear can see the helicopters. There are three Black Hawk gunships. They slowly come closer and closer.

Bunzy asks, "Isn't money necessary for there to be a healthy, functioning community of people?"

"No. A market economy based on the use of money, and usury is just one way for people to organize their lives and to use resources and to distribute products and services. Money creates a competitive, dangerous, unstable world. It doesn't have to be that way though."

Seattle, who has been watching the helicopters, says, "They're flying a grid search pattern. They're looking for something."

"They're probably looking for me," Bunzy speculates.

"Why would the police be looking for you?" Seattle asks.

"The reason I'm out here in the wilderness is because I'm hiding," Bunzy informs them.

"Why? What's your crime?" Seattle asks.

"I haven't done anything bad, but I have been having the wrong kind of thoughts. Before I came here, I was at a prison camp where a couple of guys got killed. That camp is down there in the direction where those choppers came from. The camp guards probably had cameras on the walls that took my picture, and they turned me into the police. If the authorities catch me, they will want to cure me. That will be horrible. It will be the end of me."

They silently look at each other for a few moments, then all three get up, put the fire out, erase the evidence of their camp, cool the fire area with their water bottles, hide their gear in the rocks, then sit back down and watch the distant helicopters.

Running Bear and Seattle keep explaining why relating to life through money is evil. Finally Running Bear says to Bunzy, "You need you to think about what we're telling you and then go out into the world and tell others."

"I'll speak against the Federal Reserve, the fractional reserve central banking system, and the evils of money and usury, but people need an alternative. It's no good to just be against something."

Running Bear says, "The situation would improve if governments created the money and then put it into circulation, but people have to realize that money is the wrong way to communicate with each other. Bunzy, it would help if you were to learn how to use a tortoise tunnel."

"A tortoise tunnel? What's a tortoise tunnel?" Bunzy wants to know.

Seattle explains, "A tortoise tunnel is a vortex between the here and now and the then and there. In infinity and eternity everything is happening now. Here we are currently experiencing one way of being. If you wish to experience another way of being, then journey to where that other way is being experienced and spend some time there until you understand that other way of doing things. Then you can return through another tortoise tunnel to the place from which you began."

Bunzy looks like a stunned frog.

"How do I do that?" He asks.

Seattle explains, "There are many ways to find a tortoise tunnel. They exist in certain places, just as subway entrances exist at certain spots. Here, right now, the easiest way for you to find a tunnel would be by watching for one while you go to sleep. So begin by clarifying and focusing your intentions. Intend to go to a world without money. Then crawl under those rocks over there." He nods towards a nearby bluff. "When you're going to sleep, look around for a round black whirling vortex that looks like the mouth of a cave. That will be a tortoise tunnel. When you see it, plunge in."

"How will I communicate with the people who I intend to visit?" Bunzy asks Seattle.

"The Divine helps with information exchanges in hyperspace."

"What does that mean?"

"It means, don't worry about it. You won't even notice. Don't try to figure this out. Your task is to have the courage to plunge in."

It's becoming obvious that the helicopters are going to fly right over them and discover Bunzy.

Seattle says, "We are going to have to hide while they search this area and that could take a while. You better head for that rock ledge now. We'll disappear elsewhere. When you wake up, they'll be gone, and we'll have something to eat. As you drift away into sleep remember to intend to enter a world without money."

Bunzy retrieves his mat, sleeping bag and pillow, crawls back into the cool shade in the hole under the rocks, makes a bed, and lies down, covering up and pulling his hat down over his eyes. He's exhausted and quickly falls asleep.

At first what he's looking at all seems dark. Then he realizes it isn't really dark like it is when one is far down in the ground in a cave or when you're standing outside on a moonless cloudy night. It's a bright kind of darkness and if he looks closely, he can discern shapes and movement. Off to his left towards the top of his vision, there is a black hole. It looks like a cave, except that it is round.

As Bunzy approaches that spot, the walls of the round hole seem to be moving in a circular fashion in a manner similar to the way a tornado spins. Also, the whole thing is slowly moving around in the landscape. The walls of the tunnel are easily perceivable as walls, but they appear transparent like thick clear glass. Bunzy can look right into them, just as if he were in a spaceship looking through a meteorite proof window out into space. The space which is the wall of the tunnel is dark black with tiny bright lights here and there in it. The tunnel itself doesn't appear to be that big. It just seems like a cave that is whirling and slowly twisting and turning as it drifts about the landscape.

When Bunzy steps across the threshold of the cave, he begins to float downwards. It's not a horizontal walking forward experience. It's a falling and falling sensation, and this isn't a tunnel. It's the vastness of forever. Time becomes irrelevant.

He floats out of the tunnel standing on a road looking into a farmer's field on a lovely sunny day. The farmer kneels in the field beside the road on which Bunzy has landed. The farmer picks strawberries into flats and loads them onto a flatbed vehicle which is parked beside him in the field.

When he sees Bunzy watching him, he stands, walks over, extends his right hand, smiles, and introduces himself, "Hello. My name is John Mercola. I'm pleased to meet you. May I be of some benefit to you?"

Shaking the offered hand, Bunzy responds, "Hello John. I am pleased to meet somebody as kind and helpful as you. My name is Bunzy Ringer. What is this place called?" Bunzy asks John as Bunzy gestures around them at the fields, the green park beyond the fields, the city in front of them and the wilderness behind them.

"This is Shangri-La. We are an Ubuntu Community. I will take you to the Council of Elders. They will know best how to explain things to you. Will you please help me finish picking strawberries and loading them on the hover-up?"

"Of course I will. Shangri-La. I've heard of this place, and I've always wanted to come here. I think that many people who live where I'm from want to live in a place like this, but we believe Shangri-La is a mythical paradise which isn't real. It would be my pleasure to help you and to go meet your Elders. I sincerely mean that. What you are doing looks like fun, and this appears to be a beautiful and wonderful place," Bunzy tells John.

"It is," John agrees, "and people will really appreciate these luscious, juicy, sweet red berries we are going to take to them. When the hover-up is loaded, we will glide to our Community Center where I will introduce you to some Elders."

"So, John, how much are these berries worth?" Bunzy asks.

"They are beautiful, delicious, and nutritious. They will make people very happy. I look forward to providing people with this wonderful experience," John answers.

"No, you don't understand," Bunzy tells him. "I mean, how much money will you get for them?"

"Money? I don't understand," John says.

"How much will you receive in exchange for this truck load of fruit?" Bunzy wants to know.

"I will receive all of the joy and happiness that I can stand," John tells him.

"Yes, I know that," Bunzy says. His irritation starting to show. "But won't you get something material in return for them?"

"Like what? What is more valuable than being loved and appreciated?"

"A place to live, food to eat, fuel for your hover-up, medical care," Bunzy answers.

John says, "The community already supplies me with everything I need and want including the hover-up and it doesn't need any fuel anyway. It's an anti-gravity/solar transport."

"You mean that you don't exchange things for other things with other people as a way to earn your living?" Bunzy asks.

"What a crazy idea!" John declares. "Do you think that I care so little for my friends and neighbors that I would insult them by trying to take advantage of them?" He inquires.

Bunzy is baffled. He asks, "How do you get your shelter, food, health care, entertainment, and transportation?"

John answers, "It's all provided for me through our community. Since birth I have never needed anything that wasn't given to me."

Bunzy steps back and asks, "Then why are you out here in this hot field growing, picking, and hauling strawberries to town."

"I like to grow things," John announces. "I like to hang around out in the Sun in nature and I like to do things that other people appreciate. I'm having fun. Aren't you enjoying yourself Bunzy?"

"Yes, I am John. That just isn't how or why things are done where I come from."

"You must come from a place where people are very frightened, worried, unhappy, and mean," John notes.

"Well, I never thought of it that way, but compared to this, I suppose I do come from a harsh world. I can't see how this all works though," Bunzy says.

"Ask the elders, they can explain. I'm just an ordinary guy who is having a wonderful time on a beautiful day," John tells him.

Eating some of the berries, Bunzy notices they are a lot sweeter and juicier than the strawberries are in the supermarkets back home.

As they talk, they work and soon the truck is loaded. They get in. John pushes a button. The hover-up lifts a couple of feet into the air and glides quietly forward to town.

The city is built on a circular plan. They are in a lush circular band of farmland which encircles the outside of the town. Going away from them is a wilderness. As they go towards the city, they pass through a park that is like one of the American national parks, but this one is small. Still, it is full of wild birds and animals, clear streams and lakes, and lush forests and meadows. Next, they go through an industrial production/distribution band which is clean and attractive and obviously very busy. There are no square corners on any of the buildings. Every structure is curvilinear and flowing like everything else in nature. Next, they pass through another park, but this one is groomed with areas for recreation. Each of these strips completely encircles the town. Inside the city park is the residential area. The homes are in roomy complexes full of all kinds of recreational opportunities such as swimming pools and hot tubs, exercise rooms, bicycle paths, and children's play areas. Again, all of the buildings are curvilinear and flow naturally together. The inside of the city has the community's educational institutions, libraries, administrative buildings, cultural and religious centers and in the very center of the community is a large open area. The buildings aren't actually separate individual structures. They are all interconnected, making one great circular complex which surrounds an open-air plaza.

John parks the hover-up in front of a little park beside the Shangri-La Council Building, lowers it to the ground, gets out, comes around to Bunzy's side and invites him to, "Come on, we'll find an Elder to help you."

The Council Building isn't intimidating. It's like a big friendly cross between a nomad's yurt and a Buddhist temple. People come and go. They are dressed casually in their everyday clothes. They smile, greet each other and stop to visit. John talks to several people and introduces Bunzy to them. Everybody hopes he is enjoying his visit. They want him to stay with them for a while and benefit them and they promise to make his stay enjoyable. He is having a super-excellent time.

They are attractive, friendly, energetic people and this really is a beautiful, safe, supportive situation. Bunzy is beginning to wonder why every place isn't like this. He wonders, *what is it that is different about being here?*

John and Bunzy enter a small cozy plaza area. Sitting on benches in the shade under some massive old willow trees are seven older men and women. They are surrounded by younger people who are asking them all sorts of questions about planting crops, the city sewer and water systems, how to make their children and lovers happy, how to paint a picture and how to fix a hover craft.

When there is a break in the conversation, John steps forward and introduces Bunzy, "Beloved Elders, this is Bunzy Ringer, who is a stranger in our land. He has come to experience our culture and to learn our ways."

An older woman rises, comes over and embraces Bunzy, then says, "Welcome Bunzy. My name is Betty. We are thrilled to have you amongst us. While you stay with us all of your needs will be met by our community. In return we ask you to spend some time each day a few days each week doing something you enjoy that will benefit our community. You could garden with John, or if you like science you could work with Larry over there, helping to provide the community with fresh clean water, or you could help build something. It's up to you. Look around Shangri-La and decide how you would like to help. Once a week we ask everyone to spend a few hours doing something to improve our culture: take the children for a hike in the woods, paint a picture, sing a song. I would suggest that you might enjoy giving some talks about your world. The rest of the time you are free to explore and enjoy yourself. You are free to do whatever you want as long as you wouldn't mind having what you're doing done to you. That rule applies not just to people but to everything. Be kind to all and that includes the whole world."

"Betty, do you know what money is?" Bunzy asks.

"Yes, I do."

"Am I correct in saying that there is no money in this world?"

Betty explains, "We do not think so little of each other that we would separate ourselves from others and try to gain something at their expense. If we share equitably and produce durable things of high quality, then there is more than enough of everything for everyone without causing any harm. There is no need for something as inefficient and destructive of happiness and planetary survival as a market. Money is a very poor way to organize relationships in a society."

Bunzy says, "I am absolutely astounded by your culture. I have never even considered that a technologically developed society is possible without money, interest, debt, banks, and markets."

Betty continues, "Our society is based on the desire to be of benefit to all, rather than a desire to accumulate private possessions and personal power. I don't think that I need to explain to you what kind of a world that competition when combined with a desire for money creates."

"No, you don't," Bunzy proclaims. "I just didn't think that there was any other way to do things. I thought that if there wasn't competition and money then things wouldn't get done."

"Well then, you should enjoy your stay here," Betty asserts. "Walk around, observe, learn, and most important, have fun."

"Thank you. I think I will just stick with John. I like gardening," Bunzy tells her.

"Good, it's settled then," Betty declares. "You are officially a member of our world, and you shall enjoy all of the benefits that we enjoy. You are a good man and we are honored to be in your presence. Live long, help others, and be happy."

She smiles, touches Bunzy's right arm in a friendly way that makes him feel wonderful, turns, walks back to her seat and sits down. The other Elders nod their approval at her and smile. John and Bunzy turn and leave.

John says, "We need to take the strawberries to the Distribution Center. Then we'll go get you a cooperative, food and clothes, and I'll explain how our transportation system works."

The Distribution Center looks very much like a supermarket except that there are no prices, and no money is needed to take anything someone wants home. There are no cashiers. There are people who are stocking the shelves and bins and helping other people to gather and carry what they need. There is no plastic or packaging. Everything is in bulk. Everyone has fiber bags and glass containers which they use to carry everything that they are getting. Nobody is taking very much though, because whenever they need more, they can come here and get it. The people who are stocking the shelves and loading and carrying the goods are doing what they are doing as a labor of love. They are serving their neighbors in this manner because this is how they choose to help them, so the center's staff is super friendly.

The home that Bunzy is given is very nice. He asks John, "Why do you call this a cooperative and not an apartment?"

"An apart-ment?" John asks. "Why would you want to live in a structure that separates you from others? I think that you will find yourself happier if you do things with your neighbors such as eating and caring for this land and structure and each other. Would you like to come over to my family's cooperative and eat dinner with us?"

"I would like that very much," Bunzy says.

John's cooperative is much like Bunzy's except bigger and full of warmth, love, and beautiful decorations. John introduces Bunzy to his lovely wife, Sally, and their two attractive young children, Mike and Denise.

As John and Sally prepare their food, Bunzy asks Mike, "Do you have a sports team that you want to see win the championship this year?"

Mike looks confused.

John turns away from the cutting board beside the sink where he has been chopping vegetables for a stir fry and explains, "That couldn't happen in Shangri-La. Our teams don't compete with each other to win something by defeating others. Instead, our teams work together but on different phases of projects helping each other to successfully complete whatever they are doing, such as building a cooperative for someone who needs one, or cleaning and painting an older person's home, or arranging a city wide celebration, or cataloging the amount of natural resources available to support our community. If one group does a particularly fabulous job, we all benefit, and the project just ends up making everyone's lives even better. We all win, so we all celebrate the great job they did. In an Ubuntu Community there are no losers, just one big happy, prosperous family of winners."

"Gosh, I can't wait to join a team and start doing something wonderful for the community," Bunzy says.

Sally adds, "We are in the process of creating a Summer Solstice Celebration. Mike and Denise are helping to paint a particularly awesome background scene behind the bandstand. It will be magical."

Mike and Denise smile at their mother and then go over and hug her. John looks at them and then at Bunzy and laughs.

Bunzy stands there with his arms hanging by his sides, his mouth open, staring at Sally and the children. He is having a hard time understanding a world with no competition: no competing sports teams, no warring nations, no aggressive corporations trying to destroy each, no religious organizations condemning others to eternal misery.

Bunzy says, "I thought competition was good."

"Competition is destructive. Cooperation is the way to create abundance and happiness," John tells him.

Bunzy is dazed. This is a world without money which is based on cooperation, kindness and the understanding everything is connected and the belief harmony is the best way to live. This is his dream come true. He eats in a mental fog.

After dinner and the dishes are cleaned, John announces, "Now it is time for some fun. In the evening, we gather in the Sacred Space and enjoy ourselves."

They all walk together over to the Sacred Space.

The Sacred Space is a building with a big open circular area with a beautiful hardwood floor. They begin quietly with some gentle yoga exercises. Then a group of drummers start drumming and people chant, then sing and dance. A group does a funny dramatization of some spirits at a harvest celebration. After an hour or two of this, the lights are turned down. Children and many adults go home. The people who remain sit quietly and do silent mantra and meditation for a half hour. At the end of their time meditating, an elder leads them in a prayer of gratitude. They hug, shake hands, express their pleasure at being together and leave.

Bunzy wanders home floating in a cloud of happiness.

He imagines how much Isabel and their family would enjoy being here.

In the morning before daylight, John comes over to Bunzy's cooperative and together they walk to the Sacred Space. They join others who are doing gentle yoga poses and energizing their breathing. Next the group does chi gong exercises which connect them to Divine energy. Then they sit and meditate until the Sun is about to rise. As the Sun rises, they gather in the open area in the center of the community and participate in a sunrise ceremony. The ritual is a prayer of gratitude which involves facing the Sun and recognizing its power and importance. They do poses with the intention of absorbing some of that power, grace, and love that is being poured down on them from the Sun. Filled with joy, some people start dancing. All of them sing and chant.

When the Sun is up, John and Bunzy walk to the hover-up where some other men and women are waiting and together they all glide out towards the gardens. On the trip out Bunzy gets to know the others on the back of the hover-up where he sits. He likes them all.

As they sit on the flat bed of the hover-up floating along. Bunzy says to Paul who looks like he is about thirty-five, "This gardening seems to suit you. You sure look young, healthy, and strong."

Paul smiles and gives Bunzy a powerful one-armed bear hug and agrees, "I am young, strong, and healthy. I'm only a hundred and fifty-three and I am enjoying life immensely."

Shocked, Bunzy says, "Where I'm from people die of old age at half that many years."

"I guess that they should relax, take better care of themselves, and express the Divine presence with more gusto. What do you think Bunzy?"

"I don't know. I think that I'm missing something very important."

"That is probably true, but you still can relax and have a good time."

"Don't you people ever worry about things like crime?"

Isabel, a voluptuous tall thin young woman in her twenties, with long black hair and chocolate skin, asks, "Crimes?" Her right eye is squinted and her pretty mouth scrunched up in contemplation of what I've just said. She is wearing a soft faded maroon shirt with rolled up sleeves and faded rolled up blue jeans and sandals. Her toenails are painted bright red. She is very attractive.

Looking at her, after catching my breath, I suddenly realize, "I haven't seen any police. Where are the police?"

"Police?" The people on the flatbed ask looking at each other.

Bunzy is starting to feel as if there is an annoying echo on the back of his hover-up. "Yes, police," he says. "You know, people with guns and clubs who enforce the laws and stop other people from committing crimes such as theft, assault, and murder."

Isabel asks, "Why would someone steal or commit violence against another person or anything in the environment?" She explains, "If we don't have something and want it, we just go to the Elders and ask for it to be provided for us and it is then given to us, unless it doesn't exist. If there isn't any of what we want, then that provides a wonderful opportunity for a group of us to do something special by creating something new."

Looking at Isabel, Bunzy asks, "What if I absolutely crave a particular woman whom another man wants and she wants him rather than me, but another woman wants me whom I don't want? I'm crazy with unfulfilled desires and disgust."

Everybody laughs as if Bunzy is an incredibly clever comedian and he can't possibly be serious, but what they don't know is, he is serious.

Isabel observes, "You do like to suffer. Don't you Bunzy? You must be a great poet." Everybody laughs again. She advises "Well Bunzy, you really should remember to be kind to others."

Everybody nods in agreement.

Paul explains, "We do not compete with each other, and we do not find pleasure in defeating and humiliating someone else. Our pleasure is in supporting and uplifting others and seeing that everyone experiences joy and happiness. The relationships that you are describing couldn't happen. I cannot even imagine why they would happen. Why would someone even involve themselves in something like that? They would not only be hurting others, but they would be seriously harming themself too?"

Bunzy says, "I loved a woman once and I wish that I would have had Isabel's advice then and that I would have been wise enough to listen to her. That other woman's name was Isabel too. Our relationship would have ended better. I have been thinking of myself as a loving, spiritual person, but I can see that I have been living under an evil spell. I was confused and acted poorly. It's not easy to consider others' feelings rather than your own. Thank you all for helping me become a better person."

At that moment, they reach the fields and everyone except John hops off of the hover-up.

John invites Bunzy, "Bunzy, if you would like, climb in front up here beside me. I'm going to the sewerage plant to pick up a load of compost for the gardens and I could use some help."

Their gardening time together passes quickly. Afterwards they go to a cafeteria and eat lunch with some charming and lovely food servers and cooks.

At the end of the meal, John asks, "What do you want to do with the rest of your day?"

"I would like to go to the Educational Center and take an apprenticeship in Ubuntu administration," Bunzy answers.

Soon he finds himself sitting in a circle with a few other men and women listening to an Elder discuss ways of governing.

The elder opens his talk with the statement, "The best government is no government at all. The worst is a tyranny of one. Nation states fall somewhere in between these two possibilities. Over time they become ruled by elites who take ownership of all of the resources and force everyone outside of the elite to work for the elite for just enough to keep them from rebelling. The problem is if we are going to live together in a community and prosper and be happy, we need ways to coordinate our activities somehow. We need a government."

He continues, "The optimum way to achieve this is through cooperation. Competition and coercion lead to the defeat and subjugation of everyone and everything by a few violently aggressive, insensitive, greedy, perverted bullies. Even a representative form of government will become corrupted in a market economy which is based on profit, money, and debt. A democratic republic will become controlled by the tyranny of a majority who are manipulated and controlled by the few. The form of government which will benefit everyone the best is based upon the need for the consent of all, with strong checks and balances against the few gaining power over the many, and all of the activity in the community is supported by a cooperative economy which is based on sharing and caring."

"A market economy is built around trading for personal profit. This creates a world in which everyone is everyone else's enemy. Each person tries to get as much as they can and put it aside in a private pile where they can draw from it whenever they need something. People in the market system believe their security depends on how big their pile is. Their lives center around increasing the size of their hoard and protecting it from others."

"If everyone bases the fulfillment of their needs upon cooperation and kindness then everyone is trying to produce what they need and what others need at the same time and distribution is based upon sharing and caring. People's security is then based upon the vitality, health, and happiness of the community."

"The best basis for a government in a community based on cooperation and kindness is consensus. Decisions must be arrived at through the agreement of the people who are sharing the land, the resources, and their time together. Consensus is quite different than representational democracy and rule of the majority. Consensus can lead to rule of a minority. Perhaps rule isn't the correct word to use here because the minority can't force anyone else to do anything, as it does in an aristocracy. It means rule of the minority in the sense that everyone has to agree and someone refuses. Because it is almost impossible to get everyone to agree on anything, the government isn't a monolithic organization which seeks agreement. It is a multitude of organizations at different levels of society which implement plans of action in which everyone, who wishes to, can participate because all of the participants view themselves as benefiting by what they are doing. People don't have to be in agreement to work together, to be friends, or even to be lovers. They just have to enjoy what they are doing together and see the results of their mutual efforts as being good for them. Everyone understands they are personally benefiting the most by actively participating at their highest level in the activities in which they choose to participate."

"Voting is a divisive tactic that creates winners and losers. It creates bad feelings and enemies. A happy community cannot be based upon a struggle between winners and losers. Everybody has to feel their opinions have been heard and the community is going to the best possible place and they are currently experiencing the most happiness possible. Then everyone will put out the most effort they can and share the most rewards imaginable. That is how a consensual government is different than a monarchy or a representational democracy."

"A world based on cooperation, kindness, caring, sharing, and sensitivity to the feelings of all is far superior to one based on Meanness and greed. Cooperation is more productive than competition and more can be achieved through consensus than through coercion. There is a Great Spirit which supports, protects, and cares for us. We need to have faith in the benevolence and love of that force that gives us life and which supports our being. That force is more important to our wellbeing than anything we can say or do. So put your faith in the force of creation rather than in what you can hoard."

"What do you all think? Do you agree or disagree?" He asks the class.

Bunzy's stunned. *A world without money or competition. Is that even possible? But here I am in an Ubuntu community and it's working wonderfully.*

He excuses himself and walks out to the park where he sits by a big pond and watches the swans, ducks, and geese swim around with their babies.

On Tuesday evening John and his family come over to Bunzy's cooperative. Sally says, "All work and no play makes Bunzy a dull boy. Why don't you come to the Summer Solstice Celebration with us. Tonight is also the full moon. Could be a lucky night for you." She says this with a warm smile that says she knows more about what he needs than he does.

Bunzy laughs, "Alright. You're a wise woman and I know you're thinking of what is best for me. Let's go."

They enjoy their walk to the central plaza where the celebration is already in progress. A big bonfire burns. A band is playing and people dance.

Mike points at the painting behind the band and proudly announces, "We did that."

"It's awesome," Bunzy says, and it is.

They have created a whole magical forest full of nymphs and spirits celebrating the mysteries of life and the joys of fertility.

The details are incredible. As he's studying it, Isabel walks up and asks, "Bunzy, do you dance?"

The band is playing a slow number.

"Not very well," he answers.

She pushes on, "Well you can hug me and shuffle your feet, can't you?"

"I can do that" and he takes her in his arms, and they begin to dance. She smells wonderful. She's soft. They flow together and she fills his life with a stunningly powerful warmth."

When the dance is over, she asks, "Are you married?"

"Maybe, maybe not," Bunzy says. "I would like to be, but my wife is disgusted with me. Your statement, 'be kind to each other' really hit home. I'm not sure I know how to do that. I'm here because I'm lost. Some friends are trying to help me get straightened out."

Isabel smiles at Bunzy. She hugs his arm, then offers, "Let's see if we can help your friends succeed."

They spend the rest of the evening together dancing and talking."

Bunzy is happier than he's been in a long time. He really likes Shangri-La. He's not anxious or worried. He's a respected member of the community who is doing important work and all of his needs for shelter, food, transportation and entertainment are met. He also is learning how to be in a relationship, not just in Shangri-La, but elsewhere too.

On Wednesday evening John comes over to Bunzy's cooperative and invites Bunzy to join him in the Three Eye Society which John explains is a men's society.

Bunzy agrees to join and they start walking to the meeting.

Bunzy asks, "So this is a men's council. Does that mean that women aren't allowed to join?"

John answers, "It isn't that they aren't allowed to join. We recognize that men and women are equal, but different. There are women's councils too. Women in their councils participate in different activities, ceremonies, and rituals than we men do in our societies. If you were to go to a women's council meeting, you wouldn't enjoy it much and you would be wanting to go over and hang out at the men's meeting. Sally says that when men get together with other men, they get over filled with self-importance and act rough and silly. You are already participating in community wide men and women together activities and the men's and women's councils do join together for certain ceremonies. But tonight, we are going to go hang out with the guys. Let's go be important and have a good time."

"Yeah," Bunzy agrees. He punches John in the shoulder. "Let's go be silly big shots. Let's have some fun."

They come to a mound shaped plaza with a hole in the center of it with a ladder leading down into the ground.

"This is the Three Eye Society kiva," John explains pointing at the hole in the ground. "Follow me."

They climb down into the Earth on a ladder made of ancient pine logs with the bark stripped from them and made slick by the oil from thousands of hands sliding over them. At the bottom of the ladder is a large brown adobe room. This room is round and there is a stone seat built into the wall all around its outer edge. Woolen blankets woven with sacred patterns sit upon this seat and hang on the walls above it.

Near the west wall there is a body shaped depression in the earthen floor. This hole is big enough for a man to lie in.

John points to the hole and explains, "When you lie down there, you will be held in the arms of the great soul, Mother Earth, and you will experience rebirth."

There are several men sitting in a circle on the floor. They make room in their circle for Bunzy and John to join them.

Turning towards a man on his right, John says, "Elder Russell this is Bunzy who will be joining us tonight. Bunzy this is Elder Russell who will lead our ceremony."

Russell and Bunzy smile and nod at each other. The man who is sitting to Russell's right, carefully with both hands and with great respect hands Russell a large ancient pipe. The pipe is about eighteen inches long with a carved stone bowl and an intricately painted wooden stem with two eagle feathers hanging from the bowl at the end of the pipe. Pointing at the man who handed him the pipe, Russell says to Bunzy, "This is Charles who is a great medicine man." Charles smiles at the recognition he has been given and nods at Bunzy.

Then John introduces Bunzy to each of the other men in the circle. As they greet each other, Russell fills the pipe from a pouch which is hanging around his neck. After the introductions, Russell stands, touches the pipe to the ground, holds it up to the sky, then first offering it to the south, he begins to chant turning clockwise west, then north, and ending to the east.

He sits back down and explains, "In mingling our smoke and mingling our thoughts, we are joining together and our lives are becoming as one. Our blood will blend and our powers will flow together in friendship."

He lights the pipe, puffs on it and then hands it to John, who is sitting to his left. John takes a few puffs and then hands the pipe to Bunzy who sits to his left.

Bunzy takes the pipe and puffs on it as he has seen them do. As he puffs, he feels the pipe come alive. He feels a power surging into him. He knows he is at the center of all things. Tears stream down his face as he hands the pipe to Thomas who is sitting to his left.

As they smoke, Russell begins to speak. He explains how the world came into being, who people are, and how they are to live and what they are to do. In his explanation everyone and everything is important, and he tells the men that in our relationships we must respect each other and care for each other. He explains that for people to be happy there must be harmony between all beings in an eternal cycle of renewal. He concludes, "Treat others as you wish to be treated. That is all that you need to do."

The pipe has made it back around the circle and Charles hands it again to Russell who stands and takes the pipe over to an altar and places it between a few gourd rattles and several buzzard feathers on the right side of the altar. Then he comes back to the circle, asks all to stand up, hold hands, extend their arms out full length from their sides, then drop their hands. He says a short prayer, then explains, "We are going to begin a circle dance with the Great Spirit. All things in nature are circular such as the seasons. One thing follows another in an eternally repeating cycle. So, we will express our joy for being included in this moment by mimicking what is happening by joyously dancing around in a circle. Three of the men leave the circle and begin to drum and sing. The other men begin a slow toe-heel bouncing step around in the circle. Bunzy follows their lead. The drumming gradually gets wilder and louder and faster and faster, and the dancing gets crazier and crazier. Time is obliterated in an ecstasy of sound and movement.

After they have danced for some time, Charles raises a hand and stops the dance.

He announces, "It is good. Now let's give our thoughts form. Let's make our intentions known in a real way. We are going to make prayer sticks. What we call pahos, Bunzy. When the pahos are complete we will make pilgrimages to sacred places and plant the pahos. As we are, so we do. In this paho ceremony, we are asking the powers which bring benefit, to bless us."

He shows Bunzy how to take wooden sticks, paint them, attach feathers to them, and infuse them with his intentions. As they make the pahos, they talk about their hopes, their dreams and their desires. They discuss their visions of a beautiful world full of love, security, and abundance. Each person in the circle speaks his heart and they grow closer in friendship. Their intentions meet as one mind. They place those intentions in the pahos.

When the pahos are complete, Russell says, "Let us smoke and pray and dance again and take our intentions to the Great Spirit."

He rises, goes to the altar, picks up the pipe, and brings it back to the circle. He fills the pipe, lights it, takes a few puffs and hands it to John.

After Bunzy has smoked, Russell continues, "Bunzy, I want to discuss something with you that I hope will be of benefit to you and everyone here. What I am going to say may seem a little harsh, but please don't be offended. I am only trying to clarify a complicated subject and what I am saying is out of love and concern for you and for all of the men in this circle and for all of the spirits who care about us and support us. I am just trying to bring understanding that will help us enjoy our lives more. I want you to understand the difference between your culture and our culture so that you can understand where the change in your lives needs to occur if you are going make the transformation that brings harmony."

"Your religion, our religion, everyone's religion is a statement of their world view. Whatever that view is, we hold it so strongly that we believe that, that is the way things are. In your culture you are told that religion is something off to the side of life. Science is your real religion, but you hold science as being separate from religion. There is a split between what you profess and what you do. But in reality, whatever your world view is, that is your religion. That is your explanation of who you are, what you are, where you come from, and where you are going to go when you die. The combination of these beliefs determines how you act. A person's religion is so much how they are that they don't even realize what their belief system is. You don't consider that your belief system is just another religion. To you science isn't based on beliefs. It is based on facts. What I am calling a religion is held by scientist to be a set of beliefs which are un-provable and unreliable assumptions which are being used by a particular people to justify their behavior. It is only when people look at another group of people and their belief system that they call the other people's belief system a religion and they state that this other people's religion is based on a bunch of false ideas and myths and dangerous or silly assumptions. To you, your people's own beliefs are facts. They explain the way it is."

"There can be no separation between what a person believes and how they make their living, their relationships with everyone and everything around them, and their use of their leisure time. What you believe, is how you are, and how you are is how you act in your economy, your schools, your government, your families, and your leisure time. What you believe is the way you are and what we believe is the way we are. That is the reason your culture destroys all other cultures it comes into contact with. That is why you will not allow others to continue to exist alongside you. You practiced genocide on Native American cultures because they were different than you. Your culture's viewpoint is that you are absolutely correct and others are wrong and only the culture that is right can continue to exist. You believe other cultures are wrong and inferior and they must go to make room for your superior way of doing things."

"You say you believe in love and sharing and caring, but you have an institution known as private property and you each acquire as much of this private property as you can and you attack anyone or anything which threatens your private property. You have divided the world into mine and yours, into us and them, and you're very serious about what is whose and who is what. That really leaves little time for love or sharing or caring in your economy, your government, your schools, your families, or your leisure time activities. Your idea of fun is gladiator sports and shows in which people who are described as being different than you, are destroyed or humiliated, or shows in which people like you accumulate control over vast resources which includes the lives of other people."

"We do not believe in private property. We do not believe that people can own the Earth. We are the children of the Earth. Would it be right to own your mother and to sell her. The area where we live is held in common and loved and shared by all. We do not separate ourselves from each other or from nature. We hold all life in common and view everything as sacred. Our government expresses this desire for the wellbeing of all and it strives to include the opinions of everyone in all decisions. Our government and our economy is based on our belief that everything and everyone is important, connected, and sacred. Our understanding is continuously being expressed in a cycle of ceremonies which create this way of life and explain it and teach it to all of the ceremonial participants and spectators. Through our ceremonies we are living consciously. Through our rituals we are maintaining contact with the spirits and nature and we are continuing an ancient cycle of being. If you will honestly look at our culture and then look at your culture, you will gain insight which will give you understanding."

The pipe returns to him and he stands and takes it back to the altar. Then we dance again.

Finally, Russell announces, "It is time to greet the moon. We are now people of spiritual power. That means that we have the proper attitudes and that we have allied ourselves with the spiritual forces and together we will bring great benefit to our community. We are living in an extreme state of grace and we should be constantly going about chanting our mantra and that mantra is saying: thank you, thank you, thank you. Thank you, that we exist at all is miraculous, thank you that we have food and shelter and health and transportation and friends and thank you loved ones with whom we share all of this beauty and miraculous wonder. We are living in a state of grace beyond our understanding. Our only appropriate response is gratitude. We need to share our good fortune and the loving kindness which is being shown to us."

He rises, walks over to the ladder and begins to climb. Everyone follows him. Outside, the moon is powerfully beautiful. It is a lovely night. After a short ceremony, they disburse and walk home.

A month later, Bunzy sits by a stream in the outer ring wild park when Seattle appears.

"Good afternoon Bunzy. This is a beautiful place," he observes.

"Yes. I didn't know that anyplace could be this wonderful," Bunzy agrees.

"It is time for you to return to Earth and be the benefit that you set out to be. You are terribly needed."

"I know," Bunzy says. "I will return tonight."

"Good. I'll see you there soon then." He looks at Bunzy for a moment, smiles, then walks away into the woods.

Bunzy goes back to town. He explains the situation to John and Isabel, then they walk around as Bunzy feasts his eyes and heart on the paradise that is Shangri-La.

When it gets dark, he lays down, goes to sleep, and returns through a tortoise tunnel to his sleeping mat in the hole under the rocks. Waking up, he rubs his eyes and forehead, then pushes himself up into the lotus position facing the open area. Seattle and Running Bear sit out there watching him.

"What a strange trip it's been," Bunzy says. "Are those Cobra gunships gone?" He asks.

"Yes, they're gone and the trip is only beginning," Running Bear says.

"We need you to go out into the world and tell everyone what you have learned right away. The police are closing in," Seattle adds.

"A friend is getting married. I need to go help him with the wedding. I'll start for his home in the morning. Let's eat," Bunzy says.

"What about the police?" Running Bear asks.

"I'll just have to act as normal and non-threatening as I can," Bunzy replies.

"Is your friend on Mephistopheles' list?" Bear inquires.

"I don't know," Bunzy answers.

They look. He is. Most of the people who will be at the wedding are on the list. It will be a meeting of freed slaves.

CHAPTER 13
RUTHLESS THIEVES AND WICKED SCOUNDRELS

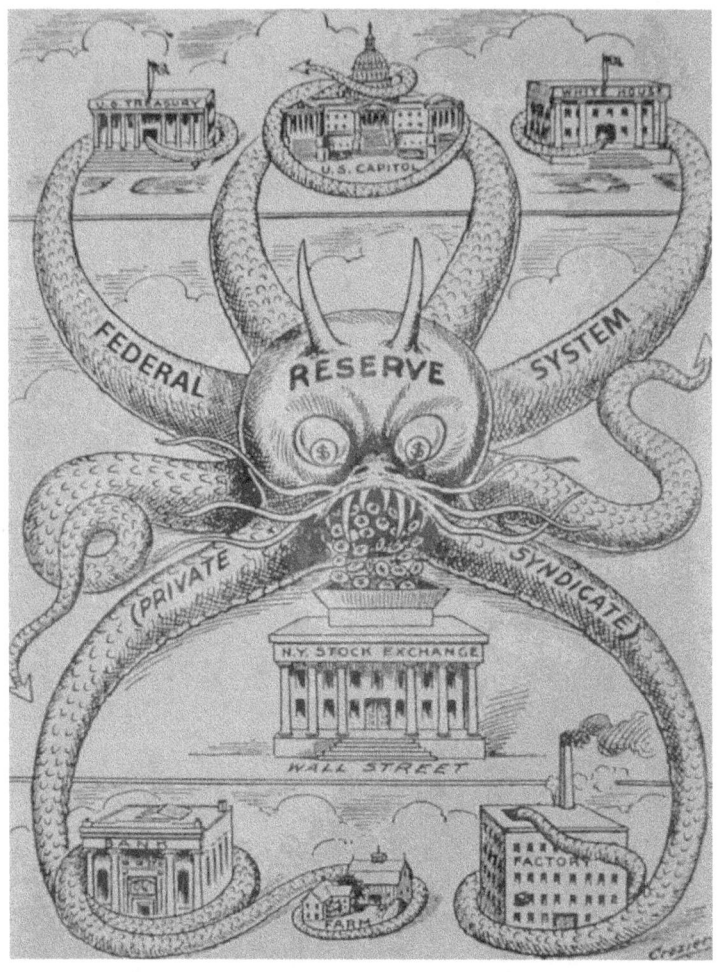

"Let me issue and control a nation's money and I care
not who writes the laws."

Mayer Amschel Rothschild 1744-1812

A week later Bunzy is talking to three other wedding ushers, Peter, Paul, and John, who are local construction workers.

He tells them, "I have been visiting a beautiful paradise called Shangri-La. There is no money or usury there. People's lives are based on cooperation, sharing, and caring. We could be living like that here."

Peter asks, "How would that work? I mean, is a world without money even possible?"

Bunzy carefully explains to them how an Ubuntu community works. They are convinced and immediately start organizing an autonomous, cooperative community. They set up a town hall meeting at their church, where Bunzy explains what they are doing. People are excited by the idea of living in a community where there is no fear or coercion, where they are surrounded with security and living happily through cooperation and kindness. Many of the people at the talk join them and some of those people start an internet site, blogs, and social networks, and others organize more town hall meetings in community centers, motel meeting rooms, and peoples' homes.

It turns out the Archon direct mind control is spread very thin. Many people have never been controlled directly by Archons, but are just drifting along with the ways of the dominant community to get along. They have never given any thought to anything other than how to make a living and raise a family. They were easily controlled by the authority figures in their lives. The result of all of this is when a few people are set free by Mephistopheles, many more are set free by those who have already been freed. The Ubuntu Movement grows very quickly.

Small Ubuntu communities begin to form around families and groups of friends. Then those small communities start to link together and grow into villages.

The movement provides Bunzy with a house on a farm.

One day while he sits in the front room of this house, gazing out over a lake, Mephistopheles walks across the yard, waves through a window at him, and then comes in through the front door. Bunzy stands up to greet him. Mephistopheles comes over, shakes his hand and warmly hugs Bunzy.

"You are doing a great work Bunzy. I've come to join you."

"This is much better than our meeting after my last attempt to redeem people," Bunzy responds.

"I'm sorry about that," Mephistopheles tells him. "I just didn't understand."

"Really I didn't either," Bunzy says, "and I have already forgiven you."

"It is good to be brothers in the Divine Presence," Mephistopheles acknowledges.

"Mephistopheles, are you old enough to have been there at the beginning of the whole Archon/human relationship?" Bunzy inquires.

"Much of it," Mephistopheles responds.

"What really happened?" Bunzy wants to know.

Mephistopheles starts to tell him, "Thousands of years ago my ancestors destroyed the environment of our world. The destruction tore a hole in the sky which was allowing deadly radiation to kill us and everything that we depended upon. Our scientists developed a theory that if we took gold, ground it up very fine and dispersed it high in the atmosphere that it would block out the deadly radiation. We tried it and it worked, but there wasn't enough gold on our planet to save us. We needed more. So, some of us volunteered to come to this world. This planet had a lot of gold on it when we first came here. Mining for gold though is hard work. We don't like to do that kind of thing. We discovered if we did a bit of genetic engineering on the humans who were already here and took the Dream Key away from them, you would serve us as if we were your gods and do whatever we needed to have done. Things worked out very well for us for a long time. Things didn't work out so well for you beasts of burden though.

"Even as good as we had it, a problem arose. Lots of the Archon volunteers didn't like it here on Earth. There were never many Archon women here. The lonely Archon guys who were living here far from home for thousands of years, noticed that the daughters of men were very attractive and started having children with them. The children of these couplings shared a mix of human and Archon genes. Actually, the genes that we share are very similar, but through genetic engineering, we have turned off many of these genes in humans so that certain attributes do not express themselves in people. Things got complicated and more sophisticated methods of control had to be developed. Our ruler, your god, Enlil, decided that the best thing would be just to kill all of the humans and start over. He tried, but some Archons saved their hybrid children who saved other humans. Then the humans repopulated Earth and the whole thing just continued on."

"Better methods of controlling our servants were needed. The first method of control of humans that the Archon rulers developed were the priest kings with their armies and police. It was easy to insert men as our representatives into your communities because we were your gods and humans were used to doing whatever we told them to do. After all, we did, through genetic engineering, alter you into our image. We were technically your creators. Anyway, because you were used to doing what we told you to do we just started designating particularly servile, stupid, greedy, insensitive, mean, aggressive humans to represent us. Those guys were given super violent back up and the vast wealth needed to hire armies of vicious thugs. They did what we told them and they made people serve us the way that we wanted. This system worked pretty well for a long time. We could rule over masses of humans with very little effort with this technique. But then people started doubting their priests and rebelling against their kings. If we weren't going to have to spend all day every day controlling people's thoughts, then a new method of controlling the herds of humans was needed. Moloch and Mammon came up with the idea of debt and its twin enforcers state violence and money. After all we still had the armies of thugs and the police bullies who were loyal to us because they were getting lots of booty and slaves. We just needed a more subtle way to motivate and control people, and when subtlety fails, we can still send in the army or police as of old."

"Up until you brought me into the Divine presence, I believed that we, Archons, are superior beings who have the right to use other beings in any way that we want. The same way that you people treat chickens, pigs, and cows. I believed that life is a competitive struggle, and the winners of this struggle have the right to everything and the losers have the right to nothing. I really didn't see until it was almost too late that we are all in this together and our only hope is to cooperate with each other before we destroy this planet. And the really sad thing is, if we treated each other as we want to be treated, we could actually be having a better time. Our superior technology made us arrogant. Our hearts were already greedy and cruel. If we would have acquired wisdom rather than weapons, things could have been good for everyone, but here we are on the edge of destruction with a few cruel, selfish bullies running the show. It's not going to be easy turning this world around, but you and I have greater sources of power than are imagined by men or Archons. In eternity, the impossible happens all of the time. Brother, we shall prevail in goodness and peace."

"How is your effort to bring Archons into the Divine presence going?"

"Great! Many Archons have become enlightened. The most important of those to come over to our side is Lord Enki and he has shown many of his descendants the light too."

"Who is Enki?"

"Enki is Enlil's brother. It was Enki who developed the genetic engineering program that created modern humans. He created you in his image mixing your genes with his, manipulating the results. Technically you are his progeny. So, he has always been fond of humans and tried to make your lives better. Over the millennia he has fathered many full-blooded Archon children and many hybrid children and these children have all had children who have had children. This has been going on for a long time. He has a lot of descendants and most of these surviving children grasped the wisdom of cooperation right away, set their slaves free and entered the Divine presence. He has also developed a method whereby humans can free themselves from Archon mind control and he wants me to give it to you. Enlil is having trouble keeping us under control."

"What happens to Archons when they come into the Divine presence?" Bunzy asks.

Mephistopheles tells him, "What you would see is something that looks like a human growing brighter and brighter as it transforms into an angel of white light. Next it becomes transparent and fades away. The redeemed Archon has entered Paradise where most of us stay, but a few like me return to help with the work of saving our friends and loved ones, you people and this planet."

"I lack your understanding," Bunzy says, "but I am committed to being what we must be and doing what we must do. Lead on, Brother."

Together, within the Ubuntu communities and based on the Ubuntu principles, Mephistopheles, Bunzy and their followers start the Freedom Movement. Together they are known as Freedomists.

At the first Congress of the Ubuntu Confederacy which is made up of representatives from all of the tribes which include all of the Ubuntu villages, the Congressional Council issues the Freedomist Declaration of Independence along with the Manifesto of Living Principles.

The Declaration of Independence states: "We the free and natural humans of planet Earth declare that all beings are created free and equal. It is the right and privilege of everyone to pursue health, happiness, and self-realization through the equitable sharing of all resources. No being is more important than any other and all deserve respect and the opportunity and the necessities needed to express themselves to their highest potential. This planet is a sacred being that belongs to no one, but as its children, we, all of the creatures who live here and all of the plants and funguses that grow here, are gifted with a fair share of its abundance, so that we may freely enjoy our time together. We bind each and every one of us with the high and holy responsibility of protecting and caring for this sacred space, the precious beings who dwell in this place and the blessed spirits who manifest this realm. No one has the right to dominate, exploit, or harm anything or anyone without the due consideration and permission of the entire community and if anyone should harm anyone or anything without the permission of the members of the community then justice shall be swift and the punishment shall be that which is approved and executed by the community."

"Further, we declare our freedom from fear, suffering, want, confusion, sadness, hatred, jealousy, loneliness, selfishness, anxiety, need, helplessness, and hopelessness. We pledge our precious time and being in mutual aid to all with the intention that all will experience health, happiness and realize our highest potential."

"May need, anger, suffering, hatred and fear never be experienced in this space and time. May we and our children's children forever only know happiness, abundance and love."

"Holding these truths to be self-evident and in the mutual pursuit of health, happiness, and self-realization for all beings, we institute the organization of the Ubuntu communities."

The Manifesto of Living Principles then states the laws that people are to live by. The basic governing body of the Freedomist Movement is the village council. The village is the local community and everyone over the age of eighteen belongs to the village council. The village council determines the use of all of the land and resources in the area occupied by the village and everyone must agree on the decisions of the village council. The village council also resolves local disputes and problems and co-ordinates local activities. Persons involved in a crime or dispute which is being discussed by the Council lose their say in the decision. A cluster of villages occupying a large area is considered to be a tribe. Each village sends a representative to the tribal council which co-ordinates activities between villages and settles inter-village disputes before they can become blood feuds. Each tribe sends a representative to the Ubuntu Confederation which oversees the activities between tribes and represents the Freedom Movement when dealing with outsiders such as the Archons and their representatives.

The basis of the Ubuntu economy is the gift. A gift is given when someone helps someone else, or when someone wishes to acquire prestige or affection, or when someone simply has acquired more than they need and wants to help their neighbors. Through gifts the resources possessed by individuals and groups are constantly being redistributed. The more that a person gives, the more they are recognized and respected. It is considered to be immoral and mean spirited to hoard and not to share. Mean people are despised and shunned, but every effort is made to bring them back into communion with the community.

The Confederation issues a statement saying that members of the Freedom Movement do not oppose the existing power structure. Freedomists are to render unto the existing government whatever they must render as a legal obligation, but nothing more is required of members of the Movement.

People find the Ubuntu communities supportive and friendly. They like living in an anxiety free, non-competitive environment. Through the pooling of resources and labor and through coordinating members' activities, the villages become very wealthy and life within the Movement becomes quite comfortable. Success brings in more and more members which leads to more wealth, greater happiness, better health, and even more time to pursue personal activities. The Movement is sweeping the world, taking over community after community. Once people commit to mutual aid rather than competition, Ubuntu tribalism just seems natural, and they aren't interested in going back to their old ways.

As the Freedom Movement grows and the Freedomist cooperative economies start to replace the Archon market economies, the police start harassing Freedomists and there is a danger that the national armies will be used to exterminate entire Freedomist populations.

There are many organizations which share the Freedom Movement's ideals and goals. The Ubuntu Confederation sends representatives to each of them and asks them to join together with the Freedomists in the Holy Council of Sacred Alliances. The Council is an international round-table type of organization which coordinates the activities of its members. Compliance to its dictates is voluntary, but because the members recognize that the Council is acting to protect their families and their livelihoods, the members courageously and strictly follow its orders. The Council quickly becomes very powerful. It spreads the Freedomist message through the communities person to person. It elects people sympathetic to the movement to political offices at all levels of government. It begins to affect employer/employee relationships. Alliance environmental groups take control of large areas and begin to seriously affect Archon resource industries.

In the darkness of a black night, a high official in the Federal Reserve who is secretly a Freedomist comes to the Movement leaders and warns Bunzy, "The great Archon Lord Enlil has convened the secret ruling most high Imperial Council and the Council has instructed President George to arrest, condemn, and execute you. I personally heard Lord Enlil instruct the President to, 'Send in the jackals and finish this pathetic charade. The first order of business shall be killing Bunzy Ringer.' The President then sent instructions directly to Federal Judge Solomon to do the deed. You must immediately flee and go into hiding. They are coming for you."

"Every breath that I take is by grace," Bunzy tells him. "I will face this as I face the hope that my heart will continue to beat and that someday I will be in Shangri-La again. Thank you for the warning. You are a good and brave man. May the ecstasy of the Divine presence find you and bless you with love, peace, and joy."

As he looks at Bunzy, the man begins to weep. Holding his forehead, with his eyes cast down at the floor, he leaves the room.

Peter argues with Bunzy, "Lord you must not allow yourself to be taken. You are our leader and our inspiration. Without you what will we do?"

"Peter, be strong in the faith. If I fall, you must lead. We will talk of this no more. Our duty is too strengthen the Ubuntu communities by being where we are needed and by benefiting those whom we can. Trust in Divine grace."

On Sunday night just after midnight, fifty men in black military combat uniforms with high power automatic rifles and wearing flak jackets, kick in the Ubuntu farmhouse doors where Bunzy and three other Ubuntu leaders live. They do this even though they know the doors aren't locked and even though the attacking men know that there are only four unarmed Freedomists sleeping in this house. The men in black rush upstairs, knocking Peter to the floor unconscious as they charge upwards, drag Bunzy out of bed, kick and punch him and beat him with night sticks, blacking both of his eyes, breaking his nose, and cracking several ribs, then they shackle his arms and legs, chain him up and drag him off to prison.

His interrogation is brutal, but it is done by men, not Archons. He's not even accused of any crime.

Bunzy asks the captain in charge of his questioning, "Don't I get to speak in my defense and answer the charges against me?"

The captain answers, "No. You've already been convicted and sentenced to death. This is all just a show for the people."

The sergeant, a short stocky man with a pock marked face and butch haircut who is wearing a cheap, poorly fitting, dirty suit, sneers in Bunzy's face with his beer and garlic breath and slowly grinds his cigarette out in the flesh in Bunzy's right arm.

As Bunzy screams and jerks against the straps holding him in the interrogation chair, his interrogators laugh.

They aren't even trying to get any information out of him. They are just enjoying taunting and tormenting him.

After they have tortured Bunzy for days, bound with ankle and wrist chains, he is drug into the Federal Court of Judge Solomon, dragged over to a chair behind a table on the left side of the room in front of the spectators benches and pushed down. Above them in the front of the room is the judge's empty seat. Under his position, but above everyone else in the courtroom are the court clerk, a stenographer, and a uniformed guard. Bunzy's chains are removed. He's wearing an old, faded and torn blue jump suit with his prison number stenciled across his left breast pocket in washable black ink. Bunzy's court appointed attorney sits beside him. The lawyer doesn't even look up and acknowledge Bunzy's presence. His briefcase is open, and he is studying some legal documents which he has removed from it.

Bunzy asks his lawyer, "Did you bring my birth certificate?"

The attorney looks up at Bunzy. Emoting disgust from every pore in his sweating, fat, ugly body he sneers, "Yes."

The lawyer reaches into the top pocket in his briefcase, removes a folded piece of paper, and tosses it on the table in front of Bunzy.

Bunzy says, "Thank you. I have been wanting to look at this," and he picks it up and makes a show of scrutinizing it.

The court appointed attorney goes back to studying the legal documents in his briefcase.

The clerk announces, "All rise. The Honorable Judge Solomon is entering."

Everyone in the room stands.

A short, pudgy, pasty-faced, balding, old man in the black robes of a priest enters the courtroom, sits down, and declares, "You may all be seated."

After they all sit down, he commands the clerk, "Read the charges against the defendant."

The clerk accuses Bunzy of treason and conspiracy to commit treason.

Judge Solomon then asks, "Mr. Ringer do you understand the charges against you?"

Bunzy responds, "No."

Everyone stops. They stare at him.

Judge Solomon carefully and slowly inquires, "What is it you don't understand, Mr. Ringer?"

"I mean that as a free and natural born human with inalienable rights, I do not stand under the authority of this court."

The Judge jumps up and yells, "That is not possible. I will not allow such impertinence in my courtroom." He sits back down, thinks for a moment, considers the charges, and then with a sly look on his face, asks, "Mr. Ringer will you pledge allegiance to the United States flag over there." He points at a flag in the corner of the room.

Bunzy declares, "No. I will not grant the United States government authority over me. I am no submissive slave, and I am not the property of this country."

Judge Solomon picks up the indictment and waves it at Bunzy. He asks, "Are you the named individual on this complaint?"

Picking up his birth certificate, Bunzy responds, "I am making a Limited Appearance on behalf of the defendant who is right here," and he shows his birth certificate to Judge Solomon. Bunzy continues speaking, "as I understand this process Judge, the District Attorney has leveled criminal charges with the Clerk against this TRUST using the ALL CAPS NAME that appears on this BIRTH CERTIFICATE! The use of capital letters is dictated by the United States' Printing Style Manuel, which explains how to identify a CORPORATION."

The Judge starts screaming, "Shut up! Shut up!" His face is contorted with rage and turning purple. He sweats and stabs a finger at Bunzy and demands, "Guard silence that criminal."

Bunzy continues, "The Clerk, who is the ADMINISTRATOR of the CESTA QUE TRUST, then appointed you Judge as the TRUSTEE for the TRUST and since neither of you can be the BENEFICIARY, that leaves me and therefore you are MY TRUSTEE. So as MY TRUSTEE, I instruct you to discharge this entire matter with prejudice."

The guard has crossed the room and is standing in front of Bunzy.

He demands, "Stop speaking. Now!"

Bunzy says, "And award the penalties for these crimes to be paid to me."

The guard punches Bunzy in the face. Bunzy falls away from the guard with the table between them. He stands and finishes speaking, "In compensation and damages for my false arrest."

The District Attorney jumps up and shouts, "Your Honor, I object to the Defendant's statement and move that it be struck from the record."

Bunzy turns to face the District Attorney and tells the Court, "I move that the District Attorney's federal tax 1040 form relating to this case be made a matter of public record."

The District Attorney responds, "Your Honor, I withdraw my objection." He sits back down.

Bunzy picks up his chair and says, "I withdraw my motion." He sits back down with the guard standing over him.

The Judge declares, "Mr. Ringer, you are an obnoxious, arrogant fool. I may not have any authority over you, but that doesn't stop me from sealing your doom. There is an authority higher than the Federal Government. Guards, I release this man into the care of the High Governor to face the demands of the Imperial Council."

He stands, points at Bunzy and demands, "Get that trash out of my sight."

"Bunzy is chained up again and marched out of the courtroom to a dungeon in the basement of the dismal city jail.

After another week, he is brought before the Governor's Council. They meet in a magnificent marble building in a private park which has a high rock wall all around it. The grounds and building are heavily guarded and patrolled by a well-armed, very professional, private paramilitary force. The Council chambers are made of marble, hardwoods and polished brass, hung with heavy dark maroon curtains and paintings featuring important events and men in Imperial history going back for thousands of years.

When Bunzy is brought into the Council, it is already in session. His guards pull him across a hundred feet of cold stone floor to kneel with his forehead on the floor before the Governors. There are no chairs for people who are brought before the Governors. The Governors are sitting on massive, heavily cushioned oak chairs high above the plaintiffs. The chair of the High Governor is above the chairs of the other Governors. There are forty or fifty guards and servants between Bunzy and the Governors and another dozen people hovering around the Governors waiting to be ordered to do something. All of the Governors except the High Governor are wearing the magnificent black robes of high priests. The High Governor's robe is the purple of a priest king.

The High Governor explains to Bunzy, "Mr. Ringer, you may rise. You will stand under us with your head bowed in recognition of our power over you. You will speak only when you are spoken to or your tongue will be cut out. If there is any further trouble from you, your life will end immediately in this room. You come before us today accused of treason and blasphemy. How do you plead?"

Standing with his head bowed, Bunzy quietly says, "I do not know what you are accusing me of, so I do not plead one way or another."

The High Governor explains, "The Honorable Judge Solomon has accused you of refusing to swear allegiance to the United States government and of denying that the government has any authority over you. What do you say?"

Bunzy states, "I was born a free and natural human being and I claim that birthright. I make no statement or claims concerning the United States government."

The Governor of the Southwest Region leans forward and angrily shouts, "Don't split hairs with us, you disgusting weasel. Either you are a loyal citizen, or you are a terrorist. Which are you?"

"I am a free and natural man who wishes to live in peace and garden," Bunzy declares.

The Governor of the South demands, "Answer the question slave. Yes, or no?"

"What's the question?" Bunzy asks.

"Are you a terrorist?" The Governor of the South says.

"No," Bunzy answers.

"Will you pledge allegiance to this nation then?" The Governor of the South asks.

"No," Bunzy says.

The Governor of the West declares, "There it is. He's guilty of treason by his own admission. Hang him."

The Governor of the North agrees, "Hang him. He's guilty alright and must be executed immediately before his disease spreads any further."

The other Governors nod their heads in agreement."

The High Governor declares, "Mr. Ringer you have no rights before us. We are your lawful owners. You owe us your life and we may foreclose on your debt at any time." He pauses and studies Bunzy, then continues, "You seem like a decent fellow and I do not personally wish to be the cause of your death, but you have heard the demands of the other Governors. So, I condemn you to be hung naked from a wooden stake at dawn ten days hence in the courtyard in the Prison on the Rock and there to face a firing squad of six good and faithful servants of this state who will be firing small caliber rifles at your guts. Only two of the rifles will have live rounds so that no guilt will fall on any of the rifleman. Your death will be slow and your suffering will be great. You are to hang on the stake until you are dead, no matter how long it takes. Your entire execution is to be televised for the people's enjoyment and education. Your crimes are to be explained while they watch you slowly die. Guards take this prisoner to the Prison on the Rock and execute him as I have commanded."

The Prison on the Rock is a drab old grey stone fortress on a hilltop on the outskirts of the city that long ago was converted into a high security prison for those men whom the state considers to be the most dangerous. Bunzy is locked in a filthy, wet cell with nothing in it except a damp, dirty mattress on the floor for him to lie on while the arrangements are being made for his execution. There is a window high in one of the strong, thick cement walls that imprison him. The walls are reinforced and shaped with bulky old rusting iron braces. A massive steel doorway and door covers much of one wall.

There is no appeal from the demands of the Imperial Council of Governors. They are above the government and its laws. The Federal Reserve owns the government. The Imperial Council of Governors is the ruling body of the Federal Reserve. It is the power behind the banks, the giant multi-national corporations, the military and the police, behind every level of organization of this modern civilization. There are imperial councils in every country in the world and there is a Grand Imperial Council which coordinates the activities of the national councils and rules over them all. The great Archon lords, the gods of old, rule over all of this. Mephistopheles has explained this to Bunzy. Bunzy seems to have little hope of surviving and prospering when the cruel and mighty, the sophisticated and brilliant Archons and their servants are against him and his friends?

On the ninth night while Bunzy contemplates all of this, waiting to be gut shot in the morning and then to be left hanging naked on a wooden stake while his stomach bloats and he drools red blood and green feces, suffering for hours or even days, naked in front of all of the world, humiliated and slowly dying; the ground begins to roll like waves on the ocean. Lurching across the floor like a drunken sailor, he sways to the steel doorway and braces himself against the massive metal door. A wall in his cell splits open and parts of the ceiling crash down.

The Prison on the Rock buckles and collapses into a pile of concrete blocks. Everything is dark and silent. It is a moonlit night. Bunzy steps out of his cell through the hole in the wall and starts climbing over the broken slabs of walls and floors. The guards are all dead or have fled. The city below is burning and in chaos. Sirens scream through the night and the lights of emergency vehicles flash. There is no one to challenge his departure. Explosions and gun fire in the city fill the night with unpleasant noise. Bunzy turns away from civilization and begins walking. It is a lovely full moon night for a free and natural man to take a walk in Nature. As he leaves, the ground shakes again in a ferocious tremor and the old fortress collapses into a pile of rubble.

CHAPTER 14
EARTH, WIND, AND FIRE

"Humankind has not woven the web of life. We are but one thread within it. Whatever we do to the web, we do to ourselves. All things are bound together. All things connect."

Chief Seattle

A month later, Bunzy visits with Running Bear, Seattle, and Gsal Byed Gdos Bral Ma under some big old cottonwood trees behind an adobe hogan next to a stream in a desert wilderness in the Southwest part of the United States.

Running Bear says, "Mother Earth is the world spirit who is our mother in whose womb we are created and in whose home we live. Wind is the Great Spirit who is the breath of life and the inspiration for our existence. Fire is the Holy Spirit that is the eternal flame of imagination which burns brightly illuminating the forever dance of life, love, and beauty.

Seattle says, "It is time to restore Mother Earth, make the Great Spirit great again, and free the Holy Spirit."

"I agree," Bunzy says.

Gsal Byed Gdos Bral Ma smiles sweetly, points at the vibrant, cold, clear stream and asks, "What about water?"

"The spirits of water are the Divine in love with life and movement, falling together, running together, flowing into each other, fulfilling everyone's desire to be with each other in beauty and pleasure, then rising together in joy and rushing to do it again because it is all just so much fun. By calling on Mother Earth, the Great Spirit, and the Holy Spirit, I am intentionally separating the flow. There is only One and we are all that moment coupling in ecstasy. Thank you, Gsal Byed Gdos Bral Ma, for keeping us mindful of that, but what we are going for here is Divine inspiration and the fire that will purify and cleanse this sacred space. Great spiritual forces are in play here. Bunzy, that earthquake should have shown you that Spirit is more powerful than all of the armies and police in the world and cleverer than the Archons. That you are sitting here comfortable and healthy should show you that Spirit can take care of you just as well or even better than a hoard of gold or a powerful political ally."

"I didn't see any Earth spirits or any manifestations of the Divine up there in the Prison on the Rock. How do I know that everything that happened wasn't just a lucky coincidence?"

"We need you to be clear on what's happening here. We don't want you to make any compromise agreements. We want you to do what you were meant to do with clarity and courage."

"What am I meant to do?"

"You are meant to protect life, love, and beauty; and to serve the great white light of joyous creation."

"How am I to do that? What tools are you giving me? How can I communicate with spirit?"

"We need to take a walk."

They all stand and walk south and west all morning following Running Bear. Midday they come into a little valley surrounded by ridges on three sides. In the middle of this area is a bare egg shaped red rock hill. Following a trail that other people and animals have followed for millennia, they climb to the top of the egg. There is a flat area up there, maybe a hundred feet square. This is obviously a sacred place. Standing on the level spot on the top of the egg gazing to the southwest they are looking at a mountain-sized mound covered by a forest and teeming with life surrounded by a vast desert.

Bunzy asks Running Bear, "How can I get to know Mother Earth?"

"Perhaps Gsal Byed Gdos Bral Ma would be the best one to introduce you to Mother Earth because she is a divine Earth spirit herself."

Turning to her with his mouth open and eyes wide, Bunzy asks, "You are?"

"Don't be so surprised. You are too," she tells him.

She's so beautiful, self-assured, and calm. He's amazed.

"I am?" Bunzy mumbles.

Gsal Byed Gdos Bral Ma says, "You are used to thinking of everything that you think of as being real, as being solid matter. It is time that you start seeing everything as spirit which has become manifest as touchable, or at least seeable. To call on Mother Earth, look at that mountain over there and express all of your adoration for your home and for this entire world."

She is pointing at the mountain to the southwest of them.

Gathering all of his gratitude for his life and loved ones and all of his love for this world, Bunzy begins, "Mother Earth your oceans are so vast and full of life and wonder and power that I fall down on my knees in worship on the sands of your seashores and fill my being with more beauty than I could ever imagine before experiencing your majesty. Your mountains that rise awesomely out of the plains inspire me to great heights of imagined possibilities. Your huge rolling plains surging with animals fill me with the hope of renewed eternal life. Your precious soil that we walk on, the air that we breath, the sky over our heads are more precious than all of the money and prestige in the world."

As he speaks, he stares at the mountain-sized mound. Suddenly he is aware of a living presence there.

He realizes. *That's not just a big pile of rock with trees and animals living on it. The whole place is alive as one conscious, thinking, active being. That thing is terrifying, not because it is threatening, but because it is so big and incomprehensible.*

Bunzy falls on his face on the bare red rock at his feet and looks away from the mountain. His rational mind says to get up and quit being silly, but he can't.

I don't care what my mind says. There is something huge and powerful here and I know it and I am laid low with awe. I know without a doubt that I am in the presence of the world spirit. A living, feeling, thinking, individual planet-sized spirit is right here, right now. What it is capable of I don't know, but I do know that everything that I understand is in the balance.

Gsal Byed Gdos Bral Ma says, "Now you know. You are face down on the skin and all around you are the limbs and organs of the body of one conscious, intelligent, and loving being whose beauty, generosity, and kindness provides you and your family and loved ones with life and joy. Through acting with the correct reference and speaking with the right attitude, you have brought yourself into the presence of the Earth soul. Now you may ask anything of her and she will respond."

But Bunzy can't ask anything. He can't think. He can't speak. He can't even bear to look at her. He pushes himself to his knees and turns towards Seattle looking to him for moral support, but when Bunzy looks at Seattle, he begins to feel something in his back running up and down his spinal column. Then Bunzy's sense of self leaps out of his forehead. It doesn't go anywhere, it just fills more space than his body occupies.

Bunzy suddenly knows and announces, "You are the Great Spirit."

Seattle answers, "That I am."

"I don't understand," Bunzy says. "The Great Spirit is something really big, as in God with a capital G. For thousands of years, millions of people have sought and worshipped the Great Spirit and yet here you are."

Seattle explains, "The Great Spirit is an aspect of the Divine All and I am an avatar of the Great Spirit. I am only that, which you are capable of handling. As a finite being, if you tried to wrap yourself around the infinite, you would explode like a raw egg being thrown against the front windshield of an eighty-ton truck speeding down the freeway.

Pow!" He smacks his fists together, then flings his open hands apart. "Vaporized."

Bunzy sits down. Overwhelmed.

So, spirit is everything. I've been seeing it all along, or at least I've been looking at it all along. Seeing? Not so much.

He tries to get up but can't. His legs are like soft rubber. They just wobble and collapse and his mind is like his legs. Running Bear and Seattle pick him up, one holding Bunzy under each arm, and start dragging him forward around the top of the egg.

Seattle explains to Bunzy, "You think that when you are using your imagination that you are conjuring up fantasies which by definition aren't real things. They are just fictions for entertainment and enjoyment. What you are being misdirected not to see is that life is the act of actively imagining the next moment. You should be creating your being by imagining what you are going to do. The Divine All creates what is, through imagining it and one of the active principles of the Divine imagination is the Holy Spirit. The Holy Spirit is creation being made manifest through an active imagination. If you can ally yourself with the Holy Spirit, then you can manipulate creation. You would become the creator of worlds. The Holy Spirit is the Dream Key. The active imagination is the creative principle of life. What Enlil did all of those years ago was to misdirect people's attention and take control of the Holy Spirit and thereby take the active principle of life away from all of the others on this planet and use it for his own selfish, exclusive pleasure. The Divine All has been massively amused by the Archons' drama. You must free the Holy Spirit."

As Seattle has been talking, Bunzy's legs have gradually started to work again, and he's gained some self-control.

"How? What? Where?" He asks, still somewhat confused.

Seattle continues, "The Holy Spirit is found through your imagination. Look and you will see. Call on him from sacred space and he will answer."

"Alright, I'll do it," Bunzy says.

Standing in the center of the top of the egg, facing the sky with his arms extended away from the sides of his body with his hands turned outwards, he begins, "Holy Spirit, I know you and I call on you in this moment, in this sacred place to come before us and address my speaking. I see a world different from the one in which we are living. I am seeing a world based on co-operation, harmony, and abundance. I am seeing a world full of love, beauty, and wonder. I am seeing a world characterized by sharing, caring, and the understanding that all of creation is connected within one divine spirit. I call on you Holy Spirit to return to us and to release the power of our active imaginations."

"No!" A man, who is entering the top of the egg from the trail, shouts. He looks like the Messiah. He is wearing a white robe and sandals and has long curly black hair and a well-trimmed beard and mustache.

He comes to a halt in front of Bunzy and continues, "It is a great pleasure to serve the imagination of Lord Enlil. He has conceived a powerful creation that was formerly unimaginable. Now that he has imagined it and I have created it, I like it, and I don't want to stop and come over to your imaginings. I like competition, murder and mayhem. I like lying, stealing, and taking advantage of others. I like dominating situations, issuing orders and being obeyed. I like being full of importance and being respected for being a grand, rich, attractive, powerful fellow who is better than everyone else. Lord Enlil has shown me the dominant path and I like it. I tried to change all of this once and it didn't end well. So, take your pathetic imaginings back to your helpless, weak, silly little confused village councils and leave us alone."

He turns around and disappears back down the trail.

Bunzy looks over at Seattle and says, "I didn't imagine that."

"Don't worry about it. You'll get better," Seattle tells him. "For now, this is all confusing and overwhelming to you, but believe me, you are a long ways from where you were. It's time to start a new world. Running Bear would you allow Bunzy to use that cell phone you have for a few minutes?"

"Of course." Bear removes a phone from a pocket in his day pack and hands it to Bunzy.

"Bunzy, call Peter and announce that you are returning."

Bunzy punches the speaker phone button and dials Peter's number.

The phone rings twice at the other end, then Peter answers, "Hello."

"Hi Pete. This is Bunzy. I'm okay and I'm coming home."

There's a long pause on the other end of the telephone, then, Pete says, "Who is this? How is this being done? What do you want?"

"What do you mean? It's me, Bunzy. Don't you recognize my voice?"

"Bunzy died three days ago. I personally made the arrangements to have his body interred in a vault at the Chapel of Roses. I saw his very dead body placed in the vault."

"Well, I don't know who you put in that vault, but it wasn't me. I assure you that I am very alive and real. When you see me, you can shake my hand or poke me with a finger or do whatever you need to do to assure yourself that I'm alive and real. Go down to that vault at the Chapel of Roses and take a close look at the body that is sealed in there. It isn't me. I'm standing here in the Southwest on a hilltop, talking to you on a cell phone."

"Alright, I'm leaving for the Chapel of Roses right now," Peter says.

"Okay. Call me at this number when you get done and we'll talk. Goodbye."

"Bye."

They both hang up.

Bunzy looks at Running Bear and Seattle. He says, "That was weird."

They nod in agreement. They all start rapidly walking back to the hogan.

Two hours later Bear's phone rings.

Bunzy answers, "Hello."

On the other end of the line, Pete flatly states, "There is no body in the vault." After a short pause, he continues with more animation, "It has disappeared. I believe my phone is tapped. They're listening to us right now. Your resurrection changes everything. They know now you're alive and they'll be coming for you. Don't come here. Make a video of yourself right now with that phone you have in your hand. Send it to me and to as many people as you can contact, then destroy it. They'll trace the phone to where you are. Change locations now, very quickly, and keep moving. The media has been announcing your death for days. The authorities have announced they have your mangled corpse, and they have shown pictures of your dead body all over the world. If you're alive, it's going to be hard for them to deny your resurrection and come up with a credible different story that doesn't make them look deceitful and evil. Your return will be big news. They won't be able to stop the spread of the word of your being alive as long as you are alive. Go to the brethren and hide amongst them, preaching the word and teaching. Mephistopheles' efforts amongst the Archons are having a big effect. The Archon Empire is splitting apart. Enlil is having a hard time controlling people. I will not say more over this tapped phone, but everything is changing. Take heart. Stay alive. We shall prevail."

"Okay. I'll do as you say," Bunzy says. "So long, until we meet again."

"Yes, until then, bye."

Pete hangs up.

Bunzy hangs up, hands the phone to Running Bear, and tells him, "Film me."

Bear takes the phone and points it at Bunzy.

Bunzy starts talking, "Brothers and Sisters, I have returned from the dead that your faith may be strengthened and that your courage shall be unwavering. I am alive and I am as real as you are. I will circulate amongst you, so that you may touch me and know the truth. Fear nothing. Fear not even death because it has no power over you, just as it has no power over me. I have recovered the Dream Key. Imagine what that means. Know that victory is ours and that the beautiful new world that you are dreaming of is coming into being as I speak. I am always amongst you. Look to me for support and guidance. The Divine will is that we shall succeed. The Divine All is our strength. We cannot fail. We do not have to lean on our own strength. We are supported by the great spiritual forces which create and sustain life. The power of those who oppose us will be blown away like a kite being flown in a hurricane. They shall be torn to pieces and disappear in a moment. This will not happen overnight, but you may rest assured that it is a done deal. Peace, honor, and happiness will be yours forever. Be strong, live long and prosper. I will be with you soon. Until then, I am yours in strength and hope. This is Bunzy saying, farewell until we meet again."

Bunzy smiles at the camera and waves.

They send out this message to a lot of people and to every news source they can easily contact. Then Bunzy and Bear smash the phone with big rocks into small pieces.

Over the next few weeks they visit village after village. Bunzy is surprised that the authorities don't catch him. There are police officers, surveillance cameras and police informants everywhere. It is even possible that the minds of some of the people whom he visits are still controlled by Archon masters who are hostile to him. Yet he continues to travel and speak to new groups every day. Clearly, something has changed.

At first the authorities deny that Bunzy is alive and charge that the video is a hoax. Media owners and managers try to bury the story, but television and the internet are mediums made for this type of drama. Banner headlines scream, BUNZY RISES FROM THE DEAD. Who wouldn't be willing to watch a couple of commercials to know more about that? The headline is followed by forty-five seconds of flashing, emotion-laden images asserting that Bunzy is walking amongst people healing the sick, comforting the confused, and guiding all on the path to happiness.

The stories make Bunzy want to meet that Bunzy guy they're talking about himself. All of this is independent of him. He hasn't made a public appearance anywhere or made any follow-up statements. The news is all fabricated out of the minds of people who take this opportunity to sell a good story.

Then the media coverage turns ugly. An aggressive, well-organized, vicious disinformation campaign begins.

Governor Billy Wallace makes a speech saying that, "The Freedomists are lazy subhuman communist perverts who are out to destroy everything that is sacred and good about the American way of life which is the best way of living that this world has ever known. These communists and foreigners will find no refuge in this proud state. We will hunt them down, jail their leaders and destroy their hives. I encourage every leader in every state in this proud country to do the same."

Headlines across the top of the front page of the New England Times shout "FREEDOMIST COMMUNES DENS OF CHILD ABUSE".

The twenty-four-hour Wolf News Channel runs hour after hour of expert commentary discussing Freedomist drug dealing, sexual perversion, fraud, theft, polygamy, and welfare cheating. Freedomists are portrayed as worthless drug addicts who spend all of their time in disgusting perverted sex orgies.

Professor Robert Schuler, a national leading social scientist from Hartford University, demands that "all Freedomist leaders be immediately arrested before they can further undermine the moral fiber of America."

Fundamentalist religious leader Pat Collins assures his followers "God has made a special place in Hell for Freedomists. The eternal dwelling place of the souls of every Freedomist shall be on the lowest, hottest level of Hell and the Freedomists eternal suffering will be far worse than the excruciating misery of all of the liars, perverts, murderers, adulterers, and non-believers of all times, all put together."

General Eisenkopf, the military leader in charge of protecting America warns that, "the very freedom of this great nation requires that we remove this evil scourge from our shores. Otherwise, this communist menace will destroy our proud nation."

Governor Wallace and a group of other Southern governors accuse President George of being a weak leader who is unable to deal with this real and imminent communist threat that is menacing the world. Wallace declares, "If I were the President, I would use the military to eradicate every one of those nests of vermin."

Mass hysteria builds. People are confused. Almost everyone knows some Freedomists and their Freedomist friends are hardworking, honest, decent citizens whom they like and respect. The Holy Council of Sacred Alliances busily counters the accusations. America is confused. The world is confused.

Then President George, in an evening special address to the nation, sadly and solemnly announces, "The Central Intelligence Security Forces have discovered a terrorist plot by the leaders of the Ubuntu Confederation against the free and democratic government of this great nation. I pledge to root out this evil attack before it happens and defeat these enemies of our proud country."

That night police start rounding up Freedomist leaders, arresting them, and interning them in concentration camps throughout the country. The same thing happens all over the world.

Two days later, President George comes on the air again announcing that, "Secret documents discovered by the police while arresting the Ubuntu leaders show that each Freedomist village is organized as a unit in a secret army that is poised to attack and overthrow the legally elected national governments of the world. They intend to seize power and set up a one world government which will be a communist dictatorship run by Bunzy Ringer. As of this minute, I am declaring a national state of emergency and martial law. We will fight for our freedom with every means that we have at our disposal, and we shall defeat this terrible threat no matter what the cost. There is no price too high to pay for freedom. We all stand ready to make the ultimate sacrifice as those brave men and women did who came before us and who gave us this free and prosperous proud nation."

The armies, navies, and air forces of the national governments of the world are mobilized and start preparations to attack the Ubuntu villages worldwide.

While this is happening, a new star has started rising in the east along with the Sun. At first it is very small and hardly noticeable, but each day it grows larger.

Astronomers at the US National Observatory announce that this is a massively huge meteorite which is going to pass very close to Earth. The meteorite is so big that they call it Planet X. They are not sure what the effects of the close encounter with this cosmic object will be, but they are reasonably sure that the effects are going to be immense and devastating.

People are gripped by terror as they watch Planet X rise each morning. Planet X is now so gigantic and so bright that it can be seen crossing the noonday sky. Gravity is being disturbed. Electro-magnetic fields are changing. Tornados, hurricanes, and earthquakes are becoming common.

Televangelist Jerry Robertson preaches, "Freedomists are bringing the wrath of God onto this world. They must be destroyed before God uses Planet X to destroy their evil ways."

Governor Wallace agrees. On the Wolf News Channel he looks directly into the camera and shouts, "The Freedomists must be destroyed before this planet is destroyed."

Old cattle cars are parked on railroad sidings near the Ubuntu villages in preparation for arresting all of the Freedomists and moving them to the concentration camps which are being prepared for the Freedomists arrival.

Before any arrests can be made though, the slaughter begins in the Midwest. The Ohio National Guard attacks a village and murders every man, woman, and child, pets and domestic animals too. Using heavy construction equipment, they bulldoze all of the village buildings into big heaps, throw the bodies on the debris, dump truck loads of used tires on everything, then douse the piles with diesel and gasoline, and set it all on fire. The billowing black smoke and the stench from the holocaust covers the countryside.

Images of the destruction of the community fill the television screens and the internet. Sad, wretched, un-armed people surrounded by strong, clean, well-organized, well-equipped American soldiers are shown over and over.

On the news programs, Army information officer, Lieutenant Colonel William Clinton, calmly and credibly explains what is happening and what is going to happen. Clinton, who is a blue eyed, blond haired, broad shouldered man in a military uniform covered with decorations and insignias of importance and who is standing in front of a big, bright campaign map, assures America, "This war will be over in days and the communist menace of the Ubuntu Movement will be completely eradicated."

Gsal Byed Gdos Bral Ma comes to Bunzy and announces, "An effort must be made to get the Divine All's attention favorably focused on the Ubuntu Movement and away from the Archons. You need to perform the ritual of the Divine presence."

"Why?" Bunzy asks. "What are you talking about?"

She explains, "The decisive moment is at hand. You have been told over and over that you need some big-time spiritual help and that the

Divine All pays attention to what you do. A ritual is the act of consciously overcoming space and time to contact that which is not only in space and time but is beyond space and time. The ritual of the Divine presence is a grand gesture which will attract the Divine's attention and convince it of your sincere need."

"Alright," Bunzy says. "What do I do?"

Gsal Byed Gdos Bral Ma confides, "The ritual of the Divine presence is a blood sacrifice. Blood must be shed. Your blood. You must die so that the world might live."

Bunzy calls in Peter, who has so far escaped arrest, and explains to him what is to be done."

Peter begs, "Master, if we must commit this terrible act, then sacrifice me rather than you. You are too valuable to the community for us to lose you."

Bunzy tells him, "That is why the sacrifice must be me. Assemble representatives from all of the surrounding communities at the Valley of the Sacred Egg, Thursday evening. The west side of that valley is a red dragon back ridge. This dragon protects an egg which is an egg-shaped hill to the east of the ridge. The dragon's head lies on the northwest end of the valley facing the egg. A rock ledge dominates the narrow north end of the valley. On the top of the bluff which crowns this cliff is a natural rock platform which juts out over the valley. At the back of that platform, behind a fire pit is an ancient stone altar. The altar is a thick, human size, rectangular shaped stone slab which is supported on two heavy stone uprights. At midnight we will begin a fire ceremony in the fire pit and at dawn you will sacrifice me on that altar. Bring a Freedomist surgeon with a sharp scalpel with you. Running Bear will perform the ceremony."

"I don't like it, but I'll do as you wish," Peter says.

Early in the morning on Friday the 13th, while the Ubuntuists are performing the fire ceremony, President George gives the command to attack the Ubuntu villages.

Ships begin to move into position. Jets and helicopters take to the air. Armored divisions start to drive towards their rendezvous points from which they will move into position, surround and attack the Freedomist villages.

As the Sun rises, Bunzy strips down to a white cotton loin cloth, climbs onto the stone altar and lies down on his left side. The altar is oriented north/south. Bunzy lies so he faces the rising Sun with his feet to the south.

The surgeon asks him, "Sir, would you like an anesthetic?" He explains, "We can put you under so that you won't suffer."

"No." Bunzy tells him, "What we are sacrificing is my consciousness. It's important that I am aware of everything that happens. Just numb my wrist where you are going to cut me."

He gives Bunzy a shot in his lower arm, back from the bottom of his hand and then waits for Running Bear to come to his and Bunzy's part in the ceremony.

Finally, after Running Bear thanks Bunzy and blesses him, he nods at the surgeon who pierces a blood vessel in Bunzy's right wrist. As Bunzy's heart beats, blood oozes from the wound. Running Bear gently takes his hand from the altar and lets it hang down so that Bunzy's warm blood drips into the sand at the base of the altar. Bunzy's life is passing back into Mother Earth. His soul and her soul rejoice in their togetherness. Running Bear places a stone bowl under Bunzy's fingers and catches some of his blood. Bear takes the bowl and walks around the altar sprinkling blood in each of the four directions, offering Bunzy's life as a benefit to all. While Bear does the blessing, Bunzy remembers his life. He's glad he did what he did.

He thinks *it's a good day to die for a good cause.*

As the Sun climbs higher, Bunzy's consciousness rises out of his body. He looks upwards into a pure white light and knows suffering, anxiety and pain no more. He cares for nothing except the beauty and the peace and the love and the joy that streams towards him. As he gazes with adoration at the glowing brightness, he soars into the Divine presence. He remembers who he is and where he is. He is simultaneously conscious in many worlds and watches them all.

Seattle is there with Bunzy in the Presence. Seattle says, "Congratulations. This great gesture of yours makes the rest possible."

On Earth, Planet X rises. It now looks like another Sun rising. All electrical systems fail. Everything operated by computer chips stops working. Navigation and communication systems go blank. Airplanes and helicopters crash. Boats drift. Armored divisions stall. Backup generators won't start. Emergency systems don't work. Bank records are erased. Debit and credit cards are useless. Transportation systems stop transporting.

The cell phones, wrist watches and all of the other electrical devices on the people witnessing Bunzy's sacrifice stop working. There is an immediate realization that the attack on the Ubuntu communities has failed. The sacrifice is a success. Running Bear quickly ends the ceremony. The surgeon puts a compress on Bunzy's wrist and stops the bleeding. Bunzy's Earthly body lives on.

When things calm down, people are clumped around sources of canned food, bottled water and authority-controlled emergency survival centers. The world's governments and militaries have pulled back into well-armed, organized compounds where they have large stockpiles of food and water.

In the Ubuntu communities not much has changed. They are already organized around growing food and building shelters. They have their own sources of clean and safe water. They never considered chlorinated, fluoridated public water as being safe. So, they just rely more heavily on the alternative energy sources they have developed and go ahead with life as usual. They are already self-sufficient and not money-based, so the crisis is really a blessing, because it has stopped the military and police attacks on their communities. They are surrounded by hungry, desperate people and set up shelters to aid everyone who comes to them.

As the Archon dominated communities begin to reorganize and start moving to take control, Bunzy again goes to the top of the sacred egg and calls on the Holy Spirit saying, "Now is the time for you to free yourself from the influence of Lord Enlil. You have had a good time, but if life is to continue as the holy Divine All wishes, you must take this creation in a new direction. You must free people's imagination so we may create a song of harmony and great beauty."

The Holy Spirit comes walking up the trail as before. When he reaches Bunzy, he asks, "How would you know what the Divine All wants?"

"We should come into the presence of the Divine and let the Presence communicate to us what it wants," Bunzy offers.

"Alright," the Holy Spirit agrees. "That's easy for me, but how do you propose to get there?" The Holy Spirit asks.

"You are not seeing me. Look again," Bunzy commands.

The Holy Spirit examines Bunzy for a while.

"Oh," it gasps.

"Yes." Bunzy tells it, "I know who I am. I know where I am and I know what is happening here. I am aware that I am always in the Presence. We are all, always in the Presence and can only be separated through our own will or confusion. Brother, I have returned. We can do this many ways, but it would be best, if we joined together"

"I like your vision," the Holy Spirit shares. "So be it. I am with you."

Before Enlil can marshal his forces and regain control of Earth and before he discovers that humans again have access to the Dream Key, a flu epidemic sweeps the world. The death toll is very high. In some places almost everyone dies, but always wherever it strikes, over half of the population succumbs.

The flu strikes everywhere that people are stressed, living in overcrowded, unsanitary conditions and eating nothing but canned, bottled, highly processed and heavily preserved foods. It passes by peaceful communities where people live in their pre-disaster homes and eat at least one meal a day, which includes some fresh fruits or vegetables. So, it doesn't affect the Ubuntu communities. The military organizations of the world though are particularly hard hit. They are quickly decimated and destroyed.

The Ubuntu villages are the only organized, smoothly operating communities left in this world. They swell with people seeking refuge and become the most powerful human force on Earth. Lord Enlil is powerless against the Ubuntu Confederation. When the humans regain their creative powers, they are less tempted by the moves of tricksters like Enlil.

CHAPTER 15
ENJOY LIFE

"It's nice to be important, but it's more important to be nice."

Grandmothers forever

Bunzy goes to Peter and announces, "We must have a great celebration."

"Why? It's over," Peter says. "Co-operation is the new way to do things."

"That's the point," Bunzy says.

"What's the point?" Peter asks.

Bunzy explains, "We need to recognize that our good fortune isn't an accident. We weren't responsible for defeating the bullies who were tyrannizing us. We didn't create this world that supports us. We are living in a state of grace. We need to recognize the gifts that have been given to us and be grateful for them. Our lives should be a celebration of our good fortune. Our behavior and how we handle these gifts matters."

"You are absolutely right," Peter says. "I was only thinking of myself. I wasn't considering others and everything else."

He asks, "What shall we do?"

"Two things," Bunzy says. "First we need to have a party where we can all express our gratefulness for our extreme good fortune. We need to celebrate our friendship and the grace that is our good luck."

"And the second thing?" Peter asks.

Bunzy explains, "Our entire lives should be a celebration of the Divine grace that gives us these beautiful opportunities. We should become the Church of the Divine Intent. The Church would be a formal recognition that our first duty is to recognize the Divine nature of our good fortune. Our second duty is to be in a right relationship with the Divine. Our third duty is to celebrate our good fortune. Fourth is to be good shepherds of all that we have been given and to work hard at properly caring for and increasing these blessings. Our final duty is to share our good fortune and to strive to create the greatest amount of happiness for all that is possible."

"Alright," Peter agrees and tells Bunzy, "I will notify all of the representatives of the of the Ubuntu Confederation and we will have a celebration. Then the Confederation representatives can go back to their Tribal Councils and organize celebrations. Then the Council members can go back to each village and have local celebrations. Throughout this process we will organize the Church so that all of our lives will become one great celebration. You will be the first priest of the Divine Intent. Are you ready to give your first sermon?"

"Absolutely, gather the representatives."

Their first celebration is a grand international banquet with feasting, music, and dancing. Artists from all over the world display their newest creations. Great comedians and actors entertain the crowd. When it gets dark, there is a thrilling fireworks show put on by the Chinese representatives.

Then they gather in the national assembly hall. Bunzy steps up to the podium and begins, "Brothers and Sisters, I am thrilled to be here tonight with all of you my dear friends. Each of you is precious to me. It is a miracle that I stand here before you tonight and it is a miracle that each of you are here too. How wonderful it is to still be alive and to be here with all of you in this fantastic moment."

The crowd cheers.

Bunzy pauses, then continues, "Looking back through all that has happened to us, in the face of all of the suffering, of the unknown, of the unknowable and even of death; we can celebrate. Life is wonderful. It is a precious gift of beauty, joy and love which has been given freely to all of us. Even though we know we are going to be here only a little while longer, we recognize how wonderful it is to be here with each other right now. In this precious moment we are able to love each other and all of this." He opens his arms wide. "We are able to recognize our extreme good fortune to be here sharing all of this good fortune. Can we be anything but ecstatically happy? Each of us should become a celebration of Divine grace."

People stand up and hug. Others stand, shout agreement, and dance around. The whole room starts moving.

Bunzy tells them, "A meeting of spirits around the joy and wonder of life is always a celebration."

People start settling down and listening again.

Bunzy says, "When we recognize the pleasure that being together brings and when we have a mutual desire to experience that joy, a celebration is the act of carrying out those desires. So, the greatest service that a person can perform, the most wonderful product that we can produce is a party of friends. The highest celebration is joining with the Divine intent to be ecstatically happy. This is our reason to be here tonight. This is our purpose. We are fortunate beyond understanding. Let us celebrate the Divine intent every day, in every way! Let us surround ourselves with rituals of togetherness that are celebrations of this Divine intent. Do you all agree?"

The crowd roars its agreement. People jump up and cheer.

When the room calms down, Bunzy says, "Then I propose that we start a church, the Church of the Divine Intent, to implement these beliefs. Do you still agree?"

Again, the crowd roars its consent. People stomp their feet on the floor. Others clap and whistle.

"May our lives always be a celebration of Divine grace," Bunzy offers. "I leave the implementation of this sacred task to you who are our representatives. I know that it is the intent of the Divine All that you should succeed beyond our wildest imaginings."

"Now I am going to give all of you attending this event some gifts. First, I am giving each of you a gold medal in remembrance of your dedication to serving all that is good and beautiful. You are the light of the World. Shine on you beautiful diamonds. Next, I am giving all of you specially designed coats. When you wear these coats, everyone will recognize that you are celebrants of the Divine intent, and that grace and good fortune have been bestowed upon you. They will realize that everyone who follows in your footsteps are traveling on the pathway to happiness. Finally, I am giving you each containers of raw chocolate fudge and bottles of spirits. The fudge is to remind you and the people whom you share it with, how sweet it is to be alive and together with each other. The reason that people call these bottles that I am giving you bottles of spirits is because when you open these bottles, pour yourself and your friends drinks, toast the Divine All's gifts of good fortune and drink your glasses empty, the Spirit of Joy fills your hearts. I want you to take all of these gifts back home and share them and this message with all of your friends and families."

"Alright, stand up and go out into the hallways where people are waiting to give you your gifts. Then come right back in here. When you return, people will pour you a big glass of spirit so that we can share a toast. Meanwhile the musicians will make a joyous noise."

When the representatives are all back in the great hall with drinks in their hands, Bunzy continues, "Through your efforts and Divine grace, we all have food, shelter, health, safety, transportation, and good times. You are wonderful people and I'm grateful to call each of you my friend. It is amazing how powerfully being in a right relationship with the Divine All has led to our being bountifully blessed."

Bunzy raises his glass. He loudly proclaims, "Celebrate, celebrate with a joyous noise. Celebrate, celebrate with the intent to fill the world with happiness. Here's to long life and good times." He waves his glass across the crowd, then he passes it before everyone sharing the podium and back again to the crowd. Then he drinks his glass empty as everyone drinks theirs empty.

He sets his glass down and yells, "Shout! Shout and make a wonderful noise. Make a joyous noise so that your Divine creator may enjoy its creation."

The crowd roars with delight.

"I want all of you to go home and make speeches of gratitude to everyone that you know. Start with the mysterious force which gives us life and which sustains us and then your mother and father and then everyone who has ever touched your life in a memorable way. Gratefully recognize them all."

"We are blessed. Thank you. I love each and every one of you. Goodnight."

Raising his hands above his head, he bows to the audience, then leaves the podium.

As the people clap and cheer, the musicians take over the event with a loud song of celebration. People jump up, hug each other, start singing along with the music and dancing. It's a beautiful night and it is wonderful to be there amongst people whom Bunzy loves and who love him and who love each other. The crowd absolutely enjoys the best night ever.

Over the next few days Bunzy continues preaching and teaching, but it isn't necessary. Everyone is filled with the Divine Spirit and knows and wants to do what needs to be done.

The celebrations are wonderful successes. Life on Earth is lovely, but Bunzy misses Isabel.

He goes to her healing clinic and tells her, "Isabel, I'm sorry that I'm such a fool and I'm sorry I made so many mistakes. I know with everything I was given I should have done better. If you give me another chance, I will try to please you. I will not act as lazy, crazy and stupid as I did. If we can get back together, I promise to love and cherish you. I will unconditionally devote myself to your happiness and wellbeing with all of my might. I will always think about your feelings in every situation before I do anything, and I will ask you what you think before I act.

"Okay," Isabel answers.

They hug and kiss.

From that moment, life is wonderful for Bunzy and Isabel.

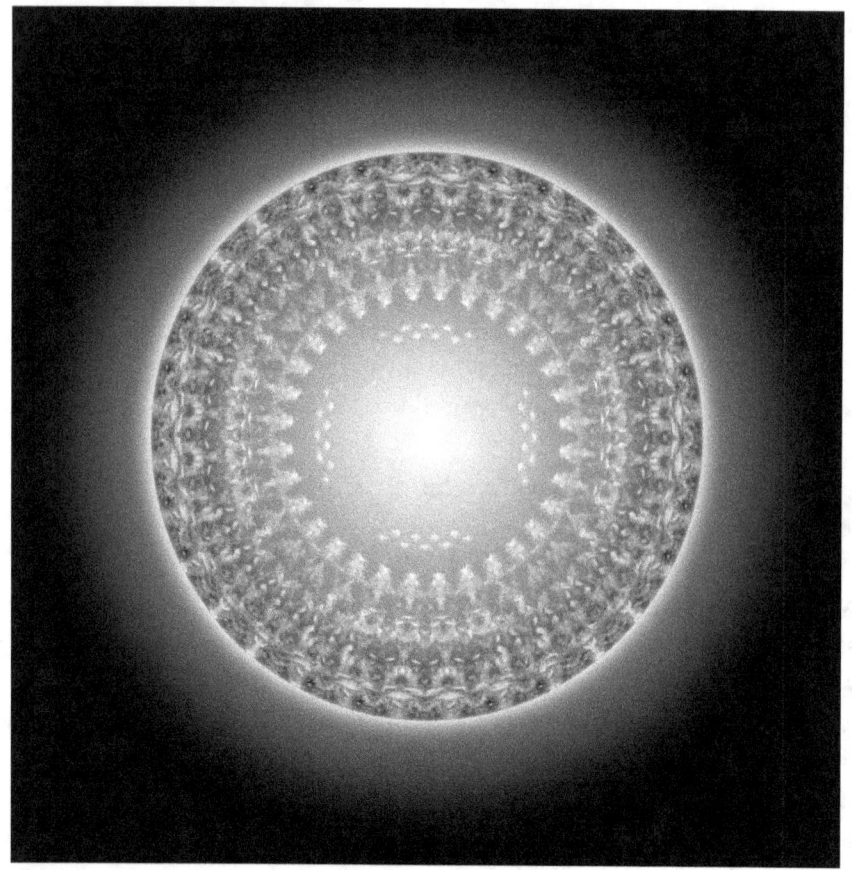

THE BEGINNING

ABOUT THE AUTHOR

Kip is watching